THE
DEAD HORSE
PAINT COMPANY

BOOKS BY EARL EMERSON

MAC FONTANA MYSTERIES
Black Hearts and Slow Dancing
Help Wanted: Orphans Preferred
Morons and Madmen
Going Crazy in Public

THOMAS BLACK MYSTERIES
The Rainy City
Poverty Bay
Nervous Laughter
Fat Tuesday
Deviant Behavior
Yellow Dog Party
The Portland Laugher
The Vanishing Smile
The Million-Dollar Tattoo

THE
DEAD HORSE
PAINT COMPANY

A MAC FONTANA MYSTERY

EARL EMERSON

WILLIAM MORROW AND COMPANY, INC.
NEW YORK

It is the policy of William Morrow and Company, Inc., and its imprints
and affiliates, recognizing the importance of preserving what has been written,
to print the books we publish on acid-free paper,
and we exert our best efforts to that end.

Library of Congress Cataloging-in-Publication Data
Emerson, Earl W.
The dead horse paint company : a Mac Fontana mystery / by Earl Emerson.—1st ed.
p. cm.
ISBN 0-688-13751-2 (hardcover)
I. Title.
PS3555.M39D43   1997
813'.54—dc21   96-29692
CIP

Printed in the United States of America
First Edition
1 2 3 4 5 6 7 8 9 10

BOOK DESIGN BY OKSANA KUSHNIR

They were still so young they hadn't
learned to count the odds
and to sense they might owe
the universe a tragedy.
—NORMAN MACLEAN, *Young Men and Fire*

THE
DEAD HORSE
PAINT COMPANY

1

THE MORGANS CHOOSE
REFRIED BEANS
FOR LUNCH

To Fontana's way of thinking, there was nothing more dishonorable than silent farting, which he had always considered sneaky in the extreme. It was with this in mind that Fontana tried to exit the station house before Les and Opal Morgan came around the corner and charged through the open bay door on a tide of freezing air—just as he knew they would when the siren on the fire station tower went off.

"Can we ride with you, Chief?" Les Morgan asked eagerly.

Nodding, Fontana stepped into his bunking boots, then gazed wistfully through the open bay doors at the headlights reflecting off the puddled streets, at the snow and rain falling in tandem.

The alarm called for a single engine company, but Fontana had decided to respond as well. When the station bell finished clanging, the dispatcher announced over the radio, "Smoke from north of the freeway. Smoke in the trees at exit forty-seven. The party reporting this said it looked like a car fire in the Denny Creek area."

After stuffing their equipment into the backseat of the chief's Suburban, Les and Opal Morgan climbed in, slamming the door too hard, as was their habit. Satan, Fontana's inherited German shepherd, watched curiously from the front seat. He hadn't quite figured out that he was in semiretirement, having received several gunshot wounds in an incident the year before.

Exit 47 was twenty miles up the highway toward Snoqualmie Pass, near the 2,500-foot level, and it had been snowing at that elevation all week. The pass itself had six feet of the white stuff.

Fontana swung the Suburban out of the building, down Alice Street, and out to Interstate 90 half a mile away. Engine 2 followed but, hampered by chains that would hold its speed below thirty-five, quickly dropped out of sight in the Suburban's rearview mirror.

Had the roads been dry, it would have taken twenty minutes to reach the location, which meant any self-respecting car fire would have burned itself out before they reached it. Certainly there would be little to save except the surrounding woods, which, because they were under heavy snow, would be pretty well protected anyway. As the town's fire chief, Fontana himself wasn't required to respond to a routine incident such as this, but he was responding now out of sheer boredom—they'd had only two alarms in the last three days—and because he wanted to make sure Engine 2 didn't get bogged down in drifts or slide off the road.

Longtime volunteers in the Staircase Fire Department, Les and Opal Morgan operated a service station around the corner, and when they had a relief man available, one or both could be counted on to show up for alarms. Nobody else had ever commented on it, but to Fontana, the Morgans, like a lot of married couples, were similar enough to be brother and sister: brown-haired, anemic, pudgy, taciturn, neckless, and unceasingly humorless. The only reason he didn't like them riding with him was that one of them had a trademark habit of farting silently. Fontana didn't know who it was, but he strongly suspected Opal; Satan usually left the room when she came in.

As he drove up the gradual slope on I-90, the rain and snow mixture on the windshield quickly turned to a solid barrage of white. The transformation seemed to happen in a fraction of a second, and the motion of a million flakes hurtling into the windshield was hypnotic. Very few drivers moved aside for Fontana's red lights, their citizenship thwarted either by fogged-over rear windows or fear of leaving the one good lane left to them.

The Morgans were fully capable of riding to exit 47 without uttering a word, either of them, but ten miles into the journey, after they'd finished suiting up, Les, a longtime fan of the obvious, said matter-of-factly, "Snowin'."

"Snowin' all right," confirmed Opal.

On either side of the highway, Mount Teneriffe, McClellan Butte, Granite Mountain, and countless other peaks were lousy with snow. Yet with the cloud cover only a hundred feet overhead, snowflakes blurring the air, and darkness falling, little of anything but the road directly in front of their headlights was visible.

When Fontana radioed to tell the King County dispatchers he was responding, they came back with "I-Ninety Command, be advised. This was reported at exit forty-seven on the north side of the highway. The caller stated it looked like it was up a side road."

"I-Ninety Command okay," said Fontana, hanging up the radio mike. He wondered how anybody had been able to see up a side road in this mess.

"There's houses up that gol-durned road," said Opal from the backseat.

"Cabins," corrected Les.

"They're houses."

"Summer cabins is all."

"Houses."

"Won't be anybody in 'em this time of year."

"That don't mean one of them ain't burnin'," said Opal.

"Don't mean one of 'em *is* burnin'," said Les.

When they were within a mile of the site, Fontana said, "Keep your eyes open. They said exit forty-seven, but people get confused."

"Can't see nothin'," said Opal from the backseat.

"Me neither," said Les.

As Fontana veered off onto the exit ramp, a coven of snowplows, four abreast, charged down the freeway on the other side of the median. Fontana veered off onto the exit ramp, proceeded up the slight incline, and took a left at a stop sign hooded with snow. "See anything behind us?" he asked.

"Nope," said Les.

"I get carsick I turn around," said Opal.

"Nothin' there," said Les. "Nothin' but snow."

"Well, I can't see it 'cause I can't turn around," said Opal.

As they skidded at the second stop sign, Fontana began to wonder if they were on a wild-goose chase. Here the road made a T: huge drifts to the left and, surprisingly, a passable track to the right. He went right. Traveling across snow packed three feet deep with more falling heavily, Fontana couldn't be sure if he was looking at another vehicle's track or mere ruts in the roadway underneath.

Now that they were on the side road, there were no other car headlights to help maintain a perspective, and the whirl of white was even more dizzying. It had been years since Fontana had driven in a snowfall this heavy. Though he was familiar with this road from hiking trips, he wasn't sure familiarity would help, for it was hard to tell if the white in front of him was eight feet distant or eight hundred feet.

Opal leaned forward, her chubby cheek alongside Fontana's, her breath smelling of chewing tobacco, a vice he had long suspected her of. Like a lover whispering secrets, she rode that way the rest of the trip. So far, except for a single blast as they were climbing into their bunking gear, the Morgans had been on their best behavior.

The two-lane road paralleled the highway for several dozen yards, then veered northeast into the trees where it climbed slightly. When they got to the narrow bridge that crossed Denny Creek, they spotted a glow ahead in the woods, a fabric of black smoke rippling up through the falling whiteness. The bridge was wooden, narrow, risky in the summer, but with snow piled on it, downright scary. They crossed it anyway, following on faith the dim indentations that might have been tracks, and were rewarded beyond the next bend with a singularly spectacular car fire.

A fifteen-foot-tall sheet of orange flame chewed at clouds of black smoke boiling off the vehicle, radiant heat melting snow all around.

As Fontana scanned the portions of the fenders that weren't blackened and blistered, he figured it for a Crown Victoria or some other domestic luxury model. The original color might have been a deep ruby. Or black. It was all orange flame and black metal now, sitting in the middle of the road on flat tires, the windows burned out.

When he stopped the Suburban and climbed out, he could feel the dry heat on his face even as the snowflakes gave him little wet kisses. He threw his jacket and helmet on, got on the radio and gave a corrected location, and then warned the engine not to cross the bridge. The dispatcher confirmed receipt of the corrected location with Engine 2, Lieutenant Kingsley Pierpont's deep, inner-city patois easily recognizable across the airwaves.

Barking, Satan leaped out of Fontana's door and circled the burning car, bounding through the snow, sinking to his shoulders in the drifts when he strayed from the roadbed. The dog was as amused by snow as the Morgans were by fire.

Without being told, the Morgans opened the back of the Suburban and each took out a thirty-pound CO_2 extinguisher. With Opal dragging hers, they approached the burning vehicle from the same direction, Opal to the right, Les to the left and, surprisingly, were able to knock down a lot of the fire. Les worked his way around the car shooting huge, noisy jets of carbon dioxide into the nooks and crannies. But even as the fire gave ground, it flared back up—an earmark of having been set with an accelerant.

With a heavy bar, Fontana began prying at the hood but was twice driven back by heat. Opal helped, and they finally got the hood up in time for Les to wash down the engine compartment, draining his extinguisher. Then, with a quiet *whoompff,* the passenger portion of the car took off again, and with both extinguishers expended, they could do nothing but stand back and warm themselves. After a bit they heard Engine 2 down the road.

Les and Opal ran to greet the engine at the bridge and came back a minute later followed by Lieutenant Pierpont, the three of them dragging a two-hundred-foot hose line. Pierpont put the nozzle on a fog pattern and knocked down the flame on the car's exterior, then stepped forward and washed out the inside. When the fire was tapped, they could see that the sheet metal and even some of the framing were warped, the seats and dash and all the windows were burned out, and colorful globs of melted plastic from taillights and bumpers lay glittering in the snow.

Standing at the rear of the vehicle, Satan began barking in a tone and attitude that Fontana immediately recognized.

"Okay, okay, Satan. We'll take care of it. Stand back," Fontana said to him just as another firefighter in full bunking clothing came around the bend. It was Heather Minerich, bulling her way up the snowy slope with a heavy extinguisher. Sandusky, who'd been running the pump on the engine, was behind her.

Lieutenant Pierpont was one of three paid regulars and the only black in the Staircase Fire Department, Sandusky was a volunteer who worked professionally in the Seattle Fire Department, and Minerich was the paid rookie. It was a tiny department, far too small for the rapidly expanding township, and it relied heavily on volunteers.

Sandusky cut what was left of the battery cables under the hood while Minerich and Pierpont worked on the smoking trunk with a pair of bars. "You see anybody when you were coming in?" Fontana asked.

"Not a soul," said Pierpont. "You?"

"Nope. Somebody was here within the last half hour, though. Wonder where they went."

"Coulda hiked off right through them trees," said Opal Morgan breathlessly, moving alongside Fontana.

"I didn't know a car could burn like that," said Les, also out of breath.

"There's five or six hundred pounds of fuel load in an automobile," Fontana said. "Not counting the gas tank. Most of it plastics. And it burns real fast. I was surprised it was still going so well when we got here."

"Cars burn like a son of a gun," said Sandusky, who never talked about it but had gotten skin grafts a year earlier after rescuing a toddler from a vehicle fire. "Whoa. Take a look at that puppy."

Fontana stepped around the group and directed the beam from his lantern inside the pried-open trunk, then got on the radio and called for the police, medical examiner, and the King County fire investigator.

"That's . . . that's awful," said Heather Minerich.

"Haven't you ever seen a crispy critter?" asked Sandusky.

"No."

"Then I guess you owe the station cake and ice cream. Why don't you try Rocky Road this time? We're getting sick of that sherbet."

"It looks like a giant burned doll. Is that really a person?"

"This Dugan's burned worse than most," said Fontana.

"Smells like pork," said Opal Morgan, stepping up and peering in. Les moved close, too. The Morgans felt compelled to enhance their reputations as the department ghouls any time they could, which was why, moving as one, they stuck their heads in the hot car trunk with the corpse and looked it over as if it were a roasted pig at a banquet.

2

THE DUGAN
IN THE TRUNK

"I don't get it," said Heather Minerich, staring inside the trunk. "How did he get in there?"

"Suicide," said Opal Morgan authoritatively, standing back and looking at Heather. "Killed hisself. It's pretty simple, you look at it."

Fontana stepped forward and shined the beam of his flashlight around the body. The corpse lay on its back, head toward the driver's side of the car, legs folded up beneath, arms elevated almost in a boxer's pose. Except for the remnants of a leather belt, a few scraps of charred cloth peeking out from under the body, and a sad-looking pair of wingtips, the clothing had mostly burned off. The belt buckle had burned loose and lay on the floor of the trunk. It wasn't a pretty sight, but then again, it didn't look enough like a human to be as gruesome as it might have been.

Fontana turned to Opal Morgan. "What makes you think it was a suicide?"

" 'Cause the car keys are right there. See 'em?" Fontana followed her chubby finger with the light beam to a small, lumpy object that turned out to be a mass of keys welded together by the heat. Opal had to almost kiss the corpse to point the keys out, a posture that didn't seem to bother her in the least.

Lieutenant Pierpont said, "Why would somebody drive out here, lock themselves in the trunk, and set fire to the car?"

"More likely they set fire to the car and *then* climbed in," said Heather.

"Why take the keys inside with you?" Pierpont asked.

"So nobody could get you out," said Opal.

"Nobody's going to get you out anyway," said Sandusky. "There's nobody out here."

"Probably got in there and changed his mind," said Les. "Got the keys out of his pocket and tried to work the lock. Hell of a deal."

"Hell of a deal," repeated his wife.

"You guys are nuts," said Sandusky. "Nobody's going to set fire to a vehicle and climb into the trunk. Who would even think up such a dumb stunt? Somebody came out here to dump a body. They killed this guy, probably in Seattle or Bellevue or maybe even California for all we know, and were driving around looking for a place to dump him where nobody would find him until next summer, and while they were driving around, the car caught fire."

"Then where are they?" asked Heather.

"I don't know," said Sandusky, lowering his voice. Everybody stopped talking and looked around at the woods and the falling snow.

"Okay," said Fontana. "Let's look around here for whatever they might have left. Satan. *Suche! Suche!*" After a quick search of the area, the dog unearthed two Amber Bock beer bottles, a wool glove, and a five-gallon gasoline can, now empty.

"That can points to arson," said Sandusky.

"Yeah, but it don't mean it wasn't a suicide," said Opal. "He douses the car real good, maybe himself, climbs into the trunk, closes it, and lights a match."

"Poof," added Les.

"God, that's terrible," said Heather. "But if it *was* a suicide, at least he was alone." She scanned the darkening woods around them. "If it *wasn't*, somebody's out here with us."

"Couldn't have gone far," said Opal.

"Probably have guns," said Les.

"And more gasoline," said Opal. Fontana's firefighters were beginning to remind him of a bunch of kids telling spooky stories around a campfire until they were all too scared to walk home.

"He wasn't dead when the fire was set," said Minerich. "Look. He was trying to get out. He was trying to push the lid up when he died. His hands are still up in the air."

"It's called the pugilistic pose," said Fontana. "Burning a body tightens the cords in the arms. A lot of burned bodies look that way, almost as if the guy was boxing."

"So he might have been dead already?"

"Possibly."

"Good. I mean, well, you know. I hate to think somebody put him in the trunk when he was alive and *then* set fire to it."

"Worse," said Sandusky. "I hate to think somebody put him in the trunk, poured gasoline all over it, then stood around and drank two Amber Bocks while they thought about torching him."

"Or while watching the car burn," said Lieutenant Pierpont.

"I don't know how much watching he could have done while it was burning," said Fontana. "He had to have gotten out quickly. The fire was still going real strong when we got here. This thing wasn't started that long ago."

"How could it have just started if we got the call when we did?" Lieutenant Pierpont asked.

"I don't know. I don't know what's going on. It took us over twenty-five minutes to get here. But I'd swear that car was only burning a few minutes when we arrived. Admittedly, it was burning hotter than a cheap chain saw. I don't know. I could be wrong, but that's the way I see it."

"You guys see tracks when you came in?" asked Lieutenant Pierpont.

"It was snowing too hard," Fontana said, as he realized it was *still* snowing too hard. Using a gloved hand he pulled out the bar propping up the trunk lid and gently let the hood back down to protect the evidence.

"We barely could see *your* tracks," said Lieutenant Pierpont.

"Somebody's trying to walk through those woods," said Fontana, "he'd better be an experienced outdoorsman, or we're going to find him next spring."

"Next spring," repeated Opal Morgan.

"S'posed to snow all night," said Les Morgan.

"Heavy," said Opal.

"Couldn't get any heavier," said Les.

"I *said* heavy."

"That's what I'm trying to tell you," said Les. "This is heavy."

"That's what I said."

■

Sandusky, Pierpont, and the Morgans headed back to Engine 2 to go home, while Fontana and Minerich waited at the scene for the police.

Once the equipment was picked up and they were alone, Heather knocked the accumulated snow off the rim of her yellow fire helmet and glanced nervously at the dark woods. She was young and tall with a lanky, loose-limbed build and a bold manner, her boldness abandoning her inexplicably on certain types of alarms—notably ripping fires and oddball stuff. She had brown eyes, short brown hair, clear skin, and had endeared herself to the volunteers by matching their off-color stories with equally crude tales of her own.

"You think there's somebody out there?" Heather asked.

Fontana looked at the dog, who'd been snapping at snowflakes in the headlights. "*Suche!* Satan! *Suche!*"

When Fontana pointed to the woods, Satan began tracking, then went off the road on the east side. A few minutes later the dog crossed the road fifty yards up. Fontana was knowledgeable enough to work Satan, but not knowledgeable enough to be an expert about what the dog could or could not do. He knew the dog could follow a perp through water, but this was different. There had to be three or four inches or more of fallen snow on top of any track that had been laid. Plus, the truck thermometer said it was sixteen degrees. Some of the water they'd poured onto the car was already frozen.

"I hate to think about him being alive in there. I hope he wasn't."

"Me too, Heather."

■

It was almost an hour before Jennifer Underhill from the King County Fire Investigation unit showed up. By then the King County Police had taped off the scene and were taking pictures, although in all the falling snow Fontana had a feeling the film would reveal little more than a blur of flakes.

Jennifer Underhill, in rubber boots, coveralls, mittens, and a small hard-hat that made her shoulder-length hair flair out like a clown's, trudged over to where Fontana was standing at the rear of the car. "What do you have?"

"*You* have it. I'm just securing the scene."

Fontana raised the trunk lid and propped it open. "Oh, boy," she said. "You find any ID?"

"Haven't looked." He explained what they'd seen on arrival and gave her the time frames.

"What's up this road?" Jennifer Underhill asked. "I've never been up here before."

"A campground. Some cabins. The trailhead for three or four popular summer hikes. It's possible people snowshoe up here or backcountry-ski. I'm not sure."

"What else?"

"You take this road far enough, it goes all the way to the pass. Fact is, this used to be the old highway to Eastern Washington."

"This little thing?"

"Hard to believe, isn't it?"

Before they left, Fontana, Satan, and one of the King County officers took a long hike up the road to the Denny Creek campground area, to the cabins. Neither they nor Satan detected much of interest. They saw no vehicles or any signs that any vehicles had passed by.

3

AN OLD ENEMY
SURFACES

Back in town, Fontana drove the two miles from the station to his home, then, on foot, negotiated the narrow trail through the shrubbery and trees next door, exchanged greetings with Mary, his full-time landlord and part-time baby-sitter, and walked home with his son. Nine years old, mop-haired, and motherless, Brendan was a genius in Fontana's eyes the way an only child frequently can be to a parent. He was full of beans and curiosity, a steadfast collector of odd facts and small dead animals, which he dutifully and ceremoniously buried under markers in the backyard.

Rain dimpled the sluggish river alongside the dike, yet two hundred feet up the mountainside it was snowing heavily. One of the reasons Fontana had decided to rent this place was that there were only a handful of houses in this tiny enclave, none visible from his.

He recalled thinking when he first saw it that he'd stepped into paradise. With Little Gadd and the river a stone's throw away, the dike and flat woodland to the south, the view was as opulent and lush as that in any national park.

Before moving here from the East, he'd been a firefighter in a large metropolitan department, then an arson investigator for the same department—a job he'd felt he was born to—and eventually a captain in operations. After the death of his wife, he began looking for a haven, a town where he could mellow out and recover from the traumas of both his personal life and his career, a post where mechanized monopolies and computerized corporations could motor on past and he wouldn't smell any of the exhaust. He'd applied for the position of fire chief in Staircase and was confirmed a month later.

Staircase had seemed like a small town doped on the narcotic of a minor depression, which was exactly what he'd been looking for; yet it seemed the minute he relocated, traffic picked up, real estate prices boomed, and some damn fool built a McDonald's out by the highway. At only thirty miles distant along I-90, Staircase was one of the last unspoiled commutes into Seattle, which made every building contractor, investor, realtor, plumber, cement hauler, land developer, tractor operator, and water witch handler in the Northwest even more intent on spoiling it. At least that was how Fontana saw it.

For a long while Fontana didn't have a telephone, but depending only on his pager and portable radio for fire calls at night had been cumbersome and unreliable, so now the only modern amenity he lacked was a television, a situation that, if other aspects of his life didn't, branded him an eccentric.

Wednesday morning when Fontana dropped his son off at Staircase Elementary, the streets were still wet from a midnight squall. The radio reported a strong possibility of snow flurries.

When he arrived at the station, Roger Truax and Mo Costigan greeted him, Roger in a suit and Mo in a tight skirt and high heels that knotted up her calves. Truax tried to hide his baldness by combing the twelve-inch-long hair that grew above his ears across his scalp and had a habit of whipping stray locks into place using a snapping motion of his neck. In the past, he'd displayed an uncanny accuracy that was much talked about among the volunteers.

Truax, an ex-captain from the Tacoma Fire Department, was

the town's safety director, a part-time job he applied a full-time fanaticism to. Recently Fontana discovered that he and Truax had applied for the position of chief at the same time, which might account for Truax's tendency toward backstabbing.

Roger was a large, soft man with cheeks that pinked up when he least wanted them to, serving as accurate lie-detectors, infallible signals of stress, chagrin, or prurient interest. When he wasn't conspiring with Mo Costigan, Roger was dreaming about parlaying his position as safety director in one of the smallest towns in the state into a state senator's seat or maybe even something more grand. Truax's ambition was as limitless as his prospects were limited.

Short, stocky, despotic, Mo Costigan was the town mayor when she wasn't running her small accounting firm in Bellevue. She and Truax looked particularly pleased with themselves this morning, which caused Fontana to glance over his shoulder to see if his dog had died.

Roger, who normally had a rather gloomy disposition, had been almost giddy the past couple of weeks. He'd finagled a spot on the planning committee for a national fire conference in Seattle the following weekend and had been squiring out-of-state fire dignitaries around the area for the past few days—boasting and lying and charging his meals to the town's account.

Truax fixed his vacant blue eyes on Fontana and said, "Heard you lost a victim in a car fire yesterday."

Fontana looked over Mo's shoulder into the next room and saw three people from the King County Fire Marshal's Office, Jennifer Underhill among them.

"What's going on, Mo?"

"Mac, you had a dead man in a car last night."

"We had something. Nobody's confirmed it was a man yet. It might have been an orangutan."

"It not only was a man," said Roger, "it was—"

"We need to talk to you," said Mo, stepping forward and grasping Fontana by the arm. Hugging the back of his wrist against herself, Mo walked him up the stairs to the classroom across from the main bunk room. Roger followed, as did the threesome from the King County Fire Marshal's Office. When Fontana nodded greetings to them, the two men returned cold expressions, and Jennifer Underhill threw him a covert look he could not decode.

Still holding his arm, Mo walked him to a chair next to a table near the front of the room and perched on the edge of the table after he sat down. She crossed her legs and patted him on the shoulder the way one might comfort an injured child. Staring at Fontana, Truax leaned against the blackboard with his arms crossed, the back of his dark suit mopping up chalk marks. Underhill and one of the King County people sat to one side while the last county fire investigator, a man named Crossworthy, went to the front of the room, placed his forearms on the lectern, and said, "Somebody close that door."

Underhill got up and closed it.

Still breathing heavily from the short climb up the stairs, Crossworthy grunted, then cleared his throat. He was a swarthy man with three chins and black hair that crept down his neck and crawled up the backs of his hands like a genetic experiment gone bad. He gave Fontana a dour look. "Tell us about the car fire yesterday," he said. "Tell us what you saw and what you did."

It took Fontana five minutes to do this, with another five minutes to respond to questions thrown at him by Crossworthy, Roger Truax, and the second male investigator, whose name he never did learn. Throughout this, Jennifer Underhill said nothing, and Mo remained uncharacteristically quiet. Mo's perfume was almost overpowering, and her nylons made whispering noises as she swung her crossed leg back and forth rhythmically. Unaccountably, she had started rubbing Fontana's back, then switched to petting him on the shoulder. It occurred to him to ask her to stop, but he decided he rather liked it.

When the questions about the car fire began to peter out, Crossworthy narrowed his gray eyes and said, "Didn't you work in a fire department back east?"

"Sure. Everybody knows that. Eighteen years."

"I understand you worked Fire Investigation for a number of years, too."

"That's right. You knew that."

"Ever run into a man named Edgar Callahan?"

Fontana grew silent for a moment. "There was an Edgar Callahan in my old department."

"You did know him, then."

"Chief Callahan? Everybody knew him. He was a deputy chief when I was with the department. A regular ballbuster. A leather-lungs from the old school. Last I heard, he was about to be appointed top dog."

"So he was chief of your old department?"

"Not as of a month ago. He might be now."

"And what were your thoughts on his appointment?"

"It doesn't affect me one way or another. What's going on?"

All eyes in the room were on Fontana. "That burnt toast in the car last night." Crossworthy said.

"That was Edgar Callahan?"

"We're checking dental work this morning, but we think it was him."

"What would Callahan be doing clear the hell out here? Thousands of miles from home?"

"More to the point," said Crossworthy, "what would he be doing getting himself burned up in your district?"

"It wasn't exactly my district," said Fontana. "The volunteers up at the pass usually take care of that area."

"Maybe somebody invited him out for a barbecue," said Truax.

4

HE'D BEEN
REPORTED MISSING

Standing with his buttocks braced against the blackboard, Roger Truax cleared his throat and said, "Edgar and several others came out here to attend the conference and to give a seminar on the Dead Horse Paint Company fire. I told you about the conference, Mac. This weekend in Seattle. There'll be fire personnel from all over the country. We asked you to be on a panel, but if I recall, you said you had a Monopoly game scheduled for that day."

"I thought the conference wasn't until this weekend."

"A number of fire officers came out early. You were at that fire, weren't you, Mac? The Dead Horse Paint Company fire?" Truax thumped his rear end repeatedly against the chalkboard, small clouds of powder wafting out from behind him like silent firecrackers.

"A lot of people were at that fire."

"Probably the worst fire tragedy in my memory," said Crossworthy, waiting for Fontana to fill in the blanks.

When Fontana did not, Truax said, "We had Ed Callahan scheduled for Saturday morning. He was going to explain what really happened at the Dead Horse Paint Company."

Crossworthy looked at Fontana. "How did you get along with Callahan?" Mo was massaging between his shoulder blades in small furious circles now; the more aggressive the questioning, the faster she worked. Fontana had a fleeting thought that her pacing and rhythm gave a clue to how she'd be in bed, though he was not inclined to explore that arena with her and was now sorry the thought had occurred to him.

"I got along with him just fine. You people sure that was Callahan?"

"It was his ID, and he's been reported missing by friends staying at the same hotel," said Crossworthy. "The medical examiner told us the height and the weight was about right, although it's hard to tell about the weight. He was burned pretty good. What we need to know from you this morning is how you two got along, and where you were yesterday afternoon for the hour preceding the fire."

"I'm a suspect? I *responded* to that fire."

"All we're asking is where you were."

"I was at the station. Before that I was hiking on Mount Gadd."

"In all this snow?"

"The best time."

"Anybody see you?"

"I was the only car in the lot."

"How long had you been back at the station when the alarm came in?"

"Fifteen minutes. Maybe less. I took a shower. Wait a minute. Mo, what are you doing here?"

"We're looking out for your best interests, Mac. Roger and I are."

It irritated Fontana that Roger had known about Callahan before he did. He had never liked Truax, partly because of the expressionless look he always had on his face, partly because Roger was one of those people who always thought he knew your job better than you knew it, and partly because no matter what platitudes Truax uttered to the contrary, his every thought rotated around himself. Fontana had never seen him express empathy for anybody else. In her own way, Mo Costigan was little better.

"Mo. Roger. I need lawyers, I'll call lawyers." He turned to Crossworthy. "Do they have to be here?"

"We thought you wanted them," said Crossworthy.

"We're on your side, Mac," said Truax. "Just tell them what happened."

Fontana looked from Mo to Roger Truax and back again. Truax's cheeks were beginning to turn pink. Mo was leaning over him like a barmaid who thought being friendly would get her a tip. "This is a police investigation, for Christsake."

"I'm your superior," said Mo. "If you're in trouble, I want to stand up for you."

"If I'm in trouble, I don't need you and Roger perched on phone poles waiting for blood."

"There's no need to get sarcastic," she said, as she and Truax left the room. "I don't like that tone in your voice."

"They talk you into that?" Fontana asked Crossworthy after they'd gone.

Not a man who readily admitted mistakes, Crossworthy stared at him silently. It was Jennifer Underhill who said, "When somebody on the payroll gets questioned, they need a supervisor in the room. They said it was city policy."

"Not that I ever heard. And Truax isn't my supervisor. You have to keep your eyes open around Mo. She tends to get a little economical with the truth."

"Let's get down to elbows and assholes," said Crossworthy. "Did you know Callahan was in the state?"

"Not until you told me."

"When was the last time you had any contact with him?"

"Like I said, two years ago. When I retired from the department."

"And what did that contact consist of?"

"When I cashed out, he was the man who took my badge and bus pass, and so forth."

"What sort of exchange did you have at that time?"

"He told me I'd make a damn fine chief in a small department."

"So you were on reasonably good terms?"

"He was being patronizing. He hated my guts. He thought it was funny I was going to be chief in a place he called Downstairs, USA."

"You think he might have been in the area because of you?"

"I didn't realize it before, but I think he was in the area for that conference."

"Rather ironic, isn't it? The odds against him dying in your district must be astronomical."

"You'll have to call the mayor back and ask her about the odds. She was the math major."

"Callahan didn't like you, but how did you feel about him?"

Fontana looked at each of the three investigators. "Callahan was a dangerous man to be around at a fire. Some people thought he tried to compensate for his small physical stature by being aggressive and foolhardy as a firefighter. He didn't tolerate timidity or caution. But he didn't seem to realize times had changed. The materials in the fires we're fighting these days are more dangerous. More unpredictable. The fires are hotter. There are toxins in the smoke—arsenic, hydrogen cyanide, nitrous oxide. And gases we've never even heard of. The equipment we have to wear weighs as much as a seven-day hiking pack. Callahan was a powerful man with powerful friends. What he said went. But he didn't get it."

"Would you say he frightened people?"

"Definitely."

"He frightened you?"

"He never had any power over me," Fontana said, wondering even as he said it why he was hedging the truth. It wasn't guilt. Could it have been vanity? Edgar Callahan had been a deputy chief during Fontana's last few years in the department, and he'd done everything possible to thwart Fontana's career. As an investigator Fontana had been monomaniacal in his dedication and, consequently, extremely successful. Through a combination of hard work, natural talent, intuition, and more than one instance of bald-faced luck, he'd managed to resolve several of the worst high-profile arson cases the city had ever seen. He'd gained a national reputation in the process. Some colleagues had said Callahan's antipathy toward Fontana increased with each of Fontana's successes.

Callahan was a powermonger who divided the world into two camps—one for those who were on his side and one for those who needed to be crushed. He kept a written list of enemies, a Nixon list, and did everything in his power to make the people on that list miserable.

"Did you know Callahan had family out here? A father?"

"I didn't know," said Fontana.

"You got anything else?" Crossworthy asked, looking at the two other investigators, who both shook their heads.

"Let me ask something, then," said Fontana. "You were up there all night, or what?"

"Just about," said Jennifer Underhill softly. "We dug up some big old space heaters from somewhere and had Puget Power bring up a generator truck, then melted the snow around the vehicle that wasn't already melted by the fire."

"What'd you find?"

Underhill looked at Crossworthy and said, "Another beer bottle. All the same brand. So far there are no prints off the bottles. Callahan's ID and wallet were intact. Credit cards. The whole shebang. As for the car, it was reported stolen in Seattle yesterday afternoon about two hours before the fire. Owner routinely left the keys in it while he warmed it up. Works in the shipyard over at Todd. Those were his keys in the trunk."

As they were leaving, Crossworthy came up to Fontana and said, "You really don't think it's a hell of a coincidence this chief you knew a coupla thousand miles away who hated your guts happens to end up dead on your doorstep?"

"I didn't say it wasn't a coincidence. But if you think about it, the I-Ninety corridor is a big place. It took us twenty-seven minutes to get to the location. I wouldn't exactly call that my backyard. Dirtbags are dumping bodies up there all the time."

"But you hated him."

"I never said that. He hated me."

Jennifer Underhill hung back when the others left, waiting until Truax's deep voice could be heard addressing Crossworthy downstairs. Her face was puffy and lined, her eye shadow darker than normal, as if she'd put it on in a bad light.

"Listen, Mac. This is my case, but Cross is going to be looking over my shoulder every step of the way. He doesn't really think you had anything to do with it. He just wanted to screw with you."

"I knew that. You got a cause of death yet?"

"To be honest with you, we still haven't figured out exactly what happened. Melting all that snow didn't do a bit of good. You were first on the scene. You have any guesses about what was going on?"

"One of my volunteers said it was a suicide, and as far as I know, she could be right."

"You don't really believe that?"

"No."

"What sort of man was Edgar Callahan?"

"You're not going to hear two different stories on it regardless of who you ask. He was a total egomaniac."

"What about his friends?"

"You find some friends, send me a telegram. I'd like to frame it."

5

PICTURES OF
CALLAHAN'S WIFE

I sit in the deputy's office waiting for Chief Callahan. It is late afternoon and I look down at the sunshine in the windy downtown street, trying not to think about it but wondering why I've been called in. The secretary outside the door is missing and so is Callahan. When I arrive, I hear Callahan's voice down the hall, then some flunky tells me to go in and wait.

"Right in there, Captain Fontana."

Callahan's desk is loaded with paperwork, folders, notes, letters, cell phones, radios, a melted helmet—his probably; he wouldn't let a prize like that get away. I wonder if this is the helmet he was wearing thirteen years earlier at a ship fire in the harbor when several thousand volts of electricity surged through Callahan and two others. The others were killed, but for some reason Callahan managed to pull through with only minimal loss of function in one arm. Pundits claim the near-fatal jolt is the reason he is so mean, but Callahan has always been mean.

Along the edge of the desk are pictures—several of them looking as if they are about to get bumped off in favor of paperwork—pictures of his wife, a woman in her late forties who has lost only a bit of her bloom. The pictures are lined up in sequence, the first few of her as a teenager, the latter at her present age. It is a loving touch, the array of photos as well as the order of them, and it seems out of character for Callahan.

As I look at the desk, I recall that Callahan had a child at one time but something happened. I cannot remember what. There are no photos of a child. If there had been a death in the family, surely I would have remembered.

My week has been bad, and I am determined not to let Callahan make it worse. Callahan is sitting in for the chief of the department and he is notorious for rearranging things while sitting in, almost as notorious as the chief is for not repairing the snafus Callahan creates in his absence. Callahan likes to settle scores when the chief is out of town. Nobody quite knows why the chief lets him, though the current theory is that he's too close to retirement to care.

My recent headaches have been so severe I fear I'll have a cerebral vascular accident on the street, driving the car, in the tub where I might drown. I hope I'm too young for a CVA, but who can be sure?

The prosecutors have decided not to file charges over the Sackrison affair, and now, when the threat of a prison sentence no longer dangles over me, there's nothing Callahan can do to make me sweat. I've been sweating.

Callahan doesn't like me but I don't know exactly why. It could be any of a dozen offenses, because Callahan has a shit list as long as your arm, and once you get on his list, there is no getting off. People have retired from the department because they were on this list: firefighters, officers, even another chief. Callahan goes out of his way to dismantle careers. Knowing how vindictive he can be, firemen get spooked at the most innocent phone call from him. In this, Callahan glories. He is the king, intimidation his scepter.

Clearly, Callahan's plan now is to let me sit here and wait in the hope it will make me anxious, to let me stew over why I've been called in. I don't mind. Periods of enforced idleness, even short ones laced with tension, have been the only relaxation I've been offered recently. I've come to savor them.

The room is small, the desk battered. I drag the hard wooden bench meant for visitors closer to the window so that I can feel the sunlight on the back of my neck. After a while I realize the window is open a crack, a soft breeze perfuming the room with the musky smell of burning leaves and autumn.

My life in the past two weeks has been a muddle. There is the guilt over having killed. There is the media portraying me as an ogre. There are strangers slapping me on the back on the street, the anonymous and unwanted congratulations. There are those who, strangers too, when they realize who I am, curse me.

Again and again, I replay the night in question.

It becomes a recurring dream that awakens me in the predawn hours with its intensity and then returns in daytime as an obsession I cannot shake, a pattern that causes me to miss freeway exits, elevator floors, telephone connections. Feeling the sun on the back of my head and neck, I cross my legs and notice my socks are mismatched.

Sackrison.

The papers are full of it. Hazel Sackrison, her prison term, her life history, her death.

Five years ago we proved she routinely punished her children with a cigarette lighter. We had photos of the burn marks; testimony from the neighbors as well as from a former boyfriend; affidavits from doctors, nurses, ambulance drivers. But she was poor and pitiful and had a face full of self-loathing, and it must have fooled somebody because she was sentenced to five years, released in three, pregnant when she walked out the gates, although how she'd managed that was anybody's guess. Her other children were in foster homes and would remain in foster homes, but Hazel is free to bear more children until the cows come home. She told me that in so many words before they took her to court.

The baby is almost eighteen months old before we begin to get calls. The neighbors hear screams. They call the Child Protective Agency, but the folks there are overworked and underzealous, and Hazel Sackrison talks her way out of trouble on their first visit. Her prison record goes unnoted. The baby appears to be healthy and cared-for and fat, and after all, they cannot watch her day and night.

I can.

I abandon my own family, neglect my other duties, and huddle in a neighbor's apartment while the neighbor is at work. I sometimes sit for eighteen hours a day. I sit until the neighbor is ready for bed and asks me to leave. In the morning before dawn, I am back.

Sipping cocoa and reading novels, I sit and listen to the walls with a stethoscope, and finally one evening my vigil is rewarded when a yelp comes from next door, a yelp that quickly turns into a mother's enraged shouting and then worse. My skin crawls as I race for the door.

"That's it," says Mrs. MacCauley, whose apartment I have been using. "Listen. What is she doing to the poor child? I told you about this."

I am blind with rage. I've already sent this woman to prison once. I race into the hall and bang on the door, finding that Hazel Sackrison has left it unlocked.

The litter-strewn apartment is filled floor to ceiling with screaming. I am shouting at Sackrison, but Sackrison is wild-eyed and manic. You can see it in her bulging eyes. The way her body is stiff and jerky. But most of all you can see it in the way Sackrison tosses her child carelessly across the room and moves on me with a ten-inch knife.

She knows who I am.

She knows I am the man who investigated her eight-year-old boy because he was setting fires at school, and she knows I am the one who took her children away.

She comes at me with the knife in two hands raised over her head, yipping, and as she moves forward, I see she is pregnant once more, maybe five months along. What is the message here, I wonder? That she can produce them faster than we can rescue them?

I grab her wrists and wrestle with her, but she gets a hand free and claws at my face, bites my thumb trying to get her knife-hand loose from my grip, and before I know it I have slugged her across the side of the head with an open palm. She kicks me in the shins. She screams. I might as well be trying to drag a wildcat around. The other neighbors are in the doorway thinking I am a boyfriend gone wacko.

The burner on the electric stove is still orange-hot, and I know what she was doing with it. And suddenly, as Sackrison tries repeatedly to kick me in the testicles, she goes down. I have only hit her once, but down she goes, maybe twenty seconds after the slap. When I remove the knife from her fist, she offers no resistance.

We wait for the police and for the medical people who will attend the child and perhaps the mother. After a while, somebody realizes Sackrison is not breathing. It occurs to me that she went down more like a sack of sand falling out of a wheelbarrow than a fainting woman. Bystanders begin CPR. Forty minutes later she is pronounced dead.

She has drugs in her system—cocaine—but the cause of death is never fully determined. The press hints there is some sort of cover-up, but the coroner's office has no reason to shield me.

I am thinking about Sackrison when Chief Callahan bursts into the office on a blast of lukewarm air and the kind of synthetic bonhomie tyrants seem able to summon up for social occasions. "How you doin' there, Captain Fontana? You see that sun out there? Hell of a day. Hell of a day."

"Yes, it is."

Callahan sits behind the bales of paperwork on his desk and toys with the half-melted helmet. He eyes me over the helmet, which he holds high enough that it acts as a mask, only the top portion of his ruddy face visible. Callahan is five-six, has spindly arms and legs and a potbelly, pale-blue eyes, blond hair, what's left of it. He was probably good-looking as a young man, but by now his intensity and the depth of his distaste for humanity have been stamped into his features so that his nose is pinched and his forehead permanently furrowed, and there is something about his eyes, about the way he looks at you, that is just plain mean. Tiny and cold, his eyes seem to belong on a jackal.

"Do you know why I've called you here?" Callahan asks.

"No."

"You don't know why?"

"No."

"Do you think you're doing a good job in the Fire Investigation Division?"

"I do. Yes."

"Why do you think so?"

I begin to itemize the reasons. I know this is important so I think it through carefully and do my level best to put up an argument that is convincing. I know Callahan is thinking about transferring me. Transfers are Callahan's weapon of choice. When I am finished, Callahan tosses off a remark, having smiled and nodded throughout my spiel, and I realize he hasn't listened to a word I've said.

"Do you think beating a woman to death is doing a good job?" he says.

"I've been exonerated in the Sackrison case."

"Because they decided not to file charges? Not filing charges is a different matter from being exonerated. A different matter entirely."

I know where this is headed, and I'm not happy about it. "The prosecu-

tor cleared me. The police department cleared me. The fire department cleared me."

"I've been thinking about a new role for you." Callahan puts the helmet down and stares intently. I have seen this look before. It is the one he uses to melt subordinates into submission. People grovel before this look. "How would you like to work out at Station Sixty-one for a spell?"

"Sixty-one?"

"I think it would be good for you."

"Sixty-one's a rest home. Besides, Operations doesn't need me. Fire Investigation needs me. They're short of people and have been for a long time."

"I would think after your . . . adventure . . . you'd be ready for a quiet little station. You don't think some time out at Station Sixty-one might not do you some good?"

I do not answer.

After a long pause, Callahan says, "Actually, I haven't made a decision yet. Maybe you can convince me one way or the other."

I think about this for a while. I'm not sure I trust Callahan enough to spill my guts, but I don't want to leave the unit either. This is Callahan's invitation to grovel, and we both know it. I consider the options, gather up my resources, and begin.

"Chief, all I know is that I belong in Fire Investigation. I've gotten twelve commendations in the past four years. Three times I've been loaned out to other cities. There are people who are born to do certain things. I was born to do this. It's a rare occasion when a man finds the job he was born to. I'm asking you . . . I'm pleading with you to keep me in the unit."

"I see. Is there anything you want to add?"

"If you're thinking about the fire department, you know I'll serve the department better where I am. I wouldn't make much of an officer in Operations."

Callahan makes a big show of thinking over what I've said. He rises and walks deliberately to the door. I get up and walk with him. Callahan drapes an arm across my shoulder as if he likes me. He smells of cologne and soap and power, which all seem to mingle perfectly with the smell of burning leaves filtering into the room. "Tell you what I'm going to do. I'm going to think about this overnight. I'll make my decision in the morning. But you've put up a good argument. You've put up a jim-dandy."

As I leave, Callahan alludes to an incident that took place three days after Sackrison's death—in the midst of the subsequent media barrage, at a time when I was sleeping three hours a night, if that. Callahan had phoned asking for an update on the proceedings—it was my first contact with him since the incident—asking me to write a private report for him detailing everything that had happened as well as everything that had been said to me or by me in those three days. I calculated it was going to take two weeks to remember all of it and maybe another week to write it down. It was a report for his eyes only. I might have hung up on him. It was hard to remember for certain. I certainly didn't write the report.

A day later a transfer letter arrives at my home, the date on the letter conspicuously two days before the meeting with Callahan. I am to work at Station 61.

6

PHOTOS
IN A PLAIN
WHITE ENVELOPE

Looking for bad guys, Satan pushed his nose through the venetian blinds at the front of the fire station and let out a low growl. Fontana had been edgy recently because someone had been stalking him, and the German shepherd had taken it upon himself to personally look after Fontana's well-being.

H. C. Bailey, the police officer Fontana had spoken to about the stalker, had run the plate number and assured him she would take care of things. Now, after several days with no sign of either the woman stalking him or the Chevy Blazer she had been driving, Fontana felt somewhat foolish.

Though he would never have admitted it, having a female police officer handle the problem had made him feel somewhat emasculated, and now he was determined not to ask H. C. Bailey what happened. Besides, he had other things on his mind.

By Wednesday afternoon, not yet twenty-four hours after the discovery of Edgar Callahan's body, Fontana had already answered half a dozen phone calls from individuals still working in his old fire department back east. Word was spreading like a cold in a kindergarten.

The callers had received news of the events in Washington State from a variety of sources. It occurred to Fontana that to someone living east of the Mississippi, Seattle and Staircase were virtually the same place, and Denny Creek, twenty miles east of Staircase, might as well be the closet in Fontana's bedroom.

Carver, an old friend of Fontana's and currently a battalion chief in his former department, had posed the question Fontana knew everybody would be asking: "How could that p-p-p-possibly have happened, M-M-Mac? Out there right in your b-b-b-baili-wick? Are you sure you didn't have any c-c-c-contact with him? Maybe he was t-t-t-trying to get together with you. Maybe he called and you forgot."

"Or maybe I fried his ass and it slipped my mind? Let me ransack my brain for a minute here. No. I don't remember fry-ing him."

"Hell, n-n-n-no. That's not what I m-m-m-meant and you know it. I'm n-n-n-not . . . I never should have opened my b-b-b-big mouth. I only called to say people are talking. Anyway, M-M-Mac. I hope you g-g-g-get it all sorted out."

"It's not anything for me to sort out. All we did was respond to a call and put out the damn fire. I was as surprised as anybody to find out who it was."

"Maybe so, but people around here are t-t-t-talking. After all, Callahan was going to be appointed department chief in t-t-t-two weeks. If you're not already figuring out what happened, maybe you b-b-b-better be."

"I'm not in investigation anymore, Carver. I run a small-town department and my hands are full. Our mayor's screwier than a pubic hair. Our safety director wants my job so badly he's already had personalized stationery made up. This is just a nuisance."

"N-n-n-nuisance or not, if this never gets solved, everybody in t-t-t-town here's going to th-th-th-think you did it."

"Are you kidding me?"

"Th-th-that's what they're going to th-th-th-think, Mac."

"I suppose it *was* a hell of a coincidence."

"Anyway, maybe we'll see you on S-S-S-Saturday."

"What's on Saturday?"

"The funeral. In Seattle in some big church there. A bunch of us g-g-g-guys are flying out to p-p-p-p-pay our respects. The union's paying for it."

■

Late that afternoon Fontana was sitting in his dark office thinking about Callahan's death when Lieutenant Pierpont knocked. "Chief?"

"Yeah. Come on in." When Pierpont turned the lights on, Fontana blinked.

"Sorry," said Pierpont. "You takin' a nap?"

"I was thinking. What's up?" Fontana had his swivel chair tipped back as far as it would go without capsizing, his feet crossed on the corner of his desk.

Pierpont glanced around the office as if to confirm or deny Fontana's statement. Deliberating in the dark wasn't anything Pierpont engaged in, and judging by the look on his face, he didn't recall Fontana having done it before either.

Kingsley Pierpont was wiry and of medium build, his hair straightened and slicked back in a way most blacks had abandoned years ago. His uniforms were immaculate, starched and pressed, and his shirts probably would have stood up on their own. He'd been having woman troubles recently, and Fontana assumed he'd come to talk about them.

Instead, Pierpont handed him a white envelope and sat down in a nearby chair while Fontana took out eleven snapshots. They seemed to have been taken at a party, because aside from the main subject in each shot, there were only arms and legs and feet, no other faces. The focal point, in the first few pictures, was a semi-clothed woman, and then in the last few, a naked woman. It was the same woman, Heather Minerich, their probationary firefighter.

"Christ on a crutch. Where'd you get these?" said Fontana.

"I caught one of the volunteers with 'em."

"Which one?"

"Hawkins."

"Where'd he get them?"

"He said he got 'em from Valenzuela."

"And where'd he get them?"

"I haven't talked to him yet, but Hawkins said Valenzuela found 'em laying around Pritchard's house after that party last week. You go to that?"

"I'm not much for parties."

"Me neither. I hear there was a bunch of volunteers there. Pritchard and those others. They drink pretty heavy."

Jim Hawkins was twenty-one, short, red-haired, and somewhat excitable. He wanted to be a firefighter about twelve times worse than Fontana had ever wanted it, which was a lot. He lived at home with his mother and drove a Mustang with a souped-up engine and a rusted-out muffler.

Fontana went through the photos in order. Nobody was identifiable except Heather Minerich, who was all too identifiable, looking drunkenly pleased with all the attention she must have been getting. In one snapshot, she was handing her bra to somebody just beyond the range of the camera.

"What'd they do, get her drunk and take these pictures?" Fontana asked.

"I don't know anything about it. I just thought you should have 'em."

"What am I supposed to do with them?"

"I don't know, Chief. I didn't know what to do with 'em, either. All I know is I don't want Hawkins passing 'em around. Maybe you should talk to Hawkins. And Heather."

"And say what, exactly?"

"I don't know. Isn't there something in some supervision manual somewhere tells you how to handle a situation like this?"

"If there is, I haven't run across it. How's she doing?"

"Good. She's doing good. She gets along with everybody, 'cept that attitude of hers comes out once in a while. She can drive a rig now. But I still don't trust her at a fire. You know I had that experience where she backed out on me."

"She had an explanation."

"And I told you what I thought of her explanation. I ain't seen nothing to convince me it won't happen again."

"What's she got left on her probationary period? Five months?"

"Four. If we don't have any more fires, she'll probably make it. I see her back out again, I'm going to recommend termination. In the meantime—"

"Let me think it over. You sure you don't recognize any of these anonymous hands or feet?"

"That sofa there looks like the one in Hawkins's mother's living room."

"I thought he said the party was at Pritchard's."

"He did."

"Lieutenant, what am I ever going to do with this?"

Pierpont got up and went to the door. "I'm just glad it's not my problem."

"What did Hawkins say when you confronted him about it?"

"He said, and I quote, 'Nice tits.' "

"Oh, dear. What'd he say about having the pictures?"

"Hawkins thinks she's a lesbian trying to prove she isn't. If she wore some feminine clothes outside of work once in a while instead of those baggy old coveralls and clodhopper boots, she wouldn't be half bad, don't you think?"

"I'm trying not to think about it."

When Pierpont left, Fontana put the photographs back in order, as there was clearly a specific order, and slipped them all into the envelope. He thought about locking them up somewhere in the station, but the only secure location he could think of was his personal clothing locker, and he didn't want them in there. For want of a better place, he put the envelope in his shirt pocket.

Fontana was having coffee with the arriving night crew when H. C. Bailey came in and signaled with a tip of her head that she wanted to talk in his office. Her Sam Browne belt jangled as she closed the door behind them and gave him a stern look. A police officer for less than three years, Bailey was short, bull-jawed, feisty, and meticulous in her work. Her hair was cut short, probably at home, the uneven bangs lying across her brow like a broken comb. She said, "You know somebody named Grace Teller?"

"I don't believe so."

"Think about it. Grace Teller."

"No."

"She's the ditz was following you. She said for five days. Are you sure you don't know her?"

"Pretty sure."

"You know *anybody* in the San Francisco Bay area?"

"Not anybody named Teller."

"She sure knew a lot about you. Knew where you were from, that you were a firefighter back east, that you used to be a captain back there. She knows where you live. Blah, blah, blah. She probably knows where your kid goes to school."

"Five days? Why was she following me?"

"She wouldn't say, and I never figured it out. I wanted to run her in. Believe me, I wanted to run her in. But it wouldn't have stuck. You see her again, though, you call me. She's bad news."

"Is that all you're going to tell me?"

H. C. Bailey sighed. "Here's what I did. I ran her plates, got her name, and picked her up right here on Staircase Way. I'm in a county car with a light bar, so she knows I'm following her. She takes me to Mercer Island and all over Bellevue. Cool as a cucumber. I finally pull her over on the old highway here as she's coming back into town. Mind you, I've been tailing her for over forty-five minutes, and it's all a wild-goose chase. I pull her over in front of the lumberyard that burned down last summer, and this gal, she's got her license in her hand as I approach, both palms open and on the steering wheel like she's been through the drill a million times."

"That or watched a lot of cop shows."

"At first she denies she's been tailing you. Then she wants to know if you sicced me onto her. Wants to know if I know you, blah, blah, blah. She's curious about you, and she has a hard time concealing it even when she's talking to a cop who is about to roust her."

"Grace Teller," said Fontana. "The name doesn't ring a bell. I got a pretty good look at her the other day. I didn't know her."

"After I'd talked to her awhile, I could see she was angling for any information she could get, so I pretended I knew you real well."

"I only spotted her twice. She was following me in Issaquah.

Followed me all the way back here. A half hour later, she's parked down the street from the station. And the next day, too."

"Okay. So I call some people in Oakland where her driver's license says she lives and I get transferred around and pretty soon I'm talking to some detective in Robbery/Homicide who wants to know what she's been up to. It seems that along with the federal government they were keeping pretty close tabs on a little group she belonged to called the Army of Righteousness, linked to a couple of bombings on the East Coast and fifteen to twenty bank robberies in the Midwest which they pulled off to fund their terrorism. The feds believe there were twelve hard-core members. Grace Teller was one of them.

"We're talking soldiers. Trained with rifles, pistols, bayonets, explosives. Stay away from her, Mac. A former member of the group—an informer—and his whole family went up in a gas explosion in their home two years ago. They never brought anybody to trial."

"The Army of Righteousness?"

"They've picked up Teller twice on gun charges. They thought they had enough to charge her with bank robbery once, but the federal prosecutors wouldn't go along with it. In the meantime, maybe a year ago, she checks out of the group. Ends up in a clinic for alcoholics and recovering drug addicts in Wisconsin. That's the last anybody in the Bay area hears about her until now."

"So this terrorist group might be planning something up here?"

"They actually don't think Teller's with the group any longer."

"So why is she following me?"

"You figure it out, you give me a buzz. By the way, what's that in the envelope?"

"This?" Fontana glanced down at the envelope in his shirt pocket.

"You keep touching it. I thought maybe you had a bunch of cash in there. It's not a good idea to carry a lot of cash around these days."

"It's not cash."

"Good. 'Cause that could spell trouble."

7

EVERYBODY ALWAYS KNEW MARY ANN WAS SEXIER THAN GINGER

Thursday night after supper Fontana and Brendan played four rounds of crazy eights and then went next door to Mary's, where Brendan was to spend the night, Brendan clasping a rolled sleeping bag in his arms, chattering like a parrot as they traipsed along the short path through the shrubbery and trees between the two houses. "Mac, is there such a thing as spontaneous human combustion?"

"Where did you hear about that?"

"Bradford's great-uncle burned up when Bradford's dad was ten. But his clothes didn't catch fire. He was just sitting in his rocking chair and he burned up. They said even the chair didn't burn. Do you think that's true?"

"No. It's an urban legend."

"Bradford's dad said it happened."

"If Bradford's great-uncle burned up, it was caused by a cigarette or some other source of ignition. This is pretty ghoulish stuff for us to be talking about, don't you think?"

"Are you kidding me? We've been talking about Bradford's great-uncle at school all year. Are you sure it couldn't have happened? Bradford said he was sitting in his rocker reading about Uganda in a *National Geographic* and just burst into flames."

"It didn't happen. People don't just burn up. Why are you worried about this?"

"I'm not worried. I was just thinking. One of the kids at school said that was your old boss who got burned up in the mountains."

"I guess I should have told you about it myself. He was a chief I used to know. We found him up by Denny Creek. But it wasn't spontaneous human combustion."

"It wasn't?"

"No." They were outside Mary's door now, the site of many polished-off conversations.

"Did it hurt when he died?"

"Actually, it probably did."

"Was he a mean guy?"

"Why do you ask that?"

"On TV when somebody dies and it hurts, he's usually a mean guy."

"That's a pretty good observation. Yeah, I guess you could say old Chief Callahan was a mean guy."

After narrowly escaping a house fire last summer that had taken the life of Mary's elderly mother, Brendan had become fascinated by the thought of dying in a fire. It didn't help that he had been unusually close to the old woman or that her death had come on the heels of his own mother's demise a year and a half earlier. To a nine-year-old who'd already been through such a tunnel of grief, it must have seemed as if the chances of somebody nearby dying a violent death were right up there with the chances of getting your shoes wet on the way to school.

Nor did it help that Fontana had recently gotten into some well-publicized scrapes that might have ended his own life, scrapes that *had* ended the lives of others.

At the door of Mary's house, Fontana ruffled his son's hair, pulled the sleeping bag out of his arms, and hugged him. If this hadn't been Sally Culpepper's last few days in town, he would have trotted right back home with Brendan and canceled the evening, but Sally was leaving for Europe soon and he wouldn't be seeing her for some time.

On the drive to Sally's, Fontana was plagued with second thoughts, some of which had to do with his son and some of which had to do with Sally's tone of voice when she arranged this rendezvous. He pulled his rattletrap truck up to Sally's wrought-iron gate. Sally must have been at the control panel inside the front door of the huge white colonial because the gate swung open immediately. He parked in the garage, where meandering tourists and star-seeking reporters would not see the truck, pushed the button to close the door, and took the flagstone path behind the garage complex to the back door.

Sally slid the patio door open and gave Fontana more of a hug than he'd expected, squeezing him so tightly he almost fell over backward into the rain. He felt the ridged muscle along her back under his cool palms.

Several years earlier, under the name of Aimee Lee, Sally Culpepper had become a cult figure in the movies. Then she disappeared for two years, only to be discovered hiding in Staircase. The "discovery" came about last summer, and for a month afterward the town was inundated with tabloid reporters and gawkers. Sally had been so overwhelmed at the attention her film career had sparked, so desirous of anonymity, so upset about what had been written about her, that she'd skulked around Staircase in a disguise. Celebrity dogged her, and she wasn't sure whether to feed the animal or poison it.

Fontana thought her affection for him flowed from the fact that he'd asked her to go dancing at the Bedouin when she was running around in one of her big-woman disguises, long before he knew who she really was. Recently, to Fontana's bewilderment, she'd decided to come out of retirement and do another film, this one in Spain. She'd already been on one junket to Europe and was to leave again after the weekend for an undetermined period of time.

Sally gave him a light kiss on the cheek and walked across the kitchen to where she'd been preparing avocado dip in a small bowl. A large bag of tortilla chips sat nearby. "I know you're a sucker for chips and dip, so I found a recipe last week in Pamplona I thought you might like. I've made way too much."

"Try me."

They settled in the living room, the house quiet except for the wind howling in the trees in the back and some low music, Kenny G., oozing from hidden speakers. Fontana wouldn't have the music in his house, but it seemed to fit the white carpets, the off-white furnishings, the woman. Visible from the east and north rooms, the Snoqualmie River raged, the result of a warm front that had moved in that afternoon, dumping rain onto the snow that had been accumulating in the mountains. If Fontana had thought of it earlier, he would have driven Brendan five miles downriver and they would have experienced the spectacle of Snoqualmie Falls as the river crested, would have felt the ground rumbling beneath their feet and been drenched by the torrential spray that the falls produced when the river was at flood stage.

Sally sat on the sofa next to him, sipping a beer. She was almost uncomfortably close, smelling of soap and wildflowers and looking exactly like a movie star, her hair swept back, her makeup not at all subtle. She wore black toreador pants and an aqua V-necked sweater as thin as tissue.

"I'm going to miss you," she said. "Four weeks. Maybe six."

"You'd think they would have a shooting schedule. You'd think they'd know."

"That's not how Vladislav works. That's why he's such a great artist."

"And why you wanted to work with him?"

"I guess. I really don't know why I took the offer."

"I thought Mother Dolores was your idol."

"She still is. I only wish I could be as certain about life as she was."

On the wall in Sally's front hallway was a picture of the actress Dolores Hart. She'd starred in *Where the Boys Are* and other features, yet, when she was twenty-four, she gave up Hollywood and moved to Connecticut, where she took holy vows and became a Benedictine nun. Sally had spoken often and fondly of Hart, and now, despite swearing off movies forever, Sally had taken on a role. He wondered if she didn't admire Hart for a strength she herself did not possess. Not that it was necessarily a sign of strength to walk away from a career, even a career as mired in tabloid harassment as hers had been; it *was* a strength, however, to know one's own mind and to follow it.

"So if this film turns out, what next? Are you going to move back to L.A.?"

"I would never move back to L.A."

"What about more movies?"

"I'll just wait and see."

As they spoke, there was a moment when they looked at each other and they both knew they were thinking the same thing. Fontana put his beer on the table behind the sofa and leaned over and kissed her. It was the first real kiss they'd ever shared, and she seemed as eager for it as he, though not as surprised— in fact, not surprised at all. When she'd called the night before, he'd sensed something was different. He hadn't guessed it was this until he'd come into the house and seen the look in her eyes.

"Sally. I'm not sure—" She moved against him and they kissed again. He was thinking about all the reasons for not doing what they were going to do. He'd been celibate for a while now, and he'd found there was a certain reasonableness as well as a natural-ness to it. He couldn't explain it exactly, but it had something to do with single fatherhood, with the unresolved emotions sur-rounding the death of his wife, with a million and one guilty thoughts. Since Linda's death he'd had several quick trysts and they'd all felt as wrong as they could feel, as if they were almost illicit. In fact, this felt wrong, too—a felony compared with the other misdemeanors—largely because Sally was such a good friend that the possibility of her replacing Linda was greater.

In the end, they made love in her bed upstairs like people who knew what they were doing, like people who'd made plans.

"I was nervous," said Sally afterward. "I didn't know if you would want to."

"And now you don't respect me? I knew this was going to happen."

She laughed. "I didn't say that. Are you sorry?"

"I'd have to be without any nerves in my body to be sorry."

After a long silence, Sally put a warm palm on his chest and said, "I'm worried about Spain."

"You'll be fine. You'll be spectacular."

"It's not the role I'm thinking about. The movie's going to be okay. But I've found this life here. I have this . . . I don't know what to call it . . . this serenity, this certainty about who I am . . . my place in the universe . . . at least I *had* it. And then Vladislav's offer came along, and before I knew what I was doing I told them I'd take it."

"You can always back out."

"Not really, I can't. That would be quite unprofessional. Besides, I've signed a contract."

For the first time Fontana realized how frightened Sally was, not only of her career and the fame that had been hounding her the past few years, but of everyday life. In fact, now that he thought about it, fear seemed to be one of her major characteristics, and not unwarranted, considering what she'd been through. There had been troubles with her son, who was now out of state with a relative until Sally would return from Spain. The constant fusillades of malicious gossip in the tabloids had come close to driving her nuts. Her mother had died of a heart attack after an erroneous report of Sally's death. Now Sally was embarking on a new course, or reembarking on an old one, refashioning a life she thought had been safely tucked into a book of memories.

She whispered, "I'm going to call you every night."

"From Spain?"

"Yup."

"What time?"

"That's a good question. I didn't call the West Coast when I was there last time, so I don't know what time."

"It doesn't matter. I'll carry the phone around with me. I'll sleep with it under the covers."

She laughed, draped a leg across his hips, and mussed his hair. "That sounds cozy. Under the covers with you."

"That's where you are now."

"It's where I'd like to be next week, too. If I don't call, will you be disappointed?"

"Heck, no. I can get a sexy voice any time I want. I've got a whole sheet of nine-hundred numbers in my wallet."

"Don't tease. I need to know somebody's waiting."

"There's no doubt about it, darlin'. Besides, I'll need somebody to help take my mind off my problems."

"That's right. You found a body up by the pass. Tell me about it. He was your superior at one time?"

"He outranked me. He was never my superior."

"It was like that?"

"It was exactly like that." He told her about the car fire, about his prior associations with Edgar Callahan. "I don't know what it was about the man, but he led this charmed life. They said when he was a kid he got washed down a storm drain somewhere and came out two miles away saying he wanted to do it again. In the department he and two others had sixteen thousand volts of electricity go through them. He got up and walked away from it. The other guys were toast. Right before I left the department, he made some mistakes at a pretty big fire where nine firefighters ended up dying."

"That must have been pretty traumatic."

"For the whole department. Any other chief, that would have been the capper on his career. Not Callahan. Even though he denied it, people knew he'd screwed up, but it didn't seem to make a bit of difference to the power structure. He led a charmed life."

"Until two nights ago."

"Right."

"The television said because he had family here there would be two services, one in Seattle and one back east. If you're going to the one here, I'd like to tag along."

"You sure? You might be recognized."

"I don't care. I want to be with you."

"I would like that." Fontana rolled over and stared at the ceiling. "I think chewing out people in public was Callahan's favorite hobby."

"He ever chew you out in public?"

"Me? Yeah. Once."

"What happened?"

"Not much."

"I take it you're not sorry he died."

"You're always sorry when somebody dies, even a horse's ass."

8

A LITTLE LOWER
THAN THE ANGELS

As Fontana had grown older and as more friends and acquaintances had passed on, he came to realize that funerals performed a necessary function both for the dead and for the living, and though he continued to dislike them, he'd grown to appreciate what they accomplished.

He was hoping this funeral would bring him some peace, because the more he thought about Callahan's death, the more it disturbed him. It seemed almost a taunt for someone to have murdered the man where Fontana might find him—a taunt and a challenge. Add that to the woman who'd been stalking him last week, and he felt more than a little uneasy.

Though he genuinely preferred his private vehicle, the old fire chief's truck (a 1960, titty-pink Carryall with twenty-seven bullet holes in it, which he'd bought from the city for two hundred dollars and patched up), it was out of a sense of propriety that he chose the official chief's Suburban for the funeral.

When he and Brendan swung into her circular drive, Sally came out and exchanged cheery greetings. Fontana hadn't thought it wise to bring either Brendan or Satan, but he couldn't get a sitter, and both boy and dog had begged to come so dramatically that they were now sitting in back together.

Once in Seattle, Fontana declined Sally's offer to check a map and consequently ended up taking a couple of extra loops around Volunteer Park before zeroing in on the Episcopal church on Tenth Avenue East. Mindful of ego and etiquette, Sally said nothing more about the map.

Though they'd spoken on the phone, Fontana hadn't seen Sally since midnight Thursday when, despite her expressed wish for him to stay the night, he dressed and drove home in the rain. He hadn't been single long enough nor had he survived enough relationships as an unmarried man to have spent much time thinking through all the guidelines of sexual protocol, but he remembered once hearing somebody in a fire station talking about the distinction between going home in the middle of the night and lingering until morning; and lingering until morning, he recalled, had some sort of matrimonial stigma attached. It wasn't so much that he didn't want to commit as it was that when he did commit, he wanted to do it in a way that was other than an accident.

It was interesting, he thought, to see Sally again, for he realized their relationship had turned a corner, yet, as if by mutual agreement, neither of them gave any outward sign. Each of them smiled politely across the space between their seats.

Fontana wore a black wool chief's uniform he'd bought for formal occasions. Sally was in a dark suit. Her hair was long and dropped about her head in a manner that hid everything but the front plane of her face. He noticed a pair of large eyeglasses; she rarely left the house without some implement to hinder recognition.

Sally turned to the boy, who had on a blue blazer and a bow tie, looking with his hair slicked back as fresh as if he'd just popped out of a Christmas package, and commented on how nicely he was dressed. Brendan tried to pretend he didn't much care. It was at times like this that Fontana wished Linda were still alive to see him. In fact, he had been thinking a lot about Linda lately, imagining it had something to do with his getting serious about Sally. The other women he'd been with in the past two years hadn't made him think about Linda at all, and now that he was with one who did, it made him realize why he'd chosen the others.

"It's sunny," Sally said.

"Yes. It's just like Callahan to order up nice weather for his last day above ground."

"You, uh . . . you okay, Mac?"

"Sure."

"Funerals bum me out, too. Even when I didn't know the person." It wasn't the funeral, though. He was still thinking about Linda.

Seattle's weather had indeed cleared, the rain clouds dispersing in a whirl of midmorning cumulus and sunshine. Looking like a fuzzy zipper, a contrail ran through the largest patch of blue to the south.

Fontana parked in back of the enormous Episcopal church, let Satan out to stretch and run, then left him in the vehicle while the three of them went around to the front and mingled.

All in all, two hundred fire service personnel stood in front of the church, columns of intimidated civilians snaking through the uniforms and feeding directly into the church, where they waited to be seated by ushers in black uniforms and white gloves. Fontana recognized Seattle fire officials, as well as officers from the county departments, a gaggle of police officers, and dozens of union officials and firefighters from his old department. Having a national conference in town had bloated the attendance figures. That would have pleased Callahan, who, had he been able, surely would have taken a head count.

A slab of Lake Union was visible, glittering through the bare trees down the back side of the hill. The freeway at the bottom of the hillside could be heard but not seen. It was a beautiful day. Because there would be another service back home, Fontana was surprised to see as many old pals as he did, even though he realized they were all in town for the conference. Maybe there were going to be door prizes.

Waiting near the entrance and looking properly reverent was

a small group of bagpipe players in kilts, their insignia identifying them as being from a British Columbia department. There would come a point when they would be the center of attention and they knew it.

Fontana greeted a group of chief officers from his old department, introduced them to Brendan and to Sally, who was calling herself, "Dolores. Dolores Hart." Her funny spectacles, the way she worked her mouth when she spoke, and the change in the pitch of her voice had Brendan in stitches.

Accompanied by his ex-wife, Kingsley Pierpont suddenly showed up alongside Fontana. "We better get in there," said Pierpont. "The place is going to be bustin' out like a box of ripe melons."

"Hey, Captain! Captain!"

The call came from a man standing alone near a large maple. "Captain?" He wore leather pants and a scruffy denim vest. His hair was in a ponytail, he had large dark circles under his eyes, and didn't seem to mind in the least that his attire didn't suit the occasion.

"Why don't you all go find seats?" said Fontana, looking at Sally.

While the others went inside, Brendan shyly alongside Sally, Fontana walked across to the man in the ponytail. "Randy," he said, extending his hand. "What are you doing here?"

"We live in Seattle now. We've been house-sitting while we look for a place of our own."

"I didn't know you'd quit the department."

"Oh, hell yeah. Haven't you been following my book? I vested a year ago. Set for life. In fact, they've got me contracted to write two more of those suckers. 'Course, they won't be like *Bagpipe City*, but what the hey. They pony up the cabbage, I pony up the manuscripts."

Randy Knutson had been a firefighter on Fontana's crew for a short time back east. A year after the most disastrous public safety tragedy in their city's history, the Dead Horse Paint Company fire, Knutson had published a book about it. The book was heralded in the press, championed by the fire service trade magazines, and spotlighted in *Time* and other national publications.

Randy had been a gifted firefighter whose Achilles' heel was his total lack of ambition. He would stay up late at night and then the next day at the station spend all day trying to sneak a few winks in a chair, on a creeper under the rig, or even in the bunk room. He was an avid amateur car mechanic. He was friendly and garrulous, yet managed to make at least one enemy wherever he worked. He'd left Fontana's crew looking for greener pastures, had gone to work for an aging lieutenant who rarely drilled his men and didn't like fires. He was working for that lieutenant the night of the Paint Company fire. In fact, the lieutenant and the rest of the crew died there. Randy might have too, had he not sprained an ankle tripping over a hose line earlier in the evening.

In addition to his leather pants and ponytail, Knutson sported a gold stud in one earlobe. "Got a brand-new hog out there on the street. A real little beauty. You probably saw it on the way in."

"I didn't. No."

"Anyway, I gotta be headin' out now." Knutson lit up a cigarette and inhaled. He flicked the burnt match into the air. "I got shit to do."

"You're not staying for the service?"

"Why should I go to his funeral? He's not going to mine."

"You're here for a reason, Randy. Why not come in?"

"Too many people hate me."

"Oh, come on. This is a funeral. Nobody's going to be upset if you stick around and pay your respects."

"You don't think so?"

"No." As if it had been choreographed, two uniformed fire officers from their former department walked past and nodded. "See? They don't hate you."

"You don't know what's been going on. Have you read my book?"

"I have it. I haven't read it."

"A lot of guys who were there couldn't read it. I knew that would happen."

"I'd better get inside," said Fontana. The crowd was thinning as the final columns of mourners were sucked through the entrance.

Randy Knutson followed him, his tone surprisingly sympathetic. "You know, Callahan wasn't really that bad. He used to come into the station when he was chief in our battalion and make sneak inspections. I think my officer told him I was goofing off around the station and he wanted to catch me at it. Write me up. You know he loved that. I used to hide from him. He'd ransack the station, convinced I was asleep somewhere, then I'd come out of a closet where I'd been hiding, rumple my hair and pull my shirt out of my pants, and walk down the hall. 'Oh, hi, Chief.' Used to drive him crazy. He'd swing by late at night and play chess with me, him and me the only two swinging dicks awake in the battalion. This was the same guy. You know? Like he was trying to be bad, but underneath he was just a regular joe."

"You put that in your book?"

"I wish I had. All I put in the book was the shit. I wish I'd been decent to him. He was basically a good man who made a few mistakes and got his tit caught in a wringer."

"Is that how you see it, Randy?"

"Don't you?"

"I think he was basically a sick man who toyed with people's lives and eventually got nine people killed. In a way, it's a wonder somebody didn't murder him a long time ago."

"He was murdered, huh?" A group of mourners walking from the roadway in front of the church grounds passed them, four men and three women. "That's his wife," whispered Knutson. "She hates me."

Fontana recognized the blonde in the center of the group, in her early fifties, trim and athletic-looking, dressed in black, dark glasses blotting out her eyes. She was a tennis player, he recalled from the photos on Callahan's desk.

The widow stopped just short of Fontana and Knutson, and whispered something to one of the men alongside her. She took off her glasses, her now-naked eyes glossy with grief, the crow's-feet and forehead tight with the strain of trying not to weep. Ignoring Knutson, she said, "Captain Fontana?"

"I'm a chief in a little department out here now. You might have heard we're the ones found your husband. I wish I knew what to say. I'm very sorry."

"Yes. Thank you. I want to talk to you. After the service?"

"Sure."

"Come on in," Fontana said to Knutson, after she left. "Stand in the back if you don't want to go in. You'll feel bad if you leave now."

"Okay, but a lot of those bloodsuckers hate my guts."

Fontana found Sally and Brendan sitting a row behind Pierpont and his ex-wife. As he sat down with them, it occurred to him that the three of them together looked a lot like a family. He wondered if Brendan was thinking the same thing.

During the service he was stunned to learn that Callahan had been a Mason, had volunteered hundreds of hours each year at a children's hospital, had used his own money to fund an annual scholarship for high school girls, had been active in his church, had built furniture in his spare time. Callahan's brother, a former fire officer, spoke glowingly of Callahan's career, unheedful of the fact that his stories didn't come off as amusing or touching.

When the minister read from the Bible, the passage was from Psalms: "For thou hast made him a little lower than the angels, and hast crowned him with glory and honour."

A little lower than the angels, thought Fontana—a perfectly ironic way to describe Edgar Callahan, and maybe the rest of us, too.

9

SIX MEN
CARRYING
A LUMP OF COAL

We are walking down a long, smoky corridor. We are all breathing heavily. Nobody is speaking. Nobody has spoken for quite some time. We smell of sweat and body odor, of fear, smoke, and of fire. From time to time the night shows through gaps in the walls or where the ceiling is missing, but we stay in the corridor because that is where the dim light is.

There are six of us, and we walk together like a machine, like a large bug, left, right, left, right, left. We are carrying a load on a makeshift stretcher constructed of fiberglass pike poles with a canvas tarp wrapped around them. Our charge is on his side, in full bunkers and boots, his air mask still on his back, though the facepiece and helmet have long since melted onto his skull. From the waist up, he is unrecognizable. From the waist down, we strain to identify him. There are nine missing men, and we mentally run down the list, trying to guess in our heads who this sorry customer is. Is he a friend of ours? Is he someone we know?

Fenster says, "Captain Fontana. Look at the size of them boots. It's got to be Malone."

"It ain't Malone," says one of the others. "Malone was on the other side of the fire."

"How do you know where he ended up?"

"Malone's got tiny feet," said someone else. "Those are size tens."

"Those aren't tens."

Somebody finally claims to wear size 10, so we stop and he puts a boot up alongside one of the dead man's, and as he does so, we all look at his sooty face and realize the absurdity of trying to identify dead men by their feet.

We walk with our burden. It seems like we walk miles, but it is only a hundred yards from the interior of the warehouse, down the long corridor, through the store portion of the building, and outside to where Chief Callahan stands in the huge, broken doorway. Lights bracket Callahan, and at first we don't realize who he is. It is five in the morning. He stands with his feet spread and his hands in his bunking coat pockets, the white helmet on his head colorless to our eyes, eyes blinded by the spotlights behind him. Callahan is a fairly small man, but like a cat puffed up for a scrap, he always looks bigger than he is.

Every thirty or forty paces we stop, supposedly to rest and make sure nobody loses his grip on the stretcher, but in reality we take deep breaths, we spit, we scrutinize our cargo, and we worry. We've put a disposable blanket over the torso, but it has come loose. As we get closer to the big lights, the body becomes more and more grizzly because we can see it more and more clearly, and as this happens, we find it difficult to look away.

Outside the building hundreds of firefighters, many from other jurisdictions, many off duty, line up in a "gauntlet of pride," as the newspapers later dub it. Before we get to the gauntlet, before we make the long walk to the fire department medic unit that will carry the body of this unknown firefighter to the morgue, before that, we must pass Callahan.

10

TYPEWRITER
COWBOY

When the commotion started in the back of the church, Fontana stood up quietly and sidled down the row to the aisle, squeezed his way past the backs of uniformed men clogging the foyer, and moved toward the sound of Randy Knutson's voice.

"Get your goddamn fuckin' hands off me," Knutson shouted, to a chorus of shushing.

Another voice, one Fontana recognized instantly, gruff and deep in stark contrast to Knutson's rather high-pitched whine, said something Fontana couldn't understand. By the time Fontana had fought his way through the tight circle of onlookers, a broad-backed man in a gray windbreaker had wrapped Knutson's ponytail in one fist and was half carrying and half pushing him through the spectators toward the churchyard. Knutson, who tumbled down the front steps and sprawled on his face on the pavement, was up in a second, fists doubled and windmilling, more of a mimic than somebody actually ready to throw punches.

He calmed down immediately when Fontana put his hand on the shoulder of the man in the gray windbreaker. "Hello, Lou."

"Mac? What the hell are you doing here?"

"Same as you. Same as Randy. Came to pay my respects. Now why don't you lay off?"

"You don't have any right to throw me out," said Knutson.

"Get your ass on the highway, typewriter cowboy," Lou Strange shouted. "Before I bust you in half." Knutson turned and left before Fontana could figure out how to heal the situation.

"Why on earth did you do that?" asked Fontana.

"Just tossin' out the trash. Hey, listen. I saw you in there with a kid. Was that Brendan?"

"Yeah."

"Damn, he's grown. We better get on back in. I'll see you out here afterwards."

"You didn't have to do that to Randy."

"Yeah, I did."

▪

While the pipers marched down the aisle, while the congregation shuffled nervously and sang a hymn, while a minister who hadn't known him lauded Callahan's compassionate deeds and generous personality, while everyone bid a last farewell to the corpse in the sealed coffin, Fontana found himself thinking about Lou Strange's bullying, as puzzled by it as he had been by Knutson's uncustomary meekness.

In Mac's old fire department, Randy Knutson was known as a contentious and compulsive troublemaker, willing to squabble to pass the time, unfailingly eager to launch into a friendly, or even unfriendly, wrestling match. One night he single-handedly captured a rapist attempting to ply his craft outside a fire station and beat the man senseless.

As the service concluded, Fontana couldn't help thinking about Tuesday afternoon, the snow, the drifting smoke, the open trunk. It was all such a contrast to the pristine church with its marble pillars and floral arrangements, to the crisp sunshine angling through the stained-glass windows.

Though the majority of onlookers went directly to their cars, the churchyard remained littered with mourners. Fontana introduced Brendan and Sally to several uniformed members of his former department, all of whom fled like park ducks in front of a dog when Lou Strange showed up.

Wearing a windbreaker with an open-necked dress shirt underneath, Strange had a broad chest that dropped down into a solid-looking beer gut, slightly bowed legs, and powerful, hirsute arms and hands. He was a tad shorter than Fontana's five-ten, fifty pounds heavier, and probably could have pushed him around on a football field without much trouble. He had pale blue eyes that would have looked stunning in the movies. Covering most of his mouth, his heavy mustache was infused with the same gray that was shotgunned through his thick hair. In his mid-fifties, he could have passed for older.

He was a most unlikely womanizer, yet that's what he'd been, discarding, in the time Fontana had known him, four wives and scores of girlfriends.

"Bet you never dreamed you'd see this many assholes from back home," said Strange. He'd shaken hands with Brendan as if he were a grown man but had taken a slow and careful measure of Sally, sizing up her glasses and face-concealing coiffure. "I know you from somewhere?"

"I don't believe so," Sally said. "I'm sure I would remember."

"Lou was more or less my mentor," Fontana said. "In my early years. They sent Lou over to my station to straighten me out."

"You'll have to tell me about that," said Sally, giving Fontana a loving look.

"Hell. They sent me over because you asked for me after the explosion. Asked who you wanted on your new crew, and you must've had a hissy fit or something, because you said me. Hell if I know why. Anybody straightened anybody out, it was you straightened me out."

"You taught me everything I know," said Fontana.

"Taught you to cuss. You didn't need no teachin' beside that. You were about the smartest young cocksuckin' firefighter I ever laid eyes on. Excuse my French, ma'am." He looked down at Brendan. "Your dad taught you to cuss yet?"

"No, sir."

"Well, he sure as fuck better get started." Strange had a habit of chewing on his shaggy mustache while he let his words sink in, but he stopped chewing to laugh at his own feeble joke. Brendan was trying not to giggle. "When I was your age, I could make a longshoreman blush and a preacher shit in his sock. I got a joke I'll tell you later, kid, about a chicken and a chest of drawers. Damn it, Mac. I haven't seen you since—"

"The Paint Company funerals. And you better not tell that joke."

"Oh, it ain't the version you heard. I found myself a cleaned-up version for women and children and parsons. I'm all cleaned up. Wouldn't say shit if I had a mouthful. I guess that was it, wasn't it? Where we last saw each other. The Paint Company funerals. Wasn't that a load of bullshit?"

"It was bad. What are you doing out here?"

Strange grinned. "Came out to make sure Callahan was dead."

"Now I know that's not true."

"Truth is, I got myself a motor home. Sold the sailboat and got myself a Bounder. Been drivin' across the country doin' nothing but drinkin' coffee and making shadows. Fact, I was going to look you up this week."

"Come on out. We've got a spot for a motor home. We can catch up on old times."

"Staircase, is it? I heard you were out there bein' a sheriff or some gol-darned thing."

"I'm a chief. There's only three paid members, which makes it a little like running Station Forty-six back home."

"You must be happier'n a pig in a puddle."

"Just about."

"Did he make a nice little sizzling sound? Our old friend?"

Fontana said nothing. "Come on, Brendan," said Sally, taking the boy's hand. "I saw some squirrels down in the parking lot. Let's go check them out."

After they were out of earshot, Fontana said, "How do you feel standing around at the funeral of a man you hated as much as Callahan?"

"You didn't like him much either, if I recall."

"I don't think anybody liked him."

Lou Strange's grin broadened underneath his mustache. "Bury your fuckin' enemies and die happy. That's what they say. I just wish I could get all the rest before my time comes."

"Like Randy Knutson?"

"He should've been in the box with Callahan. Together, the two of them would make a terrific worm farm."

"There was a time when you two were fishing buddies."

"I guess you didn't read that book'a his?"

"Couldn't stand the thought of it."

"I couldn't scratch up the twenty bucks to pay for it, myself. *Lost* my fuckin' library card. But people told me what was in it. Hey. Look at Callahan's widow. Check out the pins, huh?"

She was standing outside the church with a pair of older women and several men who had all been in the front row of the service. "Come on," said Fontana. "Let's not be talking about the widow's legs at her husband's funeral."

"You're right." Strange looked sheepish. "I'm better than that."

"Where you been, anyway, Lou?"

"The truth or the official version?"

"The truth, of course."

"After the Paint Company fire, I crawled into a bottle till I about died. Oh, I'm on the wagon now. You can't drive that fuckin' Bounder drunk. 'Course we both of us knew old-timers who drove rigs drunk. That was the old days. Iron men and wooden ladders. These days the men are wooden and the ladders are all made out of aluminum so the weak sisters can carry them." Once again he glanced in the direction of the group surrounding Callahan's widow. "Uh-oh. She's comin' over here. We've got about twenty seconds to try to look sad over that cocksucker bein' underground. I can't do it, man. I'm outa here."

Lou left, but the widow reached Fontana so quickly he couldn't be sure she hadn't heard Lou's last words. Fontana felt his face turning warm.

11

LARS WON'T
TELL ME NOTHING

She stepped in front of him and stood clutching her tiny black purse at her waist, a petite blonde, her graying hair cut to shoulder length, narrow shoulders, a sun-lined face that was lighter around the eyes from long hours in sunglasses. She appeared to be in her early fifties, and as she stood quietly appraising him, he was glad Strange had left, for there was a brittleness to this woman that was deeper than grief.

"Chief Fontana?"

"Mrs. Callahan. It's a pleasure to see you again. I can't tell you how sorry I am about the circumstances."

"Thank you. Don't I know the man you were just speaking to?"

"Louis Strange."

"Didn't he lose a brother at the Dead Horse Paint Company?"

"He was one of two people who lost a brother there."

It almost seemed as if she wasn't listening to his reply, was watching Strange instead. After a moment she said, "I understand you were the one who found Ed on Tuesday."

"Several of us found him."

"Will you talk straight, Chief?"

"Call me Mac. Yes, of course I will."

"My husband had a lot of respect for you. Did you know that?"

"I guess I didn't."

"Things changed with Ed in the last few years. There were very few people he respected, but he respected you."

For a moment or two, Fontana wondered whether she was confused, or perhaps deliberately concocting this story to flatter him. Maybe she believed it. "That wasn't my take on the situation," he said. "But what can I do for you?"

"He said you were the best investigator the department had."

"He transferred me out of Investigations."

"He did? I didn't know that."

"Yes. Well . . ."

"I want you to tell me how he died. I've been spoon-fed the official version, but you were there."

"I don't know if I can talk to you about this."

Her voice, reedy at best, took on a slight tremble. "Whatever you have to say can't possibly be as bad as what's been going on in my imagination. They said 'smoke inhalation.' But that's a catchall, isn't it? Something to keep the next of kin sedated with a false peace?"

"Not necessarily."

"I *need* to know how he died."

"If you heard 'smoke inhalation,' you know more than I do."

"I've been living with the possibility of his dying in a fire for over twenty-five years, and then this came out of left field. I need to picture it so that I can deal with it."

"He was found in a car up in the mountains. He was in the trunk. The car was on fire when we got there. From the look of the fire, an accelerant had been used. It was an odd place for a car fire, on a deserted back road in the middle of a snowstorm just to the left of nowhere."

"They told me some sort of foul play might have been involved, but nobody said anything about the trunk of a car."

"I hate to be the one to tell you."

"No, no. People are tiptoeing around trying to spare my sensibilities, as if I have any sensibilities after all the war stories Ed brought home over the years. I'd much rather know. Why was he in the trunk?''

"That's the big question. Last I heard, nobody knew."

"I want you to be my emissary. Find out what happened."

"Mrs. Callahan, I'm not—"

"Joyce. Call me Joyce. I understand you've hired yourself out for things like this before. I have insurance money, investments, the pension . . . The only thing on my mind right now is finding out what happened to Ed."

"I can't take your money for doing what the county will do as a matter of course. Trust me on this. Wait a few weeks, and the county will tell you what happened."

"You don't really think so."

"Yes, I do."

She thought about it for a few moments. Near the parking lot, Fontana could see Brendan balancing on a low concrete wall, Sally nearby.

"He was burned pretty badly?"

"Badly enough I didn't know who he was."

"Oh, Jesus."

"Joyce. If they say he died of smoke inhalation, that's how he died. People go to sleep. In fact, I've heard it described as peaceful."

"I've heard it described that way too, but gone is gone. And somebody did it. I want to know who. Did they tell you they found alcohol in his bloodstream?"

"No."

"I don't know why his brother Lars would mention that to me and not say anything about Ed being in the trunk. Lars spoke to the investigators out here, but for one reason or another he won't share the information with me. He's just like Ed that way. But the alcohol angle bothers me. Ed had an awfully high tolerance for alcohol. They said he was legally drunk, but point ten in his bloodstream wouldn't have impaired Ed in the least."

Fontana gazed across the churchyard at Lars Callahan, older brother of Edgar. If he wasn't sharing information with the widow, it was more likely a power trip than it was to spare her grief. Neither of the Callahan boys was the type to spare anyone grief.

Lars was a huge man, well over six feet, easily more than three hundred pounds. As an officer he'd been authoritarian and dictatorial, liked by a few, feared by a few, laughed at by a few, regarded much the same as his brother was, though he'd retired a captain while his brother had been destined for loftier appointments and a wider sphere of damage. Then too, Lars had not been as brainy as his brother and consequently not as frightening, not as tenacious nor half as devious.

Arms folded, Callahan glowered across the turf at Fontana with that familiar, heavy-browed, almost simian look that so strongly resembled his smaller, dead brother's. For just a twinkling, Fontana fancied it *was* Ed Callahan staring at him from across the lawn. "What did he tell you?"

She glanced at the group, and as she did so, the sunlight caught the pupils of her eyes and the little etched wrinkles around them so that Fontana thought he knew what sort of life she'd lived. Every once in a while, a face told him something about the owner, and he thought he was looking at such a face now. Joyce Callahan was a spirited soul who'd triumphed over difficulties and found what? He couldn't tell. Contentment? "You really want me to tell you what Lars said?"

"Sure."

"He thinks you were involved in Ed's death. Thinks it was no coincidence you were first on the scene."

"You believe I was involved?"

"It doesn't take a genius to realize you wouldn't kill my husband and then arrange it so you were first on the scene. Besides, if Lars is voting Republican, I'm for the Democrats. He flies United, I book on American. For years he tried to talk me into sleeping with him. What he wanted was to spite Ed."

"You ever tell your husband?"

"Ed wouldn't have believed me. I guess Lars knew that and realized I would never tell."

"That's too bad."

"Oh, I never took it too seriously."

"No. I meant that your husband wouldn't have believed you."

She didn't bother to think about what Fontana had said. "You know, Mac, I've had enough medical problems—and my parents both died young—that I've always assumed I would go before Ed, unless, of course, he went in a fire, so it's extremely disquieting to be standing here at his funeral. I'm having a hard time believing this isn't all a bad dream."

"I had that feeling when my wife died."

"That's right. I forgot. I'm sorry about your wife. That wasn't very long ago, was it?"

"Well, it wasn't four days ago."

The warmth of the sunshine on their black clothing was soothing as they took each other's measure. Though Fontana felt a stab of guilt for thinking it, he had the feeling there was a certain needy sensuousness lurking beneath the widow's cool and studied exterior, behind her blue ice-chip eyes. "So," she said, "are you going to tell me the details of his death?"

"We found him off the freeway to the pass on the Denny Creek Road. That's about fifty miles from Seattle. The vehicle plates were missing, and the car was stolen. It was pointing toward the highway, as if it had been heading out of the woods. There was a heavy snowfall. As heavy as I've seen. The car was still burning when we got there. The trunk was locked. For whatever it's worth, he had the keys inside with him. A couple of my people speculated it might have been suicide."

"Not Ed."

"That's what I told them. The last I heard, they didn't know how the fire started or what he was doing in the trunk. But it's an even guess from the charring and the way it was burning that a flammable liquid was involved. You said you heard he died of smoke inhalation. That's the first I've heard of it, but it sounds about right."

"It's just so odd. Ed flies out here for a convention. The next afternoon his brother phones me with this. It's just . . . Can you tell me something else?"

"What would that be?"

"Can you tell me what *you* think happened?"

"It would be pure speculation."

"That's what I need now. Some good old southern-fried speculation. I can't get a straight answer out of Lars or the county people. Don't you see? I need somebody to tell me what *might* have happened. This is all so inconceivable. I need a handle for it."

Fontana put his hands in his pockets and looked around at the thinning crowd. On the street, fire engines were starting their loud, diesel motors. A line of cars was filing out of the parking lot in back. "I won't say I haven't thought about this. Maybe he was walking down the street and saw something fishy going on with the stolen car, and the thieves hijacked him along with the car. Maybe some Dugan was riding around in the stolen car, saw your husband on the street, and decided to rob him."

"Ed wouldn't suffer anybody pushing him around."

"Still, they might have overpowered him, thrown him in the trunk, and driven him out on I-Ninety. Set the vehicle on fire thinking nobody would find it in a snowstorm."

"With Ed inside?"

"There are people around who would do that."

She thought about it for a few moments. "The police said there was no money in his wallet. They said his watch was gone. His rings removed. It's more evidence that counters Lars's theory that it was personal. Don't you think? Your robbery scenario sounds more reasonable."

"It sounds reasonable to me too, Joyce. A robbery gone wrong. But if that's the case, you're well advised to let the county work it out. It's exactly the type of crime you'd want a large police organization to handle."

Joyce Callahan mulled over what he'd said. Across the lawn some members of the group she'd come out of the church with were casting wary glances their way. It was plain nobody from the little group was going to come over and fetch her, but that they all disapproved of what they were sure she was doing. "I understand from one of the King County investigators you've done freelance work since you moved out here. I'm going to hire an agent to look into my husband's death. I'd like that agent to be you.''

"Joyce, the investigator the county's assigned happens to be very conscientious and capable. I'm sure she'll get to the bottom of this.''

"She? How'd she get her job? If she was at the top of some list, that's one thing. Only I bet she wasn't. I bet she was part of a quota. I've been the wife of a firefighter long enough to know all about quotas.''

"I don't know how she got her job, but I do know Jennifer Underhill. She's a top-notch investigator. She'll get to the bottom of it. If she doesn't, you come back and talk to me. There are a lot of avenues to explore yet. Give her a chance.''

"You won't consider it?''

"I'll consider it. I don't think I'll do it, but I'll consider it.''

"I'm flying home tomorrow. Call me. You know the number. Damn it. We were planning for Ed to spend five more years as chief and then we were moving to Yuma. Five years. Will you call me?''

"If I change my mind.''

"Call me anyway.''

"Sure, Joyce.''

She strode around the walkway and back to the group, her heels making hollow sounds against the cold pavement. She quickly linked arms with Lars Callahan, then was swallowed by the group. Fontana watched them move away like the broken parts of a dragon after a Chinatown parade and wondered whether he would ever call her. He wondered why she thought he knew her number, as if he and Callahan had been friends.

When he crossed the low-cropped grass toward the parking lot, a broadly smiling black man in a blue ski jacket approached from the corner of the church. "Hey, man. Funny seein' you here.''

"Larry,'' said Fontana. "What the hell are you doing in Seattle?''

"Hey, man,'' said Lawrence Drummey, slapping Fontana's palm. "Came out for the big conference. The old man was supposed to explain what all really happened at the Paint Company, but I guess somebody got to him first. Kinda like he got my brother, ya-know-what-I-mean?''

Lawrence Drummey's brother had died at the Dead Horse Paint Company, as had Lou Strange's, and either by coincidence or design, both surviving brothers of the tragedy had shown up at the funeral.

"You been out here all week?" Fontana asked.

"Why? Am I a suspect?" Drummey grinned like a kid on his first pony ride.

12

OPEN THAT BABY UP, WE GOT ANOTHER DUGAN HEADED FOR THE UNDERGROUND

"Anybody who ever hated the man is a suspect," said Fontana.

Drummey's smile didn't expose any teeth, but it did make his mustache seem sparser as it stretched, and it cranked down his eyes until they looked like they belonged on a hamster. "Any man who ever hated him? They gonna work on this with a computer?" The two men exchanged looks and then Drummey laughed so loudly mourners turned to see what the fun was about. "I came out here 'cause I wanted to hear the old man's version of the Paint Company. Mighta been kinda interestin', hearin' his version. Ya-know-what-I-mean?"

Lawrence Drummey was short and wide, with near-black skin, powerful thighs that tugged at the seams of his slacks, close-cropped hair, and an attitude of perpetual joviality. He had already been in the department a year or two when Fontana joined, so he had twenty or twenty-one years there by now. "You still working?" Fontana asked.

"Yeah. Why? Of course I am. You hear somethin' about me, man?"

"Out here? I don't hear anything out here." But he had heard stories. That Drummey had been institutionalized in a mental hospital after the Dead Horse Paint Company fire, that he'd taken a year off work, that since the fire he'd been divorced twice and jailed too many times to count, that he was on medication prescribed by a psychiatrist.

"Come on, man. You musta heard somethin'?" Drummey urged.

"Only what the widow just now told me. That her brother-in-law thinks I did it."

"Captain Lard? Lard's almost as big a prick as Dead Ed. You ever work with Lard?"

"A long time ago."

"He was a two-dimensional zero-pucker asshole, ya-know-what-I-mean? Edgar was the full-blowed, three-D model."

"Well, he's gone now."

"And that was the widow," Drummey said, gazing across the churchyard. He said it in such a manner that Fontana was fairly certain he'd known Joyce Callahan's identity earlier. "Pretty lady."

"What are you thinking?" Fontana said.

"Me?"

"You look like you're hatching up some sort of plan."

"Me?"

"Come on, Larry."

"I'll tell you what. The son of a bitch got what he deserved. Burned to death just like my brother and all the others. Couldn't have been neater. Tried, tied, and fried."

"What do you mean by that? Who tried him?"

"Nothin'. Don't mean a damned thing. And, hey man, I saw you talking to Strange earlier. He's somebody else needs to be packed away in a box. Fact, he should be in the same box with Callahan."

"You want him dead, too?"

"Did I say dead? Just put him in the box and bury it. He don't have to be dead."

Drummey walked away without another word, seemingly in a world of his own. The vision of Strange in the coffin with the dead man had scattered too many euphoric messages through his cerebrum, like an AT&T circuit box on Mother's Day. He hadn't even said good-bye. Strange had wanted Knutson in the box with Callahan, and now Drummey wanted Strange in there, too. The box was getting crowded. Drummey had had a lot of difficulty in the department, not the least of which was his brother dying at the Dead Horse Paint Company. Before the fire, Larry Drummey had been confidant to no one. He had been disliked and mocked, so that Fontana figured his brother's death had been a double blow to him, losing both a brother and the only real friend he'd had on the job.

At the Paint Company fire, after learning his brother was one of the missing, Drummey became hysterical, wailing and flailing and throwing himself around until he'd broken two of his own fingers.

After the fire there'd been rumors about Drummey—bizarre stories about him wandering through various fire stations at night in his brother's dress uniform, stories made even more eerie because he so closely resembled his brother. He was arrested for making midnight phone calls to individuals involved in the Paint Company fire. He was also arrested at five in the morning outside Edgar Callahan's bedroom window with a shotgun and twelve shells.

After climbing into the Suburban, Fontana, Brendan, and Sally waited for the heater to start working. If he'd thought about it earlier he would have tossed Sally the keys, but he hadn't, and she and Brendan had spent the last twenty minutes in the cold waiting for him. "I'm sorry," Fontana said. "Sometimes I think I've lost my mind."

"Oh, we had a fine time, didn't we, Brendan?"

"Sure did. Mac, we heard people talking about you."

"Did you now?"

"Firefighters from your old department, I assume," said Sally. "I had no idea you were so highly regarded back there."

"A legend," Fontana kidded.

"No. Seriously. They are in awe of you."

"It's funny what rumors will do for you." He fitted the truck

into a long line of cars heading out to Tenth Avenue East, two
lines merging at the exit point like a zipper. A block onto Tenth
Avenue, Fontana spotted Lou Strange and Lawrence Drummey
talking at the curb beside a Bronco. He wondered if Strange
hated Drummey as much as Drummey hated him. A young
woman stood behind Lou, and even when he slowed so he could
look her over carefully, no one in the group noticed him, concen-
trating as they were on each other.

"Is she somebody you know?" Sally asked.

"The gal who was following me earlier in the week."

Sally twisted around, but it was too late. "You're serious? Was
that your friend with her?"

"Lou Strange."

"Dad?"

"What is it, Brendan?"

"Was I born at the time of the Paint Company fire?"

"What makes you ask?"

"Everybody was talking about it."

"You were six."

"Right before Mom died?"

"Yeah."

"Were you at the fire?"

"Yes."

"Would you tell us about it?"

"Sure. Why?"

"I just want to know."

"I'd like to know about it, too," said Sally.

"Well, it was in this huge old barn of a building that took up
most of two, maybe three, city blocks. Part of it was a brewery
warehouse years before. It had been vacant for about twenty years,
and then this consortium of middle-aged entrepreneurs got together and set up a food co-op there. Eventually they sold household items, too: plants, tools, paint. They had a stuffed horse in
the front window, which is where the name came from. The Dead
Horse Paint Company."

"So they sold house paint?" Sally asked.

"Right. The place was quite successful and kept expanding.

They cut doors through the walls of adjacent occupancies that had formerly been separate—put in fire doors and all the goodies when they were asked to.

"One night it caught fire. After that the fire inspectors descended on it in droves. They wrote so many violations, the company had to close its doors for two months while they made renovations. A week after it reopened, it caught fire again.

"It was a small fire—at first—in a twisty, deep part of the building, far from any windows or outside entrances. It was winter and the sprinkler system had been disabled because freezing weather had burst the pipes. The watchman was asleep in the office when the place caught. The fire was extinguished quickly and everybody got ready to go home. But then it rekindled.

"What happened was, in the middle of fighting the rekindle, two firefighters realized one of their crew was missing and went in to look for him. Well, they got in trouble. The fire got bigger and trapped them deep in the interior of the block. They radioed for help, but the man commanding the fire—Ed Callahan—didn't really help them the way he should have. Afterward he said they hadn't adequately explained where they were.

"Rescue crews were sent in to find the missing men. Everyone could hear the first two on the radio trying to tell where they were. They still had air, but the fire was closing in fast on their position. They dug through a brick wall, but it was the wrong wall, and all they found was a crawlspace with more brick and mortar. If they'd gone the other direction, they would have found a corridor that would have taken them out.

"Anyway, another group of five went in with two hose lines, and about two hundred feet into the building—mind you, it's all smoke and hellish heat now with a visibility about zero—a wall fell on them and disabled every one of them. By then the radio was jammed up with calls for help from both groups and several chiefs trying to take charge. The radio system became overwhelmed. In fact, not long after that, the city put in a completely new radio system.

In the end, the original two guys died, plus the five rescuers, and two more searching in the basement, who fell into a subcellar and drowned before anybody could get them out. The cellars were full of water from the fire lines upstairs. Nine dead in all.''

"Dad," said Brendan. "You were lucky."

"I guess I was."

"I take it there was some blame involved," said Sally.

"Considerable blame, more than anyone bargained for. Randy Knutson? The man I was talking to when you both went into the church? A New York publisher got the idea to have him write about the loss of the nine firefighters. He'd already written a few books about local fire history; plus he was at the fire."

"Bagpipe City?" Sally asked. "My sister read that . . . maybe a year ago?"

"Randy stumbled into a real coup. The publisher paid him a fortune and then promoted the hell out of the book, plus Randy found out things about the fire nobody else knew. He found out that the first two trapped firefighters were looking for the third member of their crew. Until Randy discovered it, everybody assumed they'd gotten lost *with* the third member of their crew. But it turned out he wasn't even on the fire ground. Without telling anybody, he hornswoggled a couple of young guys riding Aid Twenty-seven to take him to the hospital for a twisted knee. On the way to the hospital, he directed them to stop at an apartment where he said he had to pick something up. They were wet behind the ears and he was an old warhorse, so they were just intimidated enough to do it. He went into the apartment and didn't come out for forty-five minutes. It was like dominoes. The whole night. One mistake after another."

"Let me guess. The man who's funeral we just went to? He was the one the first two were looking for?"

"No. Callahan was a deputy chief. He was there, and he *was* accused of malfeasance, but the man the first two were looking for was Lou Strange."

"The man with the mustache?"

"And the foul mouth. The one standing next to the Bronco with the woman who was following me last week. Funny thing was, Lou was one of the best around. In the last few years he acquired an attitude, but still, when the bell hit, he put on the blue suit and the cape and you never saw anything like it. He put out the original fire. But some embers dropped down the inside of a wall and set off another entire set of rooms. By the time his crew panicked and went looking for him, it was going gangbusters."

"I don't understand," said Brendan. "Why didn't they just tell somebody they couldn't find him?"

"You had to know Lou. He took consummate pride in his fire-fighting prowess. In fact, I believe he took pride in the difference between the way he acted around the station and the way he fought fire. It was an act with him, but it was an act he guarded zealously. You stepped on the act, you stepped on Lou. If they'd embarrassed him by saying they couldn't find him, he would have been on them for years."

"How *did* he act around the station?" Sally asked.

"Ever see a walrus sunning himself on the rocks?"

"And this Callahan? You say he was accused of malfeasance. What was it he did wrong? He must have been exonerated if he was going to be chief of the whole department three, four years later—"

"More like two years later. Callahan was cleared because he had friends in the mayor's office. It's sick, but it's the way it is. Besides that, no official study ever pinned malfeasance on him, despite his not shutting down lines he knew were pushing fire onto crews inside. The three studies that were done glossed over his part in it. Until this week he was the luckiest son of a bitch I ever knew."

13

YOU
SLY OLD DOG

At a few minutes before eight, Fontana walked through the back doors of the Bedouin and wiped the rain and sand off his shoes on the floor mat. The Bedouin attracted people from all over the valley, as well as from Seattle and the other nearby metropolitan areas. Tonight the dance floor was less crowded than usual, which meant you could walk between the couples.

After Fontana's eyes adjusted to the dimness, he spotted some familiar faces, including one he hadn't expected. Lou Strange sat in the far room at the bar, sipping from a bottle of mineral water.

"You *are* on the wagon," Fontana said, ordering a Red Hook and edging up between Strange and a man in a brand-new cowboy hat.

"Seven months, three days, and twelve hours," Strange said, leaning his broad back against the bar, propping his elbows up as he squinted through the wide doorway into the dance area.

"It's tough, huh?"

"Worse than all of my goddamn divorces put together."

"But you're doing it."

"Badly."

"I don't think there is a badly, Lou. It's pass/fail."

"Say, who was that little number you were with at the funeral? People here in town tell me you're seeing Aimee Lee."

"That was Lee."

"Bowser! Why didn't you say something? I mean, I thought she looked familiar. That was some sort of disguise, right?"

"Only the glasses."

"Damn, man. How'd you luck into a piece like that? You send her a fan letter—instead of mailing back an autographed eight-by-ten, she shows up at your doorstep?"

"It's a long story."

"That bad, huh?" He laughed.

"It's just that she's a very private individual."

"You're in that romantic phase. You'll get over it. Damn, man. A woman like that'll knock the wrinkles right outa your dick. With the papers all over her every time she sneezes, I can see why she'd be nervous. Don't worry. I won't ask for any state secrets."

Until the Dead Horse Paint Company, Strange had been unruly, intractable, funny, lazy, lovable, indomitable. After the Paint Company, he couldn't stop talking about an uncle who'd committed suicide when Strange was a boy by lying on train tracks. In his drunkenness, Lou claimed there was a certain nobility in choosing the manner in which you were to die.

After the Paint Company funerals, Fontana had spent time with Strange, mostly while Strange drank, thinking that if he was left to himself for too long, Strange would shoot himself, for in those days a pistol was never far from his shaky hand. He'd commiserated with Lou, who had needed a lot of commiseration during that time, a period when Lou's remaining friends held secret meetings about his welfare.

It was then that Fontana, in a moment of frailty and what he now recognized as emotional panic, confessed an extramarital affair to Louis Strange. Confessing his infidelity to Lou had been a mistake. Strange had been handy, a willing ear, and Fontana, obsessed with his own problems, thought that Strange's hearing about somebody else's troubles might distract him. It was a poor excuse, the only saving grace being, Fontana hoped, that Lou was so pickled in alcohol he wouldn't remember.

"Come on, Mac. Tell me about your movie star."

"Nothing to tell."

"That's not what I heard."

"That's what I'm telling you."

"She coming around tonight? I gonna get a chance to dance with the Plaything?" he said, referring to Aimee Lee's fourth and last movie.

"I doubt it."

"But you're going to see her afterwards, right? You sly old dog. So I guess you got over your wife and all that guilt crap?"

"No, Lou. I haven't gotten over Linda. Fact is, I've tried to stay away from women lately."

"Haven't been doing a very good job, have you?"

Fontana smiled grimly. "I guess not."

"Can't blame you. I mean, how many of us get a crack at a movie star? Say, I ever tell you the one about the priest with the calcified balls?"

"She's just like anyone else, Lou, except she has a few thousand people thinking about her at any given time."

"You mean a few million. And I bet your balls ain't calcified."

Fontana shrugged.

"So you're really, uh, still having a hard time about Linda?"

"I don't know if you'd call it a hard time. But I guess I'm not over it."

"Jesus, man. It's been what? Two years?"

"And how long has it been since the Paint Company?"

"Touché."

"Time doesn't change much, Lou. I cheated. She found out. We had a fight, said things we shouldn't have said. She went out to the car. Next thing I know I'm getting a call from the paramedics saying I'd better hightail it up to the hospital."

"You don't really think it was your fault? It was a drunk driver. You're lucky she lived long enough for you to say good-bye. Mac, get some help. Somebody professional. That's how I quit drinking. Trust me on this. Promise you'll see somebody."

"Don't think I haven't thought about it."

"I'm not asking you to think about it. I'm asking you to *do* it."

Johnny Mathis was singing a tune Fontana couldn't name. He spotted several volunteers from the Staircase department dancing with their wives. Two groups in ski togs on their way back from the slopes. And in the middle of it all, H. C. Bailey cheek to cheek with a blonde almost a head taller, the other woman's eyes closed, her jaw propped against the top of Bailey's head.

"I was surprised you showed up for Callahan's funeral," Fontana said.

"It was my pleasure."

"I bet it was."

"What'd his wife say to you?"

"Nothing much."

The music in the other room concluded, and a swarm of dancers came into the bar area to order drinks, among them Mayor Mo Costigan and H. C. Bailey, who was hand in hand with her blonde. Mo buttonholed Fontana on one side while H. C. Bailey ordered two beers on the other. Sipping his mineral water, Strange focused his attention on Bailey. After ordering, she went to the ladies' room while Strange conversed with her friend, who fanned herself with her hand.

"Never expected to see two women dancing like that in a little town like this," Strange said. The blonde's reply was drowned in a cascade of laughter from two couples on the other side of her.

Mo hipped Fontana aside, snapped out an order to one of the bartenders, then stood nose to chest with him and said, "Mac, you got some business in your department you're going to have to clean up. And I mean pronto."

"What business would that be, Mo?" he said, trying to listen to Strange's discourse behind him, not quite hearing either conversation completely.

"You know what business."

"No, Mo, I don't."

Behind him, Strange was saying, "You tellin' me you never wanted to try the real thing?"

"You know exactly what I'm talking about, Mac. There's a little problem in your department, and you'd better get a grip on it before it turns into a big problem."

"Just tell me what you're talking about, Mo."

She leaned against him and spoke. "I'm talking about those pictures of Heather you have floating around."

"*I* have floating around? If they're floating around, I don't know anything about it."

"Then you better get cracking, because everybody else in town knows." Without blinking, she handed him a photograph, obviously taken from the same batch Lieutenant Pierpont had given him. In this one, Heather Minerich wore a sweater and panties.

"Where'd you get this?" Fontana said, tucking it securely away in his shirt pocket, then batting Mo's hands away as she spilled her beer trying to retrieve it.

"Damn it, Mac. Never mind where I got it. What are you going to do about it? And hand it back over."

"This doesn't belong to you, Mo."

"You think you can handle a situation like this? You ever had to deal with anything like this?"

"Actually, no, Mo. I haven't."

"Because if you can't handle it, I'd like to bring in a specialist."

"A specialist in what?" She reached for his pocket one last time, but he fended her off. "There are people out there who specialize in employees who have nude pictures of themselves floating around in the workplace? Where do you find a specialist like that?"

"Just get it cleaned up, Mac. *Before* I have to call in outside help. By the way, Bailey just now told me that woman who was stalking you last week is over there. See her?"

"Where?"

"Under the exit sign. Standing by herself."

She wasn't dressed for the weather: black leather shorts, hiking boots, and a white sleeveless shirt. Disappearing and reappearing behind a curtain of milling people, she observed the commotion around her shyly. So this was the woman who'd been following him—the same woman he'd seen chatting with Lou Strange and Lawrence Drummey that morning at the funeral.

"Bailey told me all about her, Mac. She doesn't look as if she could walk across the street by herself, much less rob a bank or scare the yellow piss out of a big, tough man like you. But the FBI says she's a cold-blooded terrorist. I'm going to talk to Bailey when she gets back from the toi-toi and see if we can't have her arrested."

"On what charges?"

"Bailey'll cook something up. Bailey said she was a bomb expert. And the cops down south think she was involved in a whole string of bank robberies. Look at her, standing over there trying to pick up men. There aren't enough men in this town to go around and she wants to horn in."

"What makes you think she's trying to pick up men, Mo?"

"Look at her!"

"Can't see her very well from here," Fontana said, putting his empty beer bottle on the bar counter and heading across the room.

"For godsakes, Mac. Don't go over there! Are you insane? You might be tough, Mac, but she's going to eat you alive. And give me back that picture!"

As he strolled across the Bedouin, another song from the jukebox started up, "April Love," by Pat Boone. He hadn't heard it in years. He made his way through couples on the dance floor and headed directly for the woman, who spotted him and began to look nervous as he drew closer. A young man to her right had been speaking to her, but she'd brushed him off with a bland show of disinterest, and when Fontana arrived, she stepped forward and clasped his hand as if she'd been expecting him. Her grip was tight and insistent, her palm moist. He hadn't intended to ask her to dance, but he went out onto the floor with her anyway.

Playing upon her obvious anxiety, Fontana said nothing for the entire number. When the tune ended and another began, they danced again as if by mutual agreement. After a few bars of the second song, she said, "You recognized me. Is that it?"

"Not in a million years."

"You know who I am, though?"

"I do now."

"The police told you. Of course they did. You're probably friendly with the police."

"The police didn't tell me."

"I'm different than I used to be."

"I know you are."

"You would have recognized my sister. She didn't change one little bit. And you don't look different either, Mac. Well, you do, actually. You look better." Although she'd done her best to make it sound normal, the word "Mac" had rolled around in her mouth like a stone, obtrusive and alien.

14

IT'S LIKE
HYPNOTIZING
A CHICKEN

Grace Strange. He didn't remember much about her. Only that her father, Lou Strange, had been divorced from her mother for ten or twelve years, and that she and her mother and sister had moved out of state—California, now that he thought about it. Her mother had been a handsome woman with a fiery temper, a full-blooded Arapaho from Colorado, but aside from her dark hair and eyes, Grace didn't look much like her. "You were always on roller skates," Fontana said.

"You remember that?"

"Yep."

"What else do you remember?"

Not much, he thought. Whenever he'd visited the house, she'd hung around the adults like a pet, not trying to mix into the rep-artee, but not wanting to leave either. It had gotten so he hadn't noticed whether she was in the room or not. She'd been small for her age, shy, easily hurt. Now she looked curiously ordinary and a little tough. Or was he imagining the latter because of what H. C. Bailey had told him about her past? "You and your father traveling together?"

"We tow the Blazer and drive the motor home. Dad wanted to see the West Coast. We've already done Montana, Idaho, part of Oregon. Did you know I had a horrible crush on you when I was a kid?"

"When the cops talked to you earlier in the week, you were going by the name of Grace Teller."

"Teller was the name of my mother's second husband. He adopted us. I guess she made him. He was a pig. Mom wanted both our last names to be the same. Funny, because three years later they separated, and now I'm Teller and she's MacDonald. I suppose the police told you all about me?"

"A little."

"My father and I are trying to get to know each other before it's too late. Traveling and taking it easy."

"Lou's always taken it easy."

"That's what he wants people to think. Did you know he's had ulcers for twenty years? They got so bad once he had to be operated on."

"Lou?"

"He probably told you the operations were for his knee or a hernia or something."

"I think I did hear that hernia story once."

"Ulcers. Dad's never had a hernia. It's only been the last few months they aren't bothering him."

"What are you two doing in this part of the country?"

"Dad wanted to see you."

"Why come out now? This exact week?"

"You mean the week Chief Callahan died? It was a total accident."

It occurred to Fontana that what she'd said could have been taken two ways, that Callahan's death was an accident, or that the timing of their arrival was an accident. "Why were you following me?"

"I wasn't."

"That's not what you told the cop who pulled you over."

"Did I say something else? I don't recall."

"Come on, Gracie. What's going on?"

"Gracie. I remember you used to call me that. It used to be like somebody playing a xylophone all up and down my spine. I swore I was going to grow up and marry you."

"You're not going to tell me why you were following me?"

"When we moved, I thought I was going to die. I had a clipping of you from the newspaper. Dad was in it, too. You were both on the roof of a burning building. You were chopping holes or something. You looked so grand together with the smoke all up around you. I kept that clipping for years and years, and then one time in school I made a charcoal drawing from it. I still have it."

"So how did you get mixed up with terrorists?" Fontana asked.

"Oh, gosh. I can't believe how bent out of shape people get. A few political ideas that don't jibe with yours and they're ready to storm the building with a SWAT team."

"You didn't belong to a terrorist group?"

As if she'd memorized the words, her voice changed, became didactical, haranguing. It was a spiel, and one she'd given before. "I belonged to a loose gathering of friends. We might have had a name for it, if that makes it political. The Army of Righteousness. Does that sound heretical? These people were my friends. My stepfather, Mike, wasn't all Mother thought he was going to be, and I ended up leaving home because of it. Let's see. The first time he put his hand in my panties I think I was fourteen. But there's no use going through that again."

"How old were you when you and your mother moved to California?"

"Almost twelve. I can't believe you didn't recognize me."

"I guess that makes you twenty-two now?"

"Twenty-three."

"And your stepfather is what happened between twelve and twenty-two?"

"The regular trouble. The more he had to drink, the worse Mike got. Completely sober, he pretended none of it happened. That was the worst part, the total bullshit hypocrisy of the guy. And then my mother, who refused to believe what was going on. So I ran away with a girlfriend and we ended up on the streets.

Ran away four or five times before I decided it was a waste of time to ever go back.''

"Then what?''

"You want to hear all this?''

"I do.''

For her part, Grace seemed pleased he was interested in her. In fact, getting her to talk had been about as easy as hypnotizing a chicken.

15

THIS IS
WHAT HAPPENS WHEN
YOU LOITER IN
BAD NEIGHBORHOODS

During the next three dance numbers, Grace Strange Teller told Fontana her life history.

Fontana couldn't help thinking that if her mother hadn't divorced Lou, if the family hadn't broken up, she wouldn't have been drawn into the vortex of lawlessness. He wondered if the thought had ever occurred to her father.

After leaving her stepfather's home in Hayward, California, Grace had lived on the streets of Berkeley for two summers in succession before finding a band of street kids to hook up with, sharing food and crashing in parks or communal pads. She and her friends shoplifted, burgled, pilfered, adopted scams to avoid payments at restaurants, sold drugs—mostly to high school kids visiting the area—and once even became desperate enough to stage an armed robbery, which she claimed they aborted before it began.

By the time she was sixteen, she was on the streets a year and a half. She had kicked a heroin habit. She had been incarcerated and released for the assault of a flower seller on Mother's Day. The juvenile detention period hadn't been all bad, because besides offloading her heroin habit there, she graduated high school.

When she was seventeen, Grace found a steady boyfriend, a tall, long-haired revolutionary from South Carolina with a thick drawl and enough emotional baggage for a troop of orphans. Though he was twenty-six, Grace was the first woman he'd ever slept with. His name was George Tchaikovsky, and he had a small car and an apartment that she and her friends were allowed access to. He was a righteous and militant politico, passionate in his beliefs and zealous to change the world.

Along with a cousin and several other radicals who'd dropped out of the University of California, Tchaikovsky formed a loose-knit group initially called the Berkeley Coalition for a New America, later the Voodoo Stick Band, and later still, after they began sticking up banks, the Army of Righteousness. Their goals, as related by Grace, were at first nebulous but later began coalescing into a loose and random pattern of attempting to shake the "establishment" out of its "complacency." Fontana didn't bother to ask what that meant.

They had, Grace admitted, committed grocery store heists in the Bay area, for which they were never charged, and then, after defecting from California, had roamed the Eastern Seaboard for six months in a caravan of cars. They robbed a farm co-op somewhere in the Midwest, though Grace refused to say where or to explain exactly what they robbed it of or whether or not anybody was hurt. From the way she told it, Fontana had the feeling somebody *had* been hurt.

"What about your little sister?" he said. "Didn't you have a sister a year or two younger? Crystal?"

Grace had been telling her story in a detached voice, as if she'd witnessed it on a television documentary, but her tone changed now. "Crystal had the same problems with Mike that I had."

"Mike was your stepfather?"

"Yes. I used to call the house every couple of weeks when I knew she'd be home from school and nobody else would be around. It was tough. I didn't want to tell her to run away because I knew how crappy the streets were. But I didn't want to tell her to stay either. Then, a year after I took off, she came to live with me at George's apartment. But she didn't like George's friends, and one night we had a fight. George was off with a couple of sisters from the movement, some political bullshit—I don't remember what. Most of the others had gone to Sacramento for a drug buy.

"Crystal and I had this huge fight on the way home from shoplifting a bunch of magazines from an AM/PM MiniMart. So here we are in the middle of the night scrapping like birds in a box, and for some stupid reason I threaten to drive her home to Mom and Mike. Then she threatens to jump out of the car. Like a dummy, I pull over and she gets out. It was a pretty bad area of town, but I was hot, so I drove off. Maybe five minutes later I came back to get her." Grace Teller stopped dancing, her body limp in his arms.

"What happened?"

"She wasn't there. It was maybe three in the morning, and when I realized she was gone, I about went nuts. The weird part was, I don't think there were more than two or three cars an hour passing through that intersection. I drove around in circles looking for her, you know, thinking she'd walked away. But how far could a person walk in five minutes? There wasn't anyplace to go. No place she could have hidden.

"After a while, I went back to George's apartment. There was always a few people hanging around, so we scrounged up a second car and went back out looking for her. I had horrible visions of what might have happened. By morning, when nobody'd seen her and she hadn't gone back to George's, we decided she'd hitched a ride home. But Mom hadn't seen her either. Two days later when she still hadn't shown up, we called the police, but because of her history of running away, they didn't take it seriously. All they wanted to do was ask me about George and his friends."

"So where was she?"

"We don't know. We never found her."

"Never?"

"No. You can about guess what must have happened. Some

creep was cruising the area and saw a fifteen-year-old girl in shorts and a halter top, stopped, conned her into his car somehow, and . . . Or forced her into it. It had to have been the first car that came along. What were the odds of a kidnapper coming by in the very first car after I let her out?"

"Grace, I'm sorry."

After some time, she said, "I guess we both made mistakes we ended up having to live with, huh?"

"What do you mean?"

"Your problem with Linda? Lou told me all about it. I always felt like we had a bond, but when I heard about that, I *knew* we had one."

Ignoring a sudden flush of indignation, Fontana said, "You don't blame your sister's disappearance on yourself, do you?"

"Three in the morning? I leave her alone on a street corner and she disappears? You bet your booties I blame myself. I've spent most of the last six years trying to figure out a way to go out in a blaze of glory. George was a revolutionary, but I was nuts, the worst in the group. At one point, I walked in on a meeting where George was trying to talk them out of eliminating me. I took a forty-five pistol out, threw it on the table, and asked who wanted to do the job."

"You didn't mean for her to get hurt. Five minutes, you said. It was a lapse in judgment, but you didn't mean for her to get hurt."

"After Crystal disappeared, George was the glue that held me together. Even today, I have this horrible feeling there's some-body right *there* . . . waiting for me the way that creep was waiting for her. I tried drugs. Booze. Sex. There wasn't anything that would make me forget. I went through this period where I wanted to hurt somebody. Anybody. I learned how to use a gun. Learned enough karate to kill. How to build booby traps. To fight with sticks. I took survival courses. Without any food or water I lived in the hills above Berkeley. I even tried to eat a cat, but all I managed to do was kill one. I was bad. For months we drove around in a car full of guns and ammunition. The trunk was full of stolen cash. We lived without the amenities, baths, phones, mail. We were hard-core. I mean, hard-core. We robbed. Stole. Dealt smack.''

"So what happened? You're not with George.''

"A cop in Sacramento shot him. They called it a routine traffic stop. The bullet went into his ear, circled around inside his skull and stopped somewhere in his brain stem. It was a rented car, but George had a gun on the seat beside him, where he always carried it. The cop said he was making a move for it, but he wasn't. It was a simple assassination.''

"So George is gone. Then what?''

"The Army stuck together for another month, and then we began squabbling, drifting off to various corners of the globe. Jim and Marsha were arrested, I heard, in Maine trying to blow up a post office. After a while, my money ran out and I decided to look up Lou. It had been so long I almost forgot what he looked like. He was drinking like a brewery rat. It took me a couple of weeks to talk him into a clinic. And then when he got out, we decided to take this trip.''

"How long have you been together?''

"Seven months. He really did need me.'' Her brown eyes turned liquid with emotion.

After they parted, Fontana watched her walk away. Bare-armed, bare-legged, looking younger than twenty-three, one of those people with a perpetually adolescent appearance to her pale flesh, to her plumpish cheeks and legs. Fontana didn't see much evidence of the rough life she'd alluded to, nothing but an old scar on her lip and a black, jail-manufactured tattoo on the web between her thumb and index finger.

Fontana was about to leave the Bedouin when Staircase's safety director, Roger Truax, caught him by the arm. He wore a fringed buckskin jacket that looked ridiculous on him. "Mac? Can I have a word with you?'' he said, his eyes as lifeless as those of a fish in the bottom of a boat.

"What's going on, Roger?''

"Well, you know I've been running this conference in Seattle all weekend. In fact, I'm on my way back out there tonight. We have a breakfast gathering I have to oversee. The thing is, Mac, there's been some talk among members from your old department.''

"What sort of talk would that be?''

"I tried not to foster this in my own conversations, but there does seem to be a current of thinking that tends to put some of the blame for that tragic business up in the mountains last week on you.''

"What are you trying to say, Roger?''

"I tried not to feed into it, but it seemed like wherever there were any people from your old department, the talk was about Callahan. Fact of the matter is, the entire conference seemed almost—well—almost obsessed with Callahan's death. A lot of people seem to be wondering what part you played in it. I tried to tell them you were a great guy, but there are rumors flying around. Some of them are downright ugly.''

"And, of course, you didn't have anything to do with them.''

"No, no, Mac. I've been putting water on the rumors, but they're heating up faster than I can cool them off. Hey, that's not a bad metaphor. Or is that a simile?''

"What are you suggesting, Roger?''

"I'm not suggesting anything. I thought you might want to know about this gossip. You know, the funny thing is, if this Callahan business isn't resolved, there are people who will always link your name to his death.''

"Thanks for reminding me of that.''

"Hey. No problem. I'm on your side.''

"You always were.''

"Darn tootin'. Hey, that's not bad either. Tootin'.''

■

The drive to Sally Culpepper's place on the river took less than ten minutes. Fontana steered through her security gates, parked in her five-car garage, and took the back path to her house. She met him at the back door wearing a white shift that extended to the floor.

Without saying a word, she led him to the sofa in the dark living room. It was warm in the house, almost as warm as the Bedouin. They could hear the wind and the rain pulsing against the windows at the back of the house.

"You smell like another woman's perfume," Sally said, caressing his rain-dampened hair.

"I've been dancing."

"I'll just bet you have."

"Jealous?"

"Not when I have you here beside me. How was the Bedouin?"

"It's still there." He told her about Lou Strange, about Roger Truax's insinuations, about his dilemma over whether to look into Callahan's death for the widow. What he was avoiding was any mention of Grace Teller; Grace was a stalker, and Sally, having been stalked, was terrified of stalkers.

"So, have you decided what you're going to do?" Sally asked.

"I don't know."

"I wish I could be here to see this through with you, but you know I'm leaving to make this movie."

"I know. In Spain. Where it rains mainly on the plain."

"I'm going to be gone longer than I thought. They're talking about four or five months. I hope this doesn't make you mad."

"Can they do that? Don't you have a contract?"

"They can't, actually, but Vladislav wants me. And I want to do this with him. I made that decision. I'm returning to films, but on my terms. And my terms right now include getting it right. So I may be gone four months. Or more."

"I'm going to miss you."

"You're not mad?"

"I'm disappointed."

She kissed the tip of his nose, her lips moist and so warm they felt hot. "I bet you are."

"Like you wouldn't believe." He kissed her, and the moment quickly grew intimate, more intimate than he'd intended. Yet somewhere in the middle of it his mind began to wander and he began thinking about things that had been said in the Bedouin, about his Linda, about his indiscretion before her death, about his recent celibacy. He'd been friends with Sally for six months, but they had waited until the week before she left to become intimate. He wondered why.

Even as he thought it over, he began to question whether he

was attracted to Sally Culpepper, his neighbor two miles upriver, or Aimee Lee, the movie star. He realized he would probably never know the answer. And if he didn't, how would she? No wonder she didn't trust anyone. Right now, except for her son who was in another state, he was the closest person in the world to her, and he didn't have a clue why.

"What's the matter?" she said.

"Nothing."

"No, something's the matter. Is it the time? It might not be that long. Besides, they won't be needing me for every bit of that. And you could visit. You could come to Spain. Oh, that would be grand. Wouldn't that be grand?"

It would, he thought, but on a movie set he'd be a fifth wheel, and besides, while he and Brendan were comfortable on his small pension and the pittance he brought in as a fire chief, there was no extra cash for flights to Spain.

"Honey, what's wrong?"

"Nothing."

"I'll be back. You know I'll be back."

"I know."

"This is my home and you're . . . I guess you're my man. I'm going to call like clockwork. You'll see." She gave him an athletic squeeze, which, for some reason, reminded him of the way Linda would sometimes hug him, as if fearful he would escape. She got up, removed her long white shift, walked in the half-light to the doorway dragging the shift along the floor behind her, stopped, looked over her shoulder at him, and said, "I'm going upstairs. You coming?"

16

SO YOU'RE THE FINE GENTLEMAN WHO SET THE POLICE ON MY LITTLE GIRL?

Brendan woke Fontana Sunday morning. "Dad. Dad. There's a big old motor home in our front yard."

It was a Bounder, Lou Strange's, judging by the cockeyed angle at which it was parked and the state the license plate had been issued in, with a Blazer parked alongside. The drapes were pulled all around, and the outriggers were down, a welcome mat and a white plastic chair set out alongside the passenger door. Fontana wondered how Strange knew where he lived, why he would block their view of the river.

Then it occurred to him. Grace knew where he lived.

Fontana and Brendan read the Sunday paper and the funnies, cooked pancakes for breakfast, and kept an eye on the yard. At nine-thirty, Grace Teller came flying out of the Bounder, hair bouncing behind her shoulders, and without looking toward the house, climbed into the Blazer, turned on the motor and windshield wipers, and spewed gravel and soggy turf from her rear wheels as she sped out of the yard. She wore the same clothing she'd had on the night before, carried only car keys, no purse.

The river was up, muddy brown and opaque and scrubbing the

banks, pushing debris downstream with its force, roaring along beneath a heavy fog that had descended on the valley during the night. Fontana had grown accustomed to the low winter clouds, the never-ending winter and spring downpours, and the way the evergreens across the river appeared so stark and deep and green against the gloom.

At ten-thirty, he left Brendan working on a school project and walked across the pine needles in the yard to the front door of the Bounder. Strange opened it before he knocked, motioning him in with a nod and a grunt, turned around, and moved deeper into his burrow.

"Got up to take a leak and couldn't get back to sleep," Strange said, tramping to the rear of the Bounder in socks and a disheveled bathrobe with a Chiquita banana sticker clinging to the backside. He took a seat on a cushioned bench along one wall and motioned Fontana to sit.

"I'm okay. Lou, this is kind of touchy, but when I invited you to stay here, I, uh . . . I didn't know you had your daughter with you."

"Yeah?" Strange's eyes were puffy, his thick hair tousled. When he scratched the stubble under his wide chin, it sounded like a rodent in an attic. "What are you trying to say?"

"She's got a history, Lou. She's been in trouble with the law."

"Not really."

"Yes, really."

"Once when she was underage, they arrested her for assault. Later they tried to pin a couple of gun raps on her and then claimed they had to let her go because of technicalities. Being innocent's always a technicality to a cop."

Fontana now recalled how Lou had always been antagonistic toward the police, which may have been because so many of his domestic difficulties with his second wife, Grace's mother, had ended with visits from the local constabulary. Of course he would take Grace's side against the authorities.

"You know about her, don't you?"

"She ain't perfect. God knows, I ain't either. But we're doin' our best, she and I. We're doin' our goddamnedest to straighten out our lives, okay? Cleaning up the loose ends and trying to pull it all together. She's needed me, Mac. And I been good for her. You realize her little sister disappeared?''

"I heard.''

"Grace never rightly got over it. You throw that disappearance in with everything else . . . well, it ain't pretty.''

"Did you know she was stalking me, Lou?''

"I don't believe that.''

Fontana explained the events that had taken place earlier in the week, but his recitation only served to incite Strange into a tantrum. Mustache flapping in the wind, he yelled, "You're the one who set the cops on my little girl?''

"I didn't know who she was, Lou. And I didn't know what else to do.''

"You set the pol-eece on my baby?''

"Yeah, your little ex-terrorist baby. And anybody else who's stalking me.''

Strange rested his arm alongside the top of the padded bench behind him and blew air through his mustache. He seemed to calm down, and then he smiled. "Women follow *me* all the time. I don't know what your gripe is. I think it's some sort of animal thing they smell on me. Something. Listen to me, Mac. Grace had some bad times, I'll be the first to admit that. I'm helping her along now. Getting her back on track, you know. Right now all she wants to do is learn how to be normal. Does that make any kinda sense?''

"Maybe you better tell her being normal doesn't include following people around.''

"Trust me, her heart is in the right spot. She's not going to hurt anybody. Just cut her a little slack, Mac. Can you do that? Cut her a little slack, and see if things don't look better to you in a few days. Believe me, you don't know the heartache this kid's been through. Lost her father when I divorced Ann. Lost her mother and then her home and a roof over her head when the goddamned stepfather tried to horse around with her. Lost her sister. Blamed that on herself. And then, just a little more than a year ago, she lost her husband. Cut her a little slack, huh?''

"Sure. Okay, Lou. Stay here for a while. We'll spend some time together. Talk over the old days. But if I see any signs of unstable behavior, I'm going to ask her to leave." Fontana moved to the door.

"You won't. By the way, old man, what's the story on your mayor?"

"Mo?"

"She off her rocker, or what?"

"Why? What happened?"

"She got a little stewed last night. We danced some, then went into Bellevue for some oysters." Strange grinned. Eating oysters on dates was an old joke with him. He liked to boast that oysters didn't improve his virility at all: "I ate twelve of the little critters one time and only eight of them kicked in."

"Don't tell me you went to bed with our mayor?"

"I woulda, but she got shitfaced and fell asleep on me. Since I quit drinkin' myself, screwing drunks just don't have the same appeal. Besides, you can't really make a move in that little bitty Porsche without getting goosed by the goddamned gear shift."

"She was driving her Porsche drunk?"

"I was driving. What's her story, anyway? That house she's got on the golf course? She married?" he said, as if the possibility had just that minute occurred to him.

"She's not married. I would have introduced you to Mo myself," said Fontana, "but I figured sooner or later you'd get even with me."

Strange laughed. "Hey, I heard some stuff about you and Aimee Lee last night. People say you followed her out here. That you've been knowin' her for years. That means you knew *her* when I knew *you.*"

"I only met her last summer."

"That's not what they're saying."

"That's what *I'm* saying."

"Oh, you mean it was a rumor, like that one about you doing in Callahan?" Fontana got up to leave, but before he got out the door, Strange managed to throw his nastiest verbal dart yet. "You been to bed with Mo?"

"No, Lou, I haven't."

"You sure? I wouldn't want to poach on your territory."

"I'd probably remember, Lou."

"In case you had plans, or something."

"No plans, Lou. Not for Mo."

"I saw you two dancing together last night. You looked kinda cozy."

"We like to dance."

■

An hour later Fontana took Brendan, two of his friends, and one of their older sisters to Snoqualmie Pass for an afternoon on the tubing hill. He'd thrown five inner tubes into the back of the city's Suburban, trusting it more than the older truck on snowy roads. But en route to Ski Acres, he found the heavy snows had long since abated, the temperature inching up into the mid-thirties, the wind picking up, the roads bare and wet. They had to wait twenty minutes on I-90 while the avalanche-control crews fired a howitzer into the hills.

After several hours of tubing, he took the kids to the Mexican restaurant in town, then dropped them off at their homes one by one. Once home themselves, Brendan fed the dog a dish of Hill's Science Diet, and Fontana filled the bath for his son.

Leaving Brendan to make bubble beards in the tub, Fontana picked up the telephone and dialed Joyce Callahan's number. Her sister answered, turning the receiver over to Joyce only after barraging Fontana with a series of paranoid questions. Clearly, the family was trying to safeguard Joyce.

"Yes?"

"This is Mac Fontana. Are you still looking for someone to investigate your husband's death?"

"I am. You interested now?"

"Yes."

"What made you change your mind?"

"Curiosity maybe. I'm not sure." He *was* sure though. People were trying to blame him for the murder, and he didn't want that added to his reputation.

"Well, I'm glad you changed your mind. I've been thinking

about it. I've got a rate figured out. A friend works for the city here and knows what the District Attorney's Office pays its freelance investigators.'' She quoted a daily rate that was considerably less than what Fontana thought fair. He told her as much, and for the next five minutes they haggled, the widow a no-nonsense businesswoman. Fontana couldn't help wondering how much of Callahan's bullheadedness had rubbed off on her.

They ended with a compromise, he to mail her a contract to sign, she to return it with a retainer. Their arrangement was no doubt technically illegal in the state of Washington, since he had no private investigator's license and wasn't planning on getting one, but the likelihood that he'd have to do anything more than talk to the county investigators and repeat their story was remote—another reason he'd let her finagle the price down.

"How long were you married?" Fontana asked.

"Seventeen years. Funny you should ask, because Ed junior called not half an hour ago. Ed's first marriage ended bitterly. In fact, he hadn't seen his son since he was a tot. He'll be at the services here tomorrow, so I'll see his son grown up, and Ed never did. Weird."

This was small talk, but the information gave Fontana another view of Callahan. Fontana had a hard time empathizing with parents who, of their own volition, didn't see their children for years, and he now found himself unwilling to give up this bias for Callahan. "What was the problem?"

"It was more involved than I can even tell you. His first wife was Chinese, and when they went through the divorce, her relatives closed ranks and jumped all over Ed. The boy became a pawn, and I suppose Ed let the trouble get the best of him."

A son he never spoke about and hadn't seen in years. An ex-wife he probably detested. A host of coworkers who didn't care if he lived or died. Callahan had his share of ghosts in the attic.

■

Tucking Brendan into bed, Fontana read him the next episode from their current favorite, *Dave Barry Does Japan*, then turned out the lights. Alone now, Fontana took his copy of *Bagpipe City* by Randolph Knutson down off the shelf and set it on the nightstand next to his bed. When he'd secured the house and checked through the front window to see what was going on in the yard—the Blazer was still missing—he climbed into bed and began skimming the book.

It gave Fontana a queer feeling to read about events he'd lived through, to see them filtered through a writer's pen, another man's imagination, to see them magnified, diminished, illuminated, and made more understandable through the written word. Knutson had done a fine job, and the only reason Fontana had never read the book before now, he realized, was sheer terror. Because he'd lived through the Dead Horse Paint Company fire and its aftermath—the funerals and the recriminations—he hadn't been able to stomach the thought of reenacting it.

He'd spent a good hour in that maze of corridors and interconnected offices and warehouse spaces thinking he was not going to get out, believing he would get lost, exhaust his air supply, or get tagged by the fire and burned beyond recognition. During a break, he recalled standing at the air wagon waiting for a fresh bottle, looking around at the sooty faces of the others. No one spoke a word.

Minutes later Captain Marshall, one of the men who had been changing air bottles alongside Fontana, entered the building through a rear entrance and died in a freak accident. It was difficult for the survivors to understand why they had lived and their compatriots had not, debilitating to imagine they'd escaped death by lottery.

Fontana had been avoiding these memories over the years, had crammed them into the smallest storage bin in the farthest receptacle of his brain. He was not unaware of how much the experience had affected him.

The Paint Company might even have been, in some convoluted way, the reason he'd been cheating on Linda with a woman he cared nothing for. As that possibility occurred to him, he realized the affair began just a month after the one-year anniversary of the Paint Company funerals. One month and one day. He'd been in a funk for weeks after the anniversary. Was the affair just an attempt to reassure himself of his own vitality?

17

NINE PREACHERS

As we speed through the vacant streets, we listen to the radio chatter. Back at the station, Ben swore one of the transmissions our scanner picked up was the crew of Engine 48 screaming they'd been overcome by flames somewhere in the interior of the building.

Ben's version is confirmed when most of the radio transmissions at the fire scene center around the whereabouts of Engine 48's crew, questioning which entrance point they'd used and how many minutes it had been since anybody had seen them.

The fire is on the far south side of town in one of the older enclaves, and judging from the messages on the radio, things are a mess. Everybody is talking at once. There are miscommunications, transmissions that should be but are not repeated, messages not received, yelling, loss of temper, radio squelch.

More than once, the dispatchers have announced only essential fire traffic will be permitted. All other transmissions are cut off by a dispatcher's curt: "Fire traffic."

During the fifteen-minute ride to the Dead Horse Paint Company, my guts begin to churn, and I attribute this not to concern over what will happen when we get there, but to the fact that I know Lou Strange is working on Engine 48. Lou isn't likely to get on the radio and report he is trapped by flames if he isn't in a serious pinch.

The fire is in an ancient complex that spans two city blocks made up of multistoried, mostly brick buildings. You can tell from the storefronts that there has been much remodeling over the years. Plenty of hidden crawl spaces for fire to hide in.

I arrive with Ben and Albert at our assigned sector and try to catch the attention of Chief Matthews, who is busy shuttling men in and out of a garage doorway that has a small amount of gray smoke coming out of it. At our feet a dozen crisscrossing hose lines run to the interior. Men are missing, and the chiefs are trucking warm bodies into the fire like pensioners pushing coins into Las Vegas slot machines.

Chief Matthews notices us, puts an arm on my shoulder and talks close to my ear. He is near to retirement and walks carefully, as if he's had some falls. Over the roaring pumpers, the chain saws, the yelling men, I strain to hear his orders.

"Listen to me, Mac. We've got three men missing and we don't have an idea in hell where they are. We think they went in from the other side around the block, but they may be anywhere. We had this fire knocked down once, but it's rekindled. Nobody knows what's in there. I've had crews running in and out, and nobody's finding jack. Follow this line here. Be careful."

After we've pulled our facepieces tight and adjusted our helmets, I direct the beam of a large lantern into the cavernous entrance, and in we go just as five stumbling figures are exiting, the low-air warning bells on their SCBAs clanging.

"Keep the line between your feet," I say to my men. "It's your ticket out of here." Ben repeats what I've said to Albert. I hear no reply, but I know from experience that Albert resents advice.

We proceed maybe twenty yards into the blackness before we encounter two firefighters manning a hose line in a narrow doorway. Inside the doorway there is a low rumble and, far in the back, flame licking the ceiling in an orange arc. Yet the passageway we walk down is relatively free of smoke.

We proceed, turn a corner, and everything is black and hot. I have to crawl to keep in touch with the hose line, to be sure we don't step into a hole or off a balcony. While we grope through the blackness, the heat begins to worsen, and bricks begin falling on us. At first they aren't falling far, but as we move along, they sound as if they've been lobbed from a plane. It is only then that I realize how tall are the walls surrounding us. I feel a sickening kind of panic for Lou and cannot shake the sense that the next object my gloved hands touch will be his dead body.

I take a glove off to test the wall beside us. It is hot on my bare palm. A tiny crack has developed and I see an orange glow on the other side. There is an inferno eight inches away from us cracking the mortar that holds the bricks in the wall.

A plume of cool air blows past me into the tiny hole as the fire sucks in every bit of oxygen it can find. Without warning, something crashes to the floor twenty yards in front, and a great blast of heat roars out into the passageway. The heat pins me to the floor on my face, and I have two thoughts: the first, that I am about to die; the second, that my men are already dead.

I hear someone struggling with a hose line, hear water gushing, but I cannot feel it. I crawl on my belly, a monster of heat riding my back. I know I am being burned because I am too hot not to be, yet I feel nothing except a strange lassitude. In fact, at one point, I stop crawling, stop moving, stop thinking. After a few moments lying on my face, something arouses me, perhaps the thought of my son, so that I begin crawling again. I can feel the skin bubbling on the back of my neck, on one ear. Albert and Ben must be nearby, but I hear nothing. I call them but receive no reply.

And then I find the hose line. Abandoned. I open it and direct it toward the heat. I try everything, a fog pattern, straight stream, but nothing seems to alleviate the searing heat. Soon clouds of steam descend on me. Albert and Ben are with me now.

We fight the fire in the passageway for another ten minutes, until the warning bells on our masks begin ringing. We try to follow the hose line out of the building, but it is buried in rubble and we lose it, get turned around on the way out, and run out of air. We're still coughing and spitting phlegm when we get to the air wagon.

I tell no one about my burns, and with all the soot and dirt on us, with the excitement in the air, nobody notices. We get our bottles changed and head back inside, as do the crews around us. The sense of urgency has never been greater. The quicker we move, the better chance of finding someone alive. But we are so tired that as we reenter the building complex we stagger.

At the entrance Chief Matthews again warns us to be careful. He says that on the other side of the block they've had a "pretty significant" cave-in. "Be careful, boys. We don't want to lose anybody else."

His words stick in our minds for most of the long, blundering journey back inside. We find the nozzle at the end of our hose line quicker this time, for the heat has diminished now, and we even manage to search three or four more rooms. It is only with a massive effort and a lot of cursing that we keep from getting turned around. When we get as deep into the interior of the complex as we can get without running out of air again, the radio chatter on the portable radio in my pocket begins to go berserk. The three of us stop in a relatively smoke-free office, leaning against desktops while we listen.

"The east end of the building. We've had a partial wall collapse on the east end of the building."

"We're digging them out."

". . . another crew in here with shovels and chain saws . . ."

"Engine Twelve, repeat your message. Engine Twelve, repeat. Engine Twelve?"

"This is Engine Forty-two. Repeat. We have men down. We need help. There is a . . ."

"Engine Twelve, repeat your message, Engine Twelve?"

"Dead Horse Command, from Engine Fifty-one. I think that's Engine Forty-two who needs help. We saw them a few minutes ago. We're going back to see if we can find them."

"Negative, Engine Fifty-one. Abandon the building. All firefighters abandon the building. This is an abandon the building call. All firefighters . . ."

". . . two men need medics and . . ." Radio static. More radio static.

The confusion on the airwaves continues. Before it is finished, a pair of firefighters have burst through a doorway behind us thinking they've made a rescue—namely us—but we ruthlessly disabuse them of the notion. They have come in from somewhere on the opposite side of the block and found their retreat blocked by flame. I tell them to stick close and we'll take them out the way we came in. We search the intertwining rooms for another five minutes before alarm bells start going off on the backpacks of our new arrivals; then we all make our way outside. Again, everybody has run out of bottled air before we get out.

Once outside, we are not allowed back in.

When we get to the rest area half a block away, we can see flames have breached the roof on another level, and on the far side of the complex flames fifty feet high are lazily licking the night sky.

We all feel lucky to have escaped the Dead Horse Paint Company's talons. Albert sits beside me, touching me like a child to prove we're still alive, talking about retiring and finding a "real" job.

The scuttlebutt in the rest area has it that three firefighters from Engine 48 are lost, and that another group of five had a wall collapse on them. Nobody on our side of the block seems to know whether the five escaped or not. After about half an hour, word comes through one of the medics that a captain on the north side of the building fell down a steep flight of steps and drowned in a basement flooded with fire department water. Later we learn this is Captain Marshall, whom I'd seen earlier. Then they find another firefighter in the water, also drowned.

I am burned and I am beginning to be woozy from the pain and I cannot help thinking about who might be dead below all that flame across the street. I feel a great sense of loss, but worse, I feel a great sense of relief. I am alive and I am ecstatic about it.

My crew and I sit on an active hose line and watch the Dead Horse Paint Company raze itself. It will be morning before they'll send us in for the bodies. Nine bodies, we are told. From experience, I know that means there will be nine separate funerals. Nine preachers.

The names filter down the fire lines in snatches, and after I tote them up, I realize Lou Strange's name is not among them. I wonder if there has been a mistake.

18

THE ANGRY MAN WITH TOILET PAPER STUCK TO HIS SHOE

It was raining so hard when Fontana took Brendan to school that there were no stray dogs on the playground, the only bikes in the rack were orphans from the day before, and a wet flag hung on the pole like a stolen shirt. Brendan's coat and lunch sack were quickly measled with raindrops as he scampered from the truck to the main doors.

When Fontana pulled into the bay at the fire station, Jennifer Underhill surprised him from behind. "Have a nice weekend, Chief?"

"There's something about going to the funeral of someone you didn't like that makes you feel guilty. How was your weekend?"

"I had to put my cat to sleep. I feel plenty guilty myself. I've got some information on the case. Can you talk?"

"Sure."

Fontana led her into his office, threw the mail and the aid reports from that weekend into a pile on his desk, closed the door, and showed her to a chair with a patch in the fabric and a pad missing on one arm—the best he could offer since Mo Costigan had placed Roger Truax in charge of furnishing the station.

Underhill wore little makeup, her hair pulled back, her blazer ironed and pants creased. She was a tall woman with substantial hip structure and a soft aspect to the flesh on her face that reminded him of a marshmallow beginning to puff up over the campfire. She was in her late thirties and had been a firefighter at one time, though he calculated it must have taken every ounce of her strength to do even the routine tasks. Then again, it was hard to know how strong a woman was by looking at her. Heather, for instance, looked like a pushover but actually was stronger than all but a few of the volunteers.

Crossing her legs, Underhill leaned against the briefcase propped in her lap. "There's lots to report. Some of it I know the implications of, and some of it I'd like to bounce off you, if you don't mind."

"Before you say anything, I need to tell you Callahan's widow hired me to tell her what happened to her husband."

"That's *our* job."

"Not exactly. Your job is to track down who killed him and to dig up enough evidence for the prosecutors to convict. Whether or not you tell her is almost beside the point. And she knows it."

"I admit I didn't much care for her. That's a horrible thing to say about someone who just lost her husband. We spoke. She seemed a little . . . frosty. I had the sense she was not going to miss him all that much."

"She misses him enough to pay money to find out what happened."

"Maybe I was wrong. Okay. Here's what we've got. Callahan was a week away from becoming the head cheese in your old department. He comes out to the fire conference this weekend, where he's scheduled to give an overview of the Dead Horse Paint Company fire, which he basically ran, right?"

"He was the incident commander. He ran it, yes."

"Scheduled to give a talk directly after Callahan is Randolph Knutson, who wrote a book about the fire, a book—I read it yesterday—that was a little less than flattering with regard to Callahan's actions. So what was Callahan likely to say at this conference?"

"Callahan was no apologist. To hear him talk about it, he ran that fire like a maestro conducting the New York Philharmonic. Knutson claims Callahan did his best to get those nine firefighters killed, that he might have lost more if certain events had gone a little differently. Callahan stands up and talks about what a god-like tactician he was, then Knutson gets up and shoots his tin-man defense full of holes with facts, statistics, quotes, and the legitimacy of a genuine *New York Times* best-seller behind him. Those two would have been worth the price of admission. Running them one after the other like that? That was wicked. Whoever thought that up?"

"You'll never guess."

"Truax?"

She nodded. "How accurate was Knutson's book?"

"I haven't read it all yet, but from what I've gotten through so far, it's dead on."

"So Callahan has been going around giving talks absolving himself, and Knutson's been going around giving talks depicting Callahan as a jackass and a killer."

"Basically."

"Did he really tell people to get in there, that they were expendable? Somebody said he struck a firefighter."

"Over the years, he struck a lot of firefighters. I don't know how he got away with it. Picking his targets carefully, I suppose. Trying to prove how tough he was. His brother was huge, and Ed was a rather small man. I think working with all of us hooligans put a serious chip on his shoulder."

"And then at the fire, after he found out a captain had gone down, he was asking people how high they were on the promotion list, as if the captain's life was just a spot to be filled on the roster? Did he really do that, Mac?"

"He did."

"And when Knutson interviewed Callahan for the book, he caught him in a number of factual errors?"

"I was actually surprised Callahan consented to an interview. He probably thought Knutson would be too intimidated to print the truth. Either that, or he'd twisted it around in his own mind so that he really believed his version and thought Knutson would too. It's hard to tell with people like him. Truax pitting those two against each other at the conference? He's lucky Callahan didn't jump all over him."

"He did. You didn't hear about it? The afternoon of the murder Callahan and Roger Truax had a loud argument at the hotel. Quite loud. Lots of witnesses. By the way, I spoke to Truax this morning before coming over here. He said he merely wanted to schedule like subjects on the same day. Said having Knutson come on directly after Callahan was just happenstance."

"Hardly."

"All I know is, he keeps asking me out."

"Roger? Roger does? Roger is married."

"He says his wife won't mind if we don't tell her. I feel sorry for her, but not enough to take him off her hands."

Fontana laughed.

"We've managed to trace part of Callahan's last day," she went on. "His colleagues at the Stouffer-Madison where they were all staying told us that just minutes after his squabble with Truax he had a heated phone conversation in the lobby. He and some others were planning an afternoon of sightseeing, riding the ferry to Bremerton and so forth, but at the last minute Callahan begged off. Said he had to meet somebody."

"Who?"

"Nobody knows."

"So there's a likelihood he wasn't abducted by strangers. That he'd been with somebody he knew."

"Or was on the way to meet them. On top of that, he told one of the desk clerks at the hotel all his troubles would soon be over. The clerk remembered him because he treated the staff poorly and because he was walking around the lobby with a piece of toilet paper stuck to his shoe. We got lucky. People remember things like that."

"Callahan frequently had a piece of toilet paper stuck to his shoe. It was a trademark."

"Really?"

Fontana smiled. "You figure out what he was doing in a stolen car?"

"That's the sixty-four-thousand-dollar question."

"I wonder if he rode the forty or so miles from Seattle in the trunk."

"As I told you before, the car was stolen in Seattle. The man it was stolen from checks out. His name is Arthur Rembrandt Huddleston."

"Rembrandt?"

"I'm not his mother. I didn't name him. I think we've excluded Huddleston from consideration. He punched a time clock at Todd Shipyard about the time that car fire was being reported."

"So what can I help you with?"

"Randolph Knutson. You know him?"

"I know him."

"What was his relationship to all these people?"

"You could speak to him yourself. He's here in the Northwest, you know. Living somewhere in Seattle."

"I saw him briefly, but he wouldn't say much. After the murder, he canceled his appearance at the conference Saturday, and he won't take our calls. You and I both know, if he doesn't want to talk there's not much we can do."

"Randy's a funny guy. Before he got in the department he worked as a clown for some outfit that did birthdays and company picnics—called Universal Clowns or something like that. Anyway, he liked to argue. His idea of a good time was starting a fight with his superior officer. Every shift. He got transferred around a lot."

"I bet Callahan loved him."

"Everybody underestimated Randy. He'd written a couple of children's books nobody ever heard of, then he wrote a book on the history of our fire department which he self-published, so when word got out that he was writing this thing on the Paint Company, people didn't pay any attention. I remember he was going around telling us he'd received half a million for the advance. Everybody thought he was bullshitting."

"You think he's on drugs?"

"I never saw any indication of drugs when I worked with him. But he looked pretty bad Saturday."

"I saw him directly after the funeral. He was dressed inappropriately and acting . . . I'm not sure how to describe it. Divorced from reality.''

"Randy's always been on the edge, but he had some trouble at the funeral that might have made him seem odder than normal. Ran into one of the principals in his book. Louis Strange.''

"Who's Strange? Which was he in the book?''

"The man who originally tapped the fire. The man who left the fire ground without authorization. The man whose crew went back into the fire searching for him and never came out.''

"How awful.''

"His daughter was following me earlier in the week. I still haven't figured that out. She's got a nasty record you might want to look up. You want to talk to them, they're sleeping in a Bounder in my front yard.''

"Maybe I will. Anybody else we should know about?''

"A man named Lawrence Drummey.''

"There was a Drummey on the list of fatalities at the Paint Company.''

"His brother. Drummey's mentioned publicly several times that Callahan should die the way his brother did. He's what you'd call obsessed.''

"Refresh my memory. I know one of them drowned and a couple had walls fall on them, and a pair got trapped in the smoke. Which one was Drummey's brother?''

"He burned to death. The fire chased them up a corridor to a dead end, and then a wall fell on them and they bought it right there. Actually, they have part of it on tape because their radios were still working. It was brutal to listen to. They played it on the news, just in case any relatives or girlfriends were going to miss out.''

"It must have been dreadful.''

"It pretty much drove Drummey into the nuthouse. He's been in and out for the past three years.''

"Where is he now?''

"Somewhere in Seattle. If you call back east, you can ask his mother.''

"I see. Do you think Knutson will talk to you? You could find out if there's anything else. I'd take it as a personal favor.''

"Sure. I'll talk to Knutson."

"Thanks, Mac. These people at the conference . . . I must have a hundred names in my notebook. They're all flying back home now that the conference is over. I've got to get to each one as soon as possible."

19

THE SECRET SMOKER

After Underhill left, Fontana quickly perused the paperwork on his desk and filled out a blank contract he took from his file cabinet. Then, braving the latest downpour, he walked to the post office and mailed the contract to Joyce Callahan. Back at the station he phoned the number Underhill had given him for Knutson, but there was no answer.

He decided to go next door.

Raising his bunking coat over his head as a makeshift umbrella, Fontana walked along the sidewalk to the permit office and climbed the carpeted stairs. He walked past Mo Costigan's office to a door marked SAFETY DIRECTOR—CAPTAIN ROGER TRUAX.

Fontana laughed each time he saw the sign. Truax was no longer a captain, but he'd been so proud of the moniker when he legitimately held it that he'd admonished people to call his wife Mrs. Captain Truax.

Roger was squatting on a too-small chair—he couldn't even furnish his own office properly—pecking away at a typewriter on a shaky stand in the corner of the small, unadorned room. Sheaves of paperwork sat on the desk and on a table along the wall. Dozens of certificates he'd collected through the years, including his high school diploma, a life-saving certificate, and an Eagle Scout award, were framed on the wall along with a photograph of Roger shaking hands with Gerald Ford and several photographs of him standing uncomfortably alongside movie and television stars. In one he was standing behind the comedian Don Rickles as Rickles operated a slot machine, clearly oblivious to both Truax and the photographer.

Using a cupped hand to hide the cigarette he'd been drawing on, Truax turned to Fontana. "Nice if you'd knock."

"I did," Fontana lied, knowing it would annoy Roger all day. "You must not have heard it. Hey, what was the idea of setting up Callahan by having Knutson come on directly after him at the conference?"

"Huh?"

"You scheduled them one after the other."

"You know, Mac, that scheduling was so tough . . . and yet the conference went off without a hitch. Even after rescheduling two hours of free time Saturday morning so people could attend the funeral, it went off like clockwork. In fact, they're thinking about having it here again in three years. If that happens, I'd like you to be more involved."

"I'm not involved at all, Roger."

"Yeah, well. You should have seen it. Every fifteen minutes I had shuttles running from the convention center to the funeral on Capitol Hill. It was Swiss precision."

"Roger, I want to ask you about your fight with Edgar Callahan."

"What fight?"

"You know what I'm talking about."

As he turned away from the typewriter, Truax's mouth began working like a landlocked grouper. Still in the chair, he faced Fontana squarely, his shirttail out, the long strands of hair on his head askew, the bald pate reflecting light from the fixture overhead. "Callahan's dead, Mac."

"I heard you and he got into it the afternoon he died. Heard you had a real dustup. Somebody said you almost came to blows."

"We didn't come to blows."

"I said you *almost* came to blows."

"I wouldn't hit anybody. You know that, Mac."

"*Almost,* Roger. I said 'almost.' "

"You know, I'm glad you came in." Truax remained seated and wheeled his chair over to his desk, where he unlocked a drawer from which he produced a small white envelope. "Do you know anything about this?"

He slid a glossy photo out of the envelope, a photo Fontana recognized immediately as having come from the same batch Pierpont had given him. It was a photo of Heather Minerich looking giggly, red-faced, naked except for a cockeyed dress hat from somebody's fire uniform, probably hers. He moved closer as if to squint at it and then quickly snatched it out of Truax's hand.

"That's my property, Mac. I need that back. Now hand that back. I can't believe I let you . . . Mo warned me you would confiscate it. Give me that back."

"Let's see the others," Fontana said.

"There are no others. You have the others. Mo warned me. I can't believe I let you do that."

"What did Callahan say to you, Roger? What got him so riled that afternoon?"

"You're not going to give me that picture, are you?"

"What picture?"

"Callahan . . ." Truax tilted back resignedly in the chair. "Callahan was PO'd because he thought I set him up to look bad. He called Knutson 'that little whiny ass' who was going to come on after him and hand everybody a pack of lies. Never called him by name. Always 'that little whiny ass.' What he wanted, I guess, was a chance to go back on after Knutson. Now give me that photo back."

"Forget it. So Callahan wanted the last word. We all want that."

"He thought he could ruin Knutson's show."

"So you made him last?"

"I had to tell him no. I couldn't squeeze the time out of the bloody schedule. I tried every which way, but the fact of the matter was, it had to be Callahan and then Knutson, no rebuttal. There was no way to get around it."

"Give me a break. You were the scheduler. You could have done anything you wanted."

"In all honesty, there was no way I could see to work it out."

"You love to wield power, don't you, Roger?"

"That was never part of my thinking. Anyway, it didn't matter, did it? Listen, Mac, that photograph you have in your pocket belongs to me. I want it back."

"I'm afraid I could never entertain the thought of giving it back unless I knew where you got it," Fontana said, opening the office door.

"I found it out behind . . . I just found it."

"Behind the station?"

"Maybe."

"In the garbage?"

"I'd lost a contact lens. Sometimes they end up in the trash."

"Give me a break. Nobody would go through the garbage for a contact lens."

"I told you where I found it. Now hand it over."

"No can do."

"You said—"

"I said I could entertain the thought if I knew where you got it. I know where you got it, and I've entertained the thought."

Fontana stepped outside, but Roger's voice was loud enough to penetrate the closed door. "What are you going to do with it? I'll make a deal with you. You show me the others, and I won't ask you for that one back."

Fontana opened the door and said, "You already asked for this one back," then went downstairs into the rain. Now that Truax had struck pay dirt in their garbage, they were going to have to get chains and padlocks—or set rattraps.

20

NEVER SPEAK HARSHLY
TO A CRYING WOMAN

For almost an hour after his visit with Truax, Fontana sat in his office with a white envelope on his desk. When he'd considered it long enough to realize he wasn't going to get any brainstorms, he called Jim Hawkins at home and was told Jim was out of town. Fontana then called Heather Minerich into his office and asked her to close the door, unsure if even that was appropriate.

Heather sat in the same chair Jennifer Underhill had warmed a little over an hour earlier, crossed her legs, and played with the half-full can of Coca-Cola she carried everywhere. He wondered if she drank twenty Cokes a day or just nursed the one.

Without preamble, Fontana scattered the contents of the white envelope onto his desk and said, "I thought you might like to comment on this."

Heather tipped forward in her chair to get a good look at the photographs. Then, still expressionless, she sorted them, using only the ring finger on her left hand, oddly the only finger on that hand that didn't have a ring, all the while moving gingerly as if afraid to leave fingerprints on the photos, assembling the prints into a number of different mosaics before she was satisfied.

He noticed she examined them with a slightly curious lift to her eyebrows, as if this were the first time she had seen them. When she was finished, she leaned back in her chair and rotated the can of Coke around in her fist, looking neither at Fontana nor at the photos.

"Did you know about these?" he asked, but she only shrugged. "You don't want to comment?"

"I, umm, I was at . . . I was at this . . . I just don't . . ." Still without looking at him, she began crying, holding her free hand in front of her eyes, then bringing up the other arm so that she could rub out her tears while still holding the Coke can, slopping a line of the sticky beverage down her bare wrist to her elbow.

Fontana decided to wait until she finished crying before saying anything further. It was a poor decision and a long wait, eight minutes by the clock on the wall, which was the only timepiece he allowed himself, since he didn't want to further humiliate her by peeking at his watch while she sobbed.

Finally, Heather said, "I guess . . . I guess I'm . . . in some major kind of trouble, do you think?"

"I don't know what to think. I *would* like to hear your story."

"I'm not in trouble?"

"I don't know. Would you like to tell me about it?"

"You're not going to fire me?"

"Not for this."

"I think you are going to fire me. That was the plan. That's what he wanted."

"That's what who wanted?"

He passed her tissues from a box on his desk. She blew her nose loudly and discarded the wadded tissues on his desktop one by one. The scene reminded Fontana of the stash of snowballs Brendan had stockpiled a couple of weeks back during their first-of-the-season snowstorm.

"Are you going to give them to me?" she asked.

"Are they yours?"

"They should be."

"Heather, can you tell me how this came about? I see legs and arms and shoes of quite a few people showing here, but no faces, and I have reason to believe some of these people are volunteers.''

''Are you going to give them to me?''

Fontana was of two minds on the issue. On the one hand, she would get them sooner or later, there was no question of that. He wasn't planning on keeping them, and they were too dangerous to be floating around where volunteers could get their hands on them. Despite all the other figures in the photos, none of which was identifiable, Fontana hadn't heard any scuttlebutt about the pictures. Kingsley Pierpont knew. Mo Costigan knew. Roger Truax knew. If others knew, Fontana hadn't been privy to it, and he was generally one of the first to hear town gossip.

Maybe he should give them to her and forget the whole thing. It was hard to know.

On the other hand, if Heather had handled herself a little more aggressively at fires, his decision might have been clearer, for she would be on probation for another couple of months and he wasn't sure she was going to pass, or even that he wanted her to pass. If they fired her, she was going to sue. She had sued other employers and was paranoid enough about this job to keep a journal—not a fact she bandied about, but one Fontana had gleaned from Mo Costigan, Heather's sometimes confidante. And recently Fontana had begun to suspect that her entrance-testing records were doctored by Mo to allow her in. If she sued, the city would need all the ammunition it could get, although what good these photographs might do in that instance, he wasn't sure.

''You're not going to give them to me?'' she said.

''I'd like you to answer a few questions first.''

''Okay.'' Her voice, now that she'd stopped crying and they were discussing the situation, was steadily shrinking.

''Is this all there are?''

''I don't know.''

''Who took them?''

''I don't know.''

''How could you not know? Is this your twin sister?''

''I was a little wasted.''

''And somebody took advantage of you?''

"I wouldn't say that, exactly."

"When were they taken?"

"Two weeks ago at this party. I think I had too much to drink."

"Whose party was it?"

"I don't want to get anybody in trouble."

"They don't seem to have any qualms about getting you in trouble, Heather, spreading these pictures around."

"I can't say."

"Here," he said, stuffing the photos into the envelope and handing them to her. "I don't know, Heather. It's not job-related, I guess, but on the other hand it is. There are only three paid firefighters here: you, me, and Lieutenant Pierpont. Until we hire more, we're it. At emergency scenes these volunteers look to all of us for guidance. We're supposed to be the pros. This is not appropriate behavior."

"I know. And it won't happen again. But what about them?"

"Who?"

"All the others."

"You mean the people at this party?" She nodded. "Tell me who they were."

"I can't."

"Then I guess nothing happens to them."

She thought about this.

"This house looks a little bit like Jim Hawkins's mother's place," Fontana went on. "I know his parents were out of town two weeks ago. Is that where the party was?"

She didn't answer.

In the end, he let Heather leave with the photos, not knowing how many of his volunteers had been involved, or what sort of implications this had for his department. Maybe it would blow over by spring. Truax would still be going through their Dumpsters, but maybe this would blow over.

21

YOU COUNT THE ODDS, YOU MIGHT FIGURE OUT YOU OWE THE UNIVERSE A TRAGEDY

Randy Knutson and his wife were house-sitting a couple of blocks off Thirty-first Avenue South, one of the main drags through the Mount Baker neighborhood in Seattle, in a gigantic box of a house painted a lazy shade of gray, Pepto-Bismol pink splashed around the windows and doors like gaudy eyeliner. The house was new and tall and built on a mound, and Fontana was relatively sure the owners of the surrounding traditional and Craftsman-style homes in this long-established neighborhood weren't thrilled about either the paint scheme or the design, which incorporated all the refinement and warmth of an airplane hangar.

Knutson's Harley was leaning on its kickstand in the open garage, oil stains blotting a piece of cardboard underneath. Taped to the wall over the workbench was a poster of a hundred or so female bicyclists standing at the starting line of a race. And in one corner of the garage a chain saw, a littering of wood chips, and an unfinished carving of an owl. Randy had always been clever with power tools.

Though it was almost noon, the house was as quiet as a Chernobyl barbershop.

Fontana parked on the sloping driveway next to a new Honda Accord and walked through the drizzle to the uncovered slab of a front porch, standing in the wet as he pressed the buzzer. Chimes sounded off somewhere in the bowels of the place.

After he'd rung three times, Fontana stepped off the porch to a stained-glass side light and cupped his hands to the clear portion of the glass. Inside he saw thick beige carpeting in the living room, a kitchen with unwashed dishes, silverware scattered on tables and countertops like dead soldiers. In the center of the kitchen floor stood an ironing board, the iron flat and unplugged. Fontana couldn't picture Randy ironing anything except money or downhill skis. In fact, Randy was famous for his wrinkled duds. What was his wife's name? Ruth? Roxanne? Rachel. Rachel had to have been ironing.

Back east Fontana had met her three or four times. She was a pretty woman with a striking figure and gentle face, a quiet, elegant female you wouldn't expect would remain at Randy's side for more than the first two minutes of the first date. They had been high school sweethearts.

In the living room, where newspapers were askew on the carpet and beer bottles stood in disorderly rows on top of them, a large brown blanket was wrapped around a bony lump on the sofa, feet poking out the end.

Fontana checked the address Underhill had given him against the numbers on the house: 3224 South Plum Street. He rang twice more, knocked loudly, stepped inside the screen, and tried the main door—which opened. "Randy? Randy?"

After a bit, a man's hoarse voice said, "I've got a gun, ratfuck."

"Randy? It's me, Fontana."

"I'll put a nine-millimeter through your gizzard. I'll mail it right through the door. I don't care."

"Randy? It's me."

"Uh?"

"Fontana."

"Stick your nose inside where I can see it."

"Only if you promise not to shoot it off."

"Captain Fontana?"

"Can I come in?"

"You alone? Come on in here. You're making the house cold. Doggone it. What are you doing here? What time is it?"

"Almost noon." Out of respect for the carpeting, Fontana removed his wet shoes, setting them under the hat stand, then dressed a chair in the kitchen with his coat.

Shrouded in the blanket, Randy Knutson stood in the center of the living room, matted hair sticking out on the left side of his head, baggy socks elongating his feet, saggy Jockey shorts and a too-small T-shirt making him look like a lost boy in a poor man's production of *Peter Pan*. At the end of his slack left arm he held a replica of a German Luger.

"Put it away, Randy."

Knutson placed the gun on a stack of magazines at the head of the couch, the only precision in the room, that stack of magazines. He yawned and slumped back down onto the couch and stared at the wall across the room. For a few moments, he seemed to forget he had a guest.

"You really need that gun?" Fontana asked, moving across the carpet in his socks. A spark jumped from his fingertip to the metal of the pistol as he picked it up. He ejected the magazine, jacked a live round out of the chamber, and set the gun back down. Randy hadn't snapped out of his coma. His back was hunched worse than it had been when he'd been a firefighter, and it had been bad enough then that people had imitated it. He must be a sight on that hog downstairs, Fontana thought. Knutson had dark sacks under his eyes, dried mucus on his teeth, dribbles of evaporating spittle on the side of his face, and a gap between his thighs and Jockey shorts that highlighted one veined testicle.

"You okay, Randy? You're not on anything, are you?"

Blinking rapidly, Knutson said, "They can test my piss any time they want."

"I wanted to see how you were."

"How do you think I am? I got run out of town. Then I got run out of a funeral. Me with the biggest literary success I ever could have hoped for, and my reward—people drive by the house and fire shots. I wanted to steel-plate the walls, bulletproof the windows, cut gun ports, shoot back at the ratfucks, but Rachel was scared. Coming out here wasn't much better. Thanks for coming by, Mac. It's nice to see a friendly face. You know how many of those joes here for the convention said they were going to visit and didn't?''

"How many?"

"A ton. Nobody dropped by except Drummey, and he popped his cork a long time ago."

"Yes, I think he probably did. Who are you house-sitting for?"

"Some judge who works in San Francisco. Got houses in the Keys, Jamaica, Mexico, the Bay area. Makes you stop and think, doesn't it? A judge. Drummey was staking out the street in front. Thought if somebody was out here from the convention and decided to shoot up my front door or kidnap the fish out of our aquarium, he'd see 'em. And then I go to the funeral and get hassled by Strange."

"If I'd had any idea Lou was going to pull that stunt, I would have had you sit with us."

"I can defend myself. I would have, too, if Strange wasn't dying of cancer."

"What?"

"That's the rumor I heard. We're not exactly close enough to discuss it ourselves."

"I hope it's not true."

"Yeah, well, whether it is or isn't, we know he didn't get cancer fighting that damned Dead Horse Paint Company fire where half the department was in there searching for him while he was out chasing pussy."

"Everybody who died there went in to save another fire-fighter," said Fontana. "They took chances they shouldn't have because they wanted to save their comrades. The funny thing was in the end there wasn't a single rescue made at that fire."

"They were all goddamn heroes. And if Callahan had had his way, there would have been more heroes. He didn't pay any attention to how many people were in trouble, just stood out there screaming for us to run in. Jesus, all those rooms and offices and hallways interconnected and the warehouse space all divided up over the years. There wasn't anyone I spoke to who went in didn't get turned around at least once. Engine Forty-four's crew stepped off a floor just before it collapsed. We could have lost more.''

"We *wanted* to go in,'' said Fontana. ''It wasn't the smart thing, but we had to make the effort.''

"I'll agree up to a point. But you were on the other side of the block. The good side. You couldn't see all the mess on the fire side. After the first few minutes, Callahan had no business sending anybody in, much less those hastily organized groups without hose lines. But you're right. The first two were looking for Lou. The rest were looking for the first two. There was nobody who died in there who didn't get into trouble looking to haul somebody else out. They were all heroes. You and me included.

"But what I was trying to say was, when I started writing the book I didn't think about the consequences. Let's face it, the papers wrote thousands of words on the Paint Company, but they never came close to the heart of it. So I thought, okay, I'll write it. But then as I was laying it out and doing my interviews, I could see how some of it was going to look bad for certain people.''

"Real bad.''

"I remember writing up notes on William Drummey and thinking his brother was going to hate me. You know, seven kids by seven different girlfriends, never married. Chasing white women everywhere. Two of his kids dying of drug overdoses before they're twenty. His pride and joy, Bill junior, in prison for rape. His other son, a gangbanger, doing time for manslaughter. Larry *gave* me his brother's diary with all the stuff about his sex life. Whores, druggies, you name it. Most of them he'd 'loan' twenty bucks to after. But Larry thought I was making his brother famous; wanted to know why I didn't give *him* more ink.

"And then Captain Marshall? His wife and kids were *glad* he drowned. Maybe I shouldn't have written about it, but I couldn't help myself. He used to slap the living shit out of his wife, even in public. Beat his kids. Five or six real bad drunk driving accidents. Got caught knocking around a fourteen-year-old hooker. I never figured out how he wormed out of that. Our old department tolerated anything.''

"There were some rough old cobs, no doubt about that."

"And then there was the way Callahan acted at the fire, yelling and screaming, and after it was all over asking Chamberlain how high he was on the lieutenant's list, because so many officers had died. What a cold bastard. The reaction to the book surprised me, because it was all stuff people knew. You knew it, didn't you?"

"Some of it. Yeah. Most of it."

"I thought they'd be a little pissed—you know, Callahan, Strange, and maybe a couple of the others—but not so pissed they'd come by my place and fire a thirty-aught-six through our front door."

"I never heard about that."

"Two nights in a row. The second night we weren't home. Had to change our phone number three times. Calls that really shook Rachel up. Told *her* they had *me*, then played tapes of a man screaming. Told *me* they had *her,* that they were going to mutilate her. I wanted to stay and fight the bastards, but Rachel was so scared she peed her pants. Hell, I never wanted anything except to make her happy. Only reason I wrote the book was because she urged me to."

"You ever find out who was harassing you?"

"The police came up blank. Callahan made a few threatening calls, but he told me who he was straight up."

"Callahan threatened you?"

"Not in so many words. The funny thing about him was, he wanted to argue, wanted to convince me what I wrote about him was wrong. He claimed he ran that fire perfectly and blamed the whole thing on Strange. I don't know what he thought was going to happen . . . like I was going to write a retraction? It's not like I went easy on that jackass, Strange. Out chasing pussy while his crew is searching for him in the fire and getting murdered by Callahan. I told it like it was, man. At least Strange had the decency to retire afterwards and turn into a good-for-nothing drunk. Callahan would have stayed in forever. I'm just glad nobody will ever have to fight another fire with either one of those bastards."

Fontana walked to a high wall of picture windows facing east.

The view from here was of the property below on the hillside, a brick house smothered in ivy, a pool alongside the driveway covered with a skin of floating leaves. "For what it's worth, Randy, I thought it was great you wrote it."

"Thanks, Mac."

"I mean it."

"You want to hear something?"

"What?"

Knutson got up off the couch and walked laboriously to the phone table, took a miniature tape out of the drawer, and inserted it into a recorder on the table. "Long time since you heard this, I bet."

It took a few moments for Fontana to recognize the tape. It brought back everything with disarming clarity. During the Dead Horse Paint Company fire, Wickersham and Snyder, coworkers of Lou Strange, had gone back inside to search for him just as the fire was rekindling. It had been a fast rekindle, the flames taking off inside a wall, spreading to a room full of flammables on the floor above. In minutes it effectively blotted out the center of the huge complex with heat and smoke. Wickersham and Snyder apparently got disoriented—they had been walking down a wide corridor with good visibility in both directions one moment, crawling on their hands and knees under a balloon of heat and smoke the next.

Soon a ball of fire was working its way down the corridor toward them, and because they'd gotten sidetracked in rooms off the main corridor, they thought they were heading out of the building when they were actually heading deeper inside.

In minutes, crews directed by Callahan came down the other end of the corridor using water streams to push the fire at Snyder and Wickersham, who immediately got on the radio and pleaded for help. This is when the tape kicked in. "Engine Forty-eight here. We're being chased by fire. Repeat. We're being chased by fire. Whoever's using hose lines in the building is pushing it at us. Engine Forty-eight. Shut down those lines."

Callahan's voice: "Engine Forty-eight. What is your location?"

"It's all ooover us! It's all . . . [indistinguishable]." Static. Then:

"Snyder's burned. He's burned bad. We're moving, but we can't find the entrance. It's getting hotter and hotter! There's fire everywhere. Somebody help us! [indistinguishable] . . . take anymore . . . those hoses! Help . . . [indistinguishable]."

The tape went on longer, mostly static and some noise that might have been someone breathing heavily into an open mike. Eventually hose lines could be heard as the crews got closer, then backed away just shy of finding the two men. No lines were ever shut down, because Callahan had sent the men on the lines in without radios and, in fact, had inexplicably ordered more lines opened after the initial contact from Engine 48. Callahan's infuriatingly calm voice continued on the tape after the panic stopped. "Engine Forty-eight. What is your location? Repeat. What is your location?"

When the bodies of Snyder and Wickersham were found, they were burned beyond recognition. Fontana hadn't listened to this for two years, but it was as chilling as if it had just happened.

Fontana knew that Knutson routinely played the tape when giving lectures, making Callahan look like a Nazi war criminal. Coming on directly after Callahan at the fire conference would have been more than merely annoying to Callahan; it would have enraged him, which Roger Truax must have been aware of, as he choreographed the conference with great deliberation.

Fontana said, "It's ghastly, but what's your point?"

"You can't honestly say you give a damn what happened to Callahan. He got those guys killed. He sat in front of that building and pushed fire onto them while they were begging him not to. He killed them. Flame-broiled the poor bastards without a second thought. You can't stand there and honestly tell me you give a shit."

"What I think is beside the point. Tell me about you and Callahan."

22

ANOTHER PICTURE
OF ANOTHER
WIFE

"You know how Callahan was. When I interviewed him for the book, the first thing he said was, 'How much is it going to cost you to get this thing published?' "

"But you felt he posed a danger to you?"

"Sure he did. One night on our front porch, right square on the mat, there was this turd, and it wasn't from a dog. That baby was the real McCoy and I'm pretty sure it was Callahan's real McCoy." Randy gave off a half smile, realizing the ridiculousness of the accusation. "Anyway, it's not like I didn't get paid for the book. It's not like we're not set up for life, man. 'Cause we are. We're only house-sitting here until we decide where to build. But you ask me if I would do it again, I'd have to think long and hard. It wasn't easy, mucking through everything that happened, interviewing survivors and relatives and watching the video of the fire, listening to the dispatch audio. Callahan lied to me at every turn."

"Tell me about this conference."

"I didn't know he was going to be there, not until I saw the program. I called up this guy out in your neck of the woods. Can't think of the name."

"Truax?"

"That's it. Liver Lips, Rachel calls him. He was working on the program committee. Fact, I think he *was* the program committee. He said he couldn't do anything about it. The programs were already printed up, Callahan was committed, I was committed."

"You were afraid Callahan would do something?"

"Not really. Even Rachel was for it. For her it was like a final head-to-head confrontation. She wanted me to lower the boom on the bastard . . . in public. Plus, it was going to sell a ton of books."

"Where is Rachel?"

"Out shopping someplace. She tries to leave me alone in the mornings. You want a beer? I feel like a beer."

"No, thanks. You see Callahan when he was here in town?"

"We had words."

"What sort of words?"

Knutson got up and, dragging his blanket like the train on a wedding gown, left the room. Fontana heard a toilet flush in another part of the house, and then he was back, too quickly to have washed his hands. At one time Knutson had been a stickler for hygiene. "Same kinda words we always had. He accused me of profiting from the Paint Company, making money over the graves of my comrades. I accused him of being the reason they were in those graves. He called me a liar. I called him a *damned* liar. Same ol', same ol'."

"Where did this take place?"

"Downtown in some hotel. You can ask Rachel when she gets back. Rachel broke it up. She's always been the voice of reason. You ever see my picture of her? Here, let me get it."

Knutson stooped and pawed like a pickpocket through a pair of crumpled jeans on the floor, coming up with a wallet from which he removed a small, plastic folder of photographs. He pulled out three photos of his hunting dogs before handing Fontana one of his wife, a studio shot. She was as pleasant-looking as Fontana remembered.

"Nice, huh?" Knutson stood close, examining the photo over Fontana's shoulder.

"Very nice," Fontana said, handing back the photo. Randy took it to the kitchen, got a beer out of the refrigerator, opened the bottle, and carried it to the sofa, where he sat heavily, sipping the beer and looking at his wife's picture.

"I don't know where I'd be without her. I really don't. Oh, I'm sorry, Mac. I forgot about Linda. I'm sorry." He got up, dragged his blanket over to Fontana, put an arm around his shoulder, and spoke close to his face. "I know how you feel, man. I really do."

"Don't worry about it." Fontana walked out from under his arm and away from the range of Knutson's sour breath. At a large picture window he picked up a pair of binoculars and focused on the snow and steel-gray rock of the Cascades forty miles distant. Whoever had previously used the binoculars had a bad left eye.

"You know," said Randy, curling his legs up beneath himself on the couch, "if you're investigating Callahan's death, I don't know anything about it."

"What makes you think I'm investigating his death?"

"You couldn't let a thing like that go by. If you're looking for the guy who offed Callahan, you should talk to Larry Drummey. He's been here two or three times in the last week. He followed Callahan out to the conference. Even bought himself a video camera so he could record it. Larry's crazy."

"I've had that feeling myself."

"He's been petitioning the state to have the Paint Company investigation reopened. He's got a petition going around to have a memorial for the black firefighters who died in the fire put up in front of city hall. Forty feet tall. He's even got an artist who thinks he's going to get the commission."

"There was only one black firefighter died at the Paint Company."

"Doodah. His brother. But you listen to Larry, it was a conspiracy to kill all the blacks in the department. He can name every black firefighter who *almost* bought it there."

"A lot of people almost bought it at the Paint Company. But it wasn't a conspiracy."

"I know that. You know that. Try and tell Larry. He'd sit here and talk to Rachel about it all day. She thought talking about all that horseshit would do him some good.''

''And you didn't?''

''I went down and worked on my wood carvings. He wanted details of the fire that weren't in the book. But he hadn't read the book. He had people tell him about the book, so he thought he knew, but he didn't. He said he was going to read it after he was off the meds. You know about him, don't you?''

''I know. Listen, I've got to go,'' Fontana said, heading for the door. ''Did you run into Callahan more than once out here?''

''We might have seen him around the convention center. They were having meetings in there all week.''

As Fontana stepped out into the rain, Knutson stretched out on the sofa like a large cat, settling in for another couple of hours. He hadn't changed much. To the consternation of his officers, he'd made a habit of sleeping in the station during the day, sometimes in a chair, sometimes flat out on a bunk. A couple of his officers wrote charges on him, but he just started sleeping on a four-wheeled creeper on the floor under the rig, which, combined with the habitual arguing, got him transferred a lot. It was a typical fire department remedy: Give the problem to somebody else.

23

AT NIGHT
WHEN ALL
THE WOMEN PHONE

At precisely nine o'clock that evening, the phone in Fontana's living room rang. Before he could get up from reading the paper, Brendan, who had been in the bathroom brushing his teeth, bounded across the hardwood floor in his socks, skidded past the phone, and snatched up the receiver while still on the fly.

"Fontana residence. This is Brendan speaking," he said breathlessly. There followed a long, one-sided dialogue between Brendan and whoever had called, Brendan grunting out the occasional yeah or nah-uh, until Fontana was out of his chair with curiosity. "It's for you, Dad," he said finally, handing over the receiver and skidding back into the bathroom.

"Hello."

"Brendan is so cute on the phone. He reminds me of Audie when he was that age."

"Sally. I really didn't expect you to call. This is wonderful. What time is it in Spain?"

"Five o'clock in the A.M. I had to get up for makeup, and I thought I'd call while they're doing my hair. How are you, darling?"

Fontana hesitated, unaccustomed to being called "darling."

"Are you there, Mac?"

"I'm fine. I'm surprised you phoned is all."

"I said I would."

"I know you did, but I guess I didn't really expect it. I figured you're putting in long hours on a movie set. You've got a lot on your mind. And there's the time difference."

"I've got you on my mind, Mac. I've been thinking about you ever since I got here. I miss you already."

"I miss you, too."

"So, what have you been doing?"

"Watching the rain. The river's going to hit flood stage sometime tomorrow."

"But it was snowing when I left."

"It's raining now. The dike looks good down here. Your place is safe. I don't know about some other parts of town. No new developments yet on the murder." But before Fontana could say anything more, a Spanish operator broke into the conversation and told them they had to vacate the line for an incoming call. Sally bid him a hasty farewell and hung up.

Several minutes later, the phone rang, and once again Brendan came dashing and then skidding across the hardwood floor in his socks. "Fontana residence, Brendan speaking." Without a word, he held the receiver out to his father.

"Sally?"

"Mac? This is Joyce Callahan. What have you found?"

"Joyce. How are you?"

"Tolerable." Her voice was businesslike and sharp. "What have you learned?"

"Not a whole lot. There are a number of people out here from our old department, and a few of them had grudges against your husband. One, a man named Lawrence Drummey, was more or less stalking him."

"Larry? He used to call here two or three times a day. We had to get a restraining order against him. He's basically harmless. You can forget him."

"Not when he flies a couple thousand miles to be near your husband."

"You have evidence he had something to do with Ed's death?"

"Not yet. I'll find out more later in the week. Then there's a man named Louis Strange. Ever heard of him?"

Her voice grew thin. "He got into a shoving match with Ed one night outside Elmo's, our favorite Italian restaurant. In fact, we never went back. It was pretty ugly."

"When was this?"

"After the book came out. After all the revisionist garbage in the newspapers. After Ed had pretty much been tarred and feathered."

"What was the shoving match about?"

"I don't remember too clearly. There was so much happening during those months. Ed and I were having dinner with one politician or another almost every night. And newspaper people. That was the rewarding side of all that trouble, the few who stayed in Ed's corner. The way I recall it, Strange wanted Ed to quit the department."

"He say why?"

"Well, Ed was supposed to make some public statements, the gist of which would have implicated Ed in those fire deaths. Of course, Ed didn't have anything to do with the deaths in spite of what was written in that horrible book. Everyone knows it was all Strange's fault."

"What was your husband's reaction?"

"I told you. They had a shoving match."

"And?"

"I thought they were going to get into a brawl, and they might have, but there were people around. Anyway, you said there were people out there. Who else?"

"Randy Knutson."

"The author?"

"Yes."

"He followed Ed out there, too?"

"He's been living here for about six months. He was on the program to talk after your husband."

"Knutson's book was full of horrible lies. You haven't read it, have you?"

"Not all of it."

"There's something else I need to get clear with you before you proceed with the investigation. Are you there?"

"I'm here."

"My husband did not commit suicide."

"Joyce, the investigators out here working for King County haven't given it a moment's thought. This is a murder investigation."

"Good. Because there are people in this town who are saying Ed killed himself. They think because of his accident with the power line years ago and all that happened over that damn Paint Company, that Ed somehow had resolved to kill himself, and that he did it out there to spare his family. That's simply not true. Ed was at the height of his career. About to be made chief of the department." She sounded as if she were trying to convince herself more than she was trying to convince Fontana.

Fontana wanted to stick to the facts, but the autopsy had found traces of paint from the inside of the trunk lid under her husband's fingernails, a finding that did not exclude locking himself in the trunk after having set fire to the car. It did indicate he'd been conscious at the time of the fire—not a pleasant thought and not one Fontana felt inclined to share with her.

On the other hand, plenty of suicidal people changed their minds. And being locked in the trunk of a burning vehicle would have been an easy thing to change your mind about. Yet, had it been suicide, why choose such a bizarre method? And in a stolen car? Could it have been a suicide disguised as something else for insurance purposes? Lingering in the back of Fontana's mind was the possibility that Callahan had purposely, out of some deeply buried remorse, chosen to die the way the men at the Paint Company had. He might have chosen the place just as carefully as he'd chosen the method.

"Joyce. How did your husband feel about the Paint Company fire?"

"He didn't feel responsible, if that's what you mean. He didn't set the fire. And *he* didn't leave his post. He was convinced he'd fought that fire with the best possible tactics and in the safest possible manner."

"What about his accident with the electrical line?"

"I'll admit it gave him problems, but they were nothing we couldn't overcome."

"Problems like depression?"

"How did you know?"

Anybody who'd ever been around Callahan knew he'd been depressed most of the time. "A wild guess. Had he seen a doctor about it?"

"Several doctors. Ed never wanted me to tell anyone about this while he was alive, but he was on medication."

"For depression?"

"Yes."

"Was he on medication when he came out to Seattle?"

"Let me look in the medicine cabinet to see if he took it with him." He could hear her walking through a house on the other side of the continent, the click of a light switch, the squeak of a cabinet door, the rattling of plastic medicine bottles. It occurred to him that it was past midnight for her and that she must have been having trouble sleeping or she wouldn't have called so late. He could sympathize. After Linda died, it had been over a year before he'd slept eight hours at one shot. "No," she came back on the line. "His medication is here."

"Should he have been taking it?"

"Ed's accident numbed up the left part of his body. He never let on how bad it was, but it was difficult for such a physical man as Ed to be forced to sit around. Once in a while he would get real low and tell me he should have died with the other two. You see, he couldn't do much of anything. Couldn't ride a motorbike anymore, and that had been his passion. He could drive a snowmobile, but he had to be careful. His sense of balance was gone. Do I think he should have been on his medication? Yes. Of course. But Ed didn't listen to me."

"Joyce, in your wildest dreams could you ever imagine him setting fire to a vehicle and then climbing in the trunk? I mean, if Ed were going to kill himself, is that a way he would ever consider?"

"I can't lie about this. Early in Ed's career they had a car fire where a man was found in the trunk of a car. Ed used to talk about it."

"Was it a suicide?"

"They never really figured it out. But don't you see? Too many people hated Ed for him to commit suicide. He wouldn't have given them the satisfaction."

And of course, one way not to give them the satisfaction was to make it appear to be a murder. "Okay. Sure. I just wish I had more to tell you."

"When will you have more?"

"I'll call at the end of the week. I may not know anything, but I'll call."

"You mean Friday? Or do you mean Saturday?"

"Friday afternoon our time."

"I guess I can wait. Thank you again for taking this on. I know you didn't want to."

"No problem." Fontana almost said "My pleasure," but caught himself. In fact, during the call he'd had to bite his tongue several times when she'd praised Callahan for one thing or another, fighting off the urge to set her straight on what sort of a fire chief her husband had been. Working for the widow was making him realize how much he'd abhorred the dead man.

■

Fontana finished reading *Bagpipe City* just before one in the morning, and as he rolled over to sleep, he wondered whether Joyce Callahan was still awake and, if she was, what delusions she was entertaining about her husband.

24

THE DEVIL'S
FIGHTING HIS WIFE

It was late Tuesday afternoon when Lawrence Drummey tripped the cowbell on the front door at the fire station in Staircase, the whispery sound of cars on wet roads outside accompanying his entrance. Having spent part of the morning on the phone trying to track him down, Fontana was somewhat startled to see him show up unbidden, though not as startled as Drummey was when he spotted Lou Strange at the rear of the station swapping war stories with a group of volunteers. Strange stopped in the middle of a dirty joke and nodded somberly toward Drummey, who gripped Fontana's hand and flashed a smile that was more theoretical than warm.

"There's my man," Drummey said. He may have been mentally unbalanced, but he still had the mannerisms and the ever-hopeful demeanor of a door-to-door salesman. "How's it goin'? You find that nasty old juju man yet?"

"Who told you I was looking for the killer?"

"I saw Randy this afternoon. You gettin' close?"

"Not so you'd notice."

"Never fear, Drummey's here. And if you're good, I might just assist you."

"Why would *you* want to find Callahan's killer?"

He burst into a paroxysm of laughter, then stepped closer and murmured, "So I can give the man a medal." Drummey laughed again and sauntered down the hallway toward Strange and the others. Fifteen feet into his journey, he turned back to Fontana and said, "Don't go away. You and I need to talk."

Strange, who had been loitering around the station all afternoon, lasted only minutes under the same roof with Drummey, exiting through the door that led into the apparatus bay. Fontana was sorry to see him go, for he hadn't seen Strange's daughter in two days and had been meaning to ask where she was before he left.

Drummey and Lieutenant Pierpont began chatting. They were the only blacks in the station, probably at that minute the only blacks in town, and they established an easy and immediate rapport Fontana found himself envious of.

A few minutes later, Fontana drove over to the grade school to line up behind all the buses and station wagons with their steamed-over windows waiting for school to be dismissed. He took Brendan home for a snack, and after hearing the highlights of his son's day—a fistfight between two girls on the playground and a school assembly featuring a Jamaican steel drum band—he walked Brendan next door on the rainy path to Mary's, where he would stay until Fontana got home from work.

When he got back to the station, Drummey latched onto Fontana in the beanery and trailed him into his office. "I thought you left."

"Had to pick up my son from school."

"That's right. You got a kid. I forgot." Drummey surveyed the small room, ignoring the swaybacked bunk and shabby desk. "You're doing pretty well for yourself."

"You wouldn't say that if you knew what they were paying me."

"You've gotta be getting more than you were back home as a captain."

Fontana shook his head.

"You're not?"

"It's a small town."

"Shit, Cap. You could make a couple hundred grand per

annum working for insurance companies. Halbert did that, and Halbert didn't have half the rep as a fire investigator you had. Why aren't you out there chasin' the bucks?''

"Halbert can't go fly fishing from his front yard.''

"Shit, man. Well, each to his own. Say, you gonna take me up there and show me where you found all this bad juju? I'd kinda like to see where Edgar P. spent his last few minutes kickin' and screamin', ya-know-what-I-mean?''

"I'm not here to satisfy your ghoulish curiosity.''

"No. I just need to see it. Get the scene in my mind.'' He tapped his graying temple with two fingers.

"Not today. It's raining. And it's apt to be raining a lot harder in the mountains.''

"That's good. Maybe it'll wash away some of that snow ya'll been having. I don't like snow. Every time I think about my brother's grave, I see it in the snow. So, when are we goin'?''

Fontana was beginning to think it might not be a bad idea to take Drummey up to the crime scene after all. Nobody had a stronger motive to kill Callahan than Larry Drummey, and it might be interesting to watch him poke around. "It'll be dark soon. How about tomorrow?''

"Dark is why I came up in the afternoon, man. Isn't this around the same time you found him? It'd be good to get up there and see it under identical—or almost identical—circumstances, ya-know-what-I-mean?''

"Maybe you're right. Okay. I've been meaning to go up there myself.'' Fontana went into the apparatus bay and removed his bunking boots from the trousers and suspenders bundle, something he rarely did, stepped into the rubber boots, which came to just below his knees, then found an extra pair for Drummey from the stores in the back room. Drummey was only five feet six inches tall but, surprisingly, had size 13 feet.

"You know what they say, man.'' Drummey grinned. "Big feet—big dick.''

"I thought it was big nose—big dick.''

Chuckling, Drummey made a play of looking at Fontana's

nose. "No, man, I don't think so. It's the feets. Always the feets."

Satan came along, hopping into the backseat behind Drummey when Fontana opened the door for him. "Hey, man. I didn't know your dog was signed up."

"Don't mind him." Fontana walked around the truck to the driver's door.

"Uh, dogs make me real uncomfortable," Drummey said, leaning forward to distance himself from the German shepherd.

"Don't worry about it. He's scared of black people."

Drummey sat up straight and smiled. "No shit?"

"He won't hurt you."

"Damn. I didn't think no dog was scared of black folks. I like that."

As the two left, Fontana was surprised to see Strange standing under the rainy overhang in front of the station smoking cigarettes with Heather Minerich and one of the medics the city contracted from Bellevue's fire department. Strange had never smoked in the old days.

■

It was raining steadily in town, but eight minutes later as they were passing McClellan Butte they saw a rainbow. Drummey, who'd been carrying on a monologue about all the angry dogs in his life, stopped for a moment, gazed at the rain and the sun together, and said, "The devil's fighting his wife. My grandma used to say that. Funny what you recall. For the life of me, I can't ever spit out my social security number, all these drugs they got me on, but I remember every word my grandma ever said. Let me tell you this, too, man. It *was* all a conspiracy. Callahan killed those guys, but Lou was the cause of the whole thing. By rights, Lou Strange should be dead, too. By rights, somebody should pour a gasoline cocktail down his throat and make him fart on a pilot light. Lou don't deserve to be walking around using up our air, man. He's bad juju."

"I know you've had a rough time of it, Larry—"

"Me a rough time? Yeah. Oh, yeah. Not as bad as my brother and them others, though."

"Why'd you really come out here, Larry?"

"I wanted to hear Callahan explain why he killed my brother. I had a whole list of questions I was going to throw at him, man."

"That was it? You came all the way out here to listen to him talk at a seminar?"

"I won't lie. I was thinkin' about killing the SOB. Sneakin' into his hotel room and puttin' him in the tub with five gallons of ethyl. Ya-know-what-I-mean?"

"Don't say things you don't mean. It's nothing to joke about."

"Or lock him in the trunk of a car and light his ass up." Drummey didn't even have all the words out before he burst into maniacal laughter. From the backseat, Satan let out a surprised bark, which cracked Drummey's laughter into silence and caused him to lean quickly forward, away from the dog, hands covering his head.

"Satan!" Fontana shouted. "Pipe down."

"Damn, that was loud." Drummey came out of his crouch cautiously. "Your dog needs some better toothpaste, man."

"He doesn't use toothpaste. He prefers salt and a Water Pik."

At several points on the drive, the south fork of the Snoqualmie was visible from the highway, as high and frenzied as Fontana had ever seen it. During the past couple of days the temperatures had warmed, and the rain had been so heavy in the mountains on top of the melting snowpack that virtually all of Western Washington's rivers were on flood alert. There was no snow left on the trees and only dirty lumps of it here and there along the highway where the snowplows had banked it up. In one area an inch of water sluiced down the roadway in a sheet.

Drummey said, "You shouldn't hang around with Lou."

"He's my friend, Larry, just like you're my friend. I won't abandon him because he screwed up three years ago. He made a mistake."

"You talk like it was an accident. They planned it together. And the hell of it was, afterwards Callahan became even more powerful and more of an asshole than ever. Fact is, that's when all the talk about him becoming the next chief started. Callahan had his own ways of greasing the skids and stopping negative talk. Had half the firefighters in the department scared shitless."

"Callahan didn't scare you, Larry?"

"Don't think he didn't try. Told me I could be out on the street without a pension, mowin' lawns and sloppin' tables. Told me he'd done it to others. But I knew about all the people who were conspiring with him, and that threw him off. I recited the facts, chapter and verse. And facts is what scares a man like that. He was afraid of me because I understood the conspiracy. I knew who was in on it. I just wish I coulda been there to hear him thumpin' the inside of that trunk, man. Hey! Isn't this the exit? Right here?"

Fontana, who had been two lanes over, swung suddenly across the highway into the far right lane and exited the freeway. "You been up here before, Larry?"

"You testing me, man?"

"How did you know where it was?"

Drummey turned and looked at the dog. "I musta seen it in the papers. Exit forty-seven, right?" When he smiled, his mouth and teeth seemed to take up the entire lower portion of his skull, and for the first time that afternoon, the occasional vacant look in his eyes seemed less vacant and more pathological.

25

KNOWING
EXACTLY WHEN
TO GO BERSERK

As they turned up the gravel road toward the crime scene, splashing through puddles where a foot of snow had been a week earlier, they crossed a small stream in the roadway, sliding as the wheels hit the mud and wet rocks. Beside him, Drummey sagged against the window, looking so stuporous and drugged, Fontana wondered if he'd swallowed some pills when he wasn't looking.

Drummey exhaled heavily and said, "I never did understand how a man could slaughter nine people and then skate. And nobody but me ever figured out Lou's real part. Makes me a little sick to think I'm the only one knows the truth."

"Lou made a stupid mistake. That was his part."

"Lou hates blacks. You talk to him. He hates us niggers. Him and Callahan both."

"Larry, it would have taken years of planning to make something like that work, and if they were trying to kill black firefighters, they blew it, didn't they? Because eight whites died in there with your brother."

"Lou hates blacks."

Fontana thought about it for a few moments. "Larry, I've known Lou off and on for twenty years. In that time I've never heard him say an unkind word about blacks."

"Him and my brother never got along."

"I don't know anything about him and your brother."

"Lou knew where your sympathies were. He kept quiet around you."

It was hard to let all those good people die without having someone to blame. Fontana knew, because he'd had the same bitter feelings, had harbored the same resentments against Callahan. He'd had more than one disparaging thought about Strange, too. An arsonist would have absorbed a lot of the fire department's internal rancor, but there had been no arsonist at the Paint Company.

"What do you want to do, Mac? Just forget about it?"

"Ultimately, that's what we all have to do, Larry."

"Like hell. I promised my brother I'd never forget. I promised I wouldn't rest until things were right."

Now that they were in the tall Douglas firs along the narrow road, it was darker, raining harder. Fontana always felt a strange ghost-town feeling when revisiting the scene of a murder, similar to feelings he had when visiting a house he'd lived in as a child; he always found the scene smaller, dingier, and somewhat divorced from his memories of it, confirming many points he suspected were only in his imagination, contradicting others he had been certain of. What made this particular murder scene worse was the fact that he was visiting it with Drummey, who may have been involved.

The closer they got, the deeper became Drummey's stupor. He grew lethargic, sleepy-eyed, taciturn, his head bobbing around on a rubbery neck. Fontana wished he had a video camera running so that he could show the tape to a psychiatrist.

"Just around this bend," Fontana said, wondering if Drummey already knew where they were headed. "Over that little bridge."

It was raining lightly now, a narrow trickle of runoff coursing down the road along a ridge of dirty, banked-up snow.

Fontana pulled to a halt near the spot where the King County

Fire Investigation crews had melted the snow around the car hulk. The vehicle had been dragged away, but there were splotches of melted rubber where the tires had been, teardrops of metal and colored plastic here and there.

Opening an umbrella, Fontana stepped around the front of the chief's truck and waited for Drummey in the drizzle. Judging by the amount of rain and the warmth of the air, he knew the rivers would be rising all night. Truax would be pleased, at long last able to issue commands as the town's safety director.

"This is where the car was," Fontana said.

Drummey began walking in a large circle around the spot, scanning the mud and broken pavement and gravel, oblivious of the wet jeweling his close-cropped hair. He'd refused the offer of an umbrella.

"What are you looking for?" Fontana asked.

"Stuff, man."

"There's not much left."

"It was still burning when you got here?"

"Yep."

Drummey looked up at Fontana. "Could you hear him pounding in there?"

"You going to keep talking like that, I'll leave you out here. I didn't like him any more than you did, Larry, but you have to respect the dead. And no, we didn't hear anything."

"He never had any respect for me or my brother after my brother died—or before. He told me Bill was a crappy firefighter. Said the reason he never came out of the Paint Company was because he panicked and knocked himself out running into a wall. That he didn't know how to fight fire and panicked. We don't owe him *anything,* least of all any damn respect."

The record, Fontana knew, showed that William Drummey and four others had been working their way down a long corridor when a brick wall collapsed on them, and while it was true that William had been found forty-five yards from the other four, nobody knew whether he'd fled in panic or had been trying to get help.

Fontana listened to the rain popping on his umbrella.

Drummey continued, "I don't know why you're sticking up for him. You didn't get along with him your own self. I heard what happened. You were bringing somebody out."

"Snyder." Fontana remembered it vividly, down to the smells, yet his memories had never been so clear or so real as they were at that moment, as if proximity to Drummey's rage was a catalyst.

■

Fontana's crew had waited until the early morning hours, when the fire had cooled enough to allow entry, only the occasional brick dropping out of the walls, although spirals of poisonous smoke still bloomed up off the debris. Then they went in with lights and stretchers to begin the grim search. Another group of six brought out the first victim while they waited for the investigators to finish with the second victim, who turned out to be Snyder, his boots half burned off, his face no face at all except for a small patch where his facepiece had kept the flames at bay a little longer. They draped the corpse with a cheap white blanket Fontana brought from one of the medic units.

Negotiating a set of debris-laden stairs, stepping over fallen timbers, over hundreds of bricks littering the pathway, they took almost thirty minutes to bundle up their comrade and then carry him to daylight.

Callahan, who'd been marching back and forth in the street, looked at their weary faces and hunched shoulders, uncovered the corpse with one swift motion, and said, "Too bad he couldn't have held out a little longer. If you pussies had another couple hours, you might have saved him."

There had been no conscious thought on Fontana's part. He merely let go his grip on the makeshift stretcher, and as it sagged, he lunged at Callahan, stumbling with him until they were both pressed up against the side of a truck. Callahan tried to slip under him, but Fontana kneed him in the head, punching downward furiously, striking helmet and shoulders and face and cheekbone. Nobody was going to blame him. In the middle of an insane situation, he had been provoked beyond the margins of sanity. And then, because nobody was going to blame him, he hit Callahan harder. Four men had to pull him off Callahan, but not before he'd closed one of the chief's eyes and loosened all of his front teeth.

Nobody ever did anything about the attack, not officially, not unofficially. Callahan, perhaps fearing his remark would be repeated in public, refused to prefer charges and, on the day he cashed Fontana out of the department, pretended to have forgotten. Everybody had forgotten until the publication of *Bagpipe City,* where the incident was rendered in full and graphic detail.

■

"You whipped his ass," said Drummey, his words bringing Fontana back to the present. "Too bad you didn't finish the fucker right there. 'Course, there were better things in store for ol' Ed."

Fontana and Lawrence Drummey stood in the light rain and thought about the fire three years ago, about the events in between, about what had happened here in the woods a week earlier. "Callahan's aide that night had a nervous breakdown," Drummey said. "Armstrong. He quit the department. They say he's fishing for halibut in Canada."

"A lot of people came out of it with nervous problems," Fontana said, gently.

26

A MOST
ELEGANT PISSOIR

Had Fontana allowed it, Lawrence Drummey would have gimped around in the rain all night. As it was, he puttered about the crime scene for fifty minutes with a borrowed battle lantern studying the ground inch by inch, working his way out from the center in a carefully considered and meticulously measured spiral, chattering the whole while to Fontana, to himself, and sometimes to the dog.

Slowly it began to rain harder. If Drummey noticed, he gave no indication of it.

While Drummey foraged, Satan nosed about the scene too and soon located a leftover pile of snow forty feet from the site, alerting Fontana with a couple of loud barks and an attitude Fontana had come to recognize. Six cigarette butts had surfaced in the rain-sodden snow like buckshot pellets emerging from the flesh of an old shooting accident. In another few hours the snow and the butts would have washed away. Fontana had no way of knowing who'd deposited them—the killer or someone from the King County team—yet they'd spotted no other detritus from the county investigators, not so much as a gum wrapper. He sealed the six butts in a plastic Baggie and dropped them into his coat pocket.

"We gotta go," said Fontana. "I have to go home and cook dinner."

"Okay, sure." But Drummey kept crab-walking around the site in a stoop.

Five minutes later Fontana said it again. Finally, after several minutes more, he said, "Listen, Larry. I'm leaving now. I'll call you a cab."

"A cab? They come out here?"

"Not that I can recall."

"Well, shit, man. I gotta go with you then."

"That's the idea." Fontana put the dog in the back, climbed into the truck, started the engine, and waited. Drummey splashed around to the driver's window.

"Look, man. I need to scout out a good tree. Ya-know-what-I-mean?"

"Sure."

Drummey walked into the woods, but when he did not reappear from the forest within a few minutes, it became painfully apparent to Fontana that he was doing just as thorough an inspection of the woods as he'd done of the road. Fontana used the department cell phone to call Mary, who agreed to prepare supper for Brendan, who then got on the phone. "What are you up to, big guy?" Fontana asked.

"Research."

"What sort of research?"

"We found a microscope Mary had in her attic. I'm checking out all your typical household germs."

"Germs are interesting."

"There's millions of them."

"I bet there are."

It was twenty-eight minutes more before Drummey showed up and climbed in, wetting the seat and the floor mats. "Hey, where does a guy take a piss around here? All that coffee I had back at the station has got my teeth floating."

"You were just in the pissoir," Fontana said, turning the engine over and heading up the road. "Should have used it when you had the chance."

"Man, I gotta take a leak. Where are you headed now?"

"We've been out this long, I thought we might as well see if there's anything up here. I'd be surprised if the county people haven't been here a couple of times already, especially since the snow melt, but I want to see for myself."

"Didn't you look up here the night you found him?"

"We walked a ways. But there was a lot of snow."

As he maneuvered the big vehicle slowly up the slope and through the woods, high beams and both spotlights on, Fontana explained that this road had once been the main highway through Snoqualmie Pass, that in the woods nearby could be found old wagon ruts along with scars on the trees where the homesteaders used ropes to lower their wagons down the steeper slopes.

Near the entrance to the Denny Creek campground he stopped and parked. Across the creek stood a cluster of summer cabins with metal roofs, unused for the most part in winter. Fontana wondered whether Jennifer Underhill had a list of the owners' names. A list might turn up something useful.

Leaving the motor and lights on, they got out and looked around, Satan rambling out of sight near the roaring creek, which was spitting dollops of water into the beams of the headlights like white hats at a military graduation. "You think they were up this far?" Drummey asked, shouting above the roar of the creek.

"Who knows?"

The heavy rain beat on the truck. The picture Drummey had put in Fontana's head of Callahan banging around inside the trunk of the burning car still bothered him. Not that it hadn't occurred to him earlier, but Drummey's giddy speculations had painted the scene in Technicolor. His mood was aggravated further by the cigarette butts, which, along with the empty beer bottles, suggested that the murderer may have stood at the edge of the trees for quite some time contemplating his prisoner in the trunk. He couldn't have hung around too long after lighting the fire because Fontana and the Morgans arrived when it was still roaring.

Someone had consumed six cigarettes and three bottles of beer. How long would that take?

Had this person soaked the car in gasoline and then stood around deciding whether or not to torch it? Did the murderer and the man in the trunk talk?

Fontana imagined Callahan making threats and trying to force his way out, banging on the inside of the trunk lid, kicking, shouting; then he would have slowly switched to deal making. There would have been no screaming until the end.

Drummey took the battle lantern and began walking up the road toward the pass. Fontana had been up there the previous summer with Brendan and knew there was nothing more than an old road full of switchbacks and potholes. It came out at the pass and was, in fact, still usable. Within minutes Drummey rounded a bend and was out of sight.

Fontana backed out of the parking area and slowly followed Drummey, headlights illuminating the rich browns and greens of the trees, making the falling bullets of rain sparkle. Satan sauntered along behind the truck.

After two hundred yards, Drummey went into the trees. When he didn't return in five minutes, Fontana moved the truck to where he'd last seen him, got out, and worked a spotlight through the tall, thin tree trunks. He saw only low branches and dense loam on the forest floor, received no answer to his calls. He hailed Satan, and a minute later the dog appeared from behind.

"*Suche! Suche!*" Fontana said, shutting off the engine and preparing to follow the dog. He exchanged the umbrella, a liability in the woods, for his helmet and left the vehicle unlocked, thinking if Drummey got back to it before he did, he'd need a warm place to recuperate.

The dog followed the track eagerly, slowing only enough to let Fontana remain in sight, wandering through the trees in a straight line for a while, then veering uphill, northeast, over hillocks and through a section of woods Fontana recognized as the old wagon trail. A few minutes later they found Drummey on the road headed in the wrong direction.

"Hey, man. I went out to take a piss and got turned around. This is a scary place. I keep thinking about big Ed, ya know? You believe in ghosts? He's probably hanging around watching us."

"He's probably somewhere else accounting for his crimes, and even if he isn't, the last thing on his mind is what we're doing in these woods." They walked down the rain-swept road, as Fontana called the dog. Damn. Getting these two into the truck at the same time was like herding cats. After a hundred yards, Fontana called again. The rain was making a loud rushing noise in the trees now. He thought he heard the dog barking back up the road in the direction they'd come from. They stopped.

Satan could be heard clearly now, his bark echoing in the canyon and the trees, louder as the rain began to abate. "Listen," Fontana said. "You're wet. You go back to the truck. I'll get Satan."

"Me too."

"Larry, you look as if you've been ejected out of a submarine. Go get warm. You don't need pneumonia."

"Sure, okay."

Fontana followed the sound of the German shepherd, knowing from the agitated barking that the dog had found something. He stepped over small rivulets bisecting the old roadway. When he found Satan, the dog was pointing into the trees at a spot Drummey had walked past only minutes before.

It was a car, almost invisible from the road. A four-door sedan, as black and charred and windowless as the vehicle they'd found Callahan in, though this was a cold scene. The trees were widely spaced here, and the ground dipped down a slight slope into a gully. When Fontana waved the flashlight, he could see scorch marks on the trees, the tops burned off in a large oval area. There had been a recent fire here, but not today, and probably not yesterday.

Boots sinking into the soft carpet of pine needles, Fontana

wended his way down the slope between the thin trees. The car had burned itself out—nobody had put any water on it—which was a message in itself.

As he got closer, he saw tracks where the vehicle had rolled off the road. It was hard to tell how long it had been here. Was it a junk car somebody had torched? An undiscovered accident? Somebody driving down from the pass who had lost control? But who would be driving down from the pass on this old road in the middle of the winter?

As he got closer, he saw the body in the backseat—blackened, just as everything in the vehicle was blackened, the skull cracked and charred and hairless, noseless, eyeless, faceless. The body was upright, sitting in the backseat. The lips were burned away and the blackened teeth formed a marred smile.

Fontana checked the car for other large objects, other bodies, found none. The rear door closest to the corpse wasn't latched completely, so when Fontana tugged on it, the door creaked three quarters of the way open before jamming on the forest loam. He took his helmet off and illuminated the passenger compartment with the flashlight. Rain trickled down his neck. Satan sniffed around the periphery of the car.

It was a small corpse, not much taller than five feet, almost no material left from the clothing, and those fragments charred and crumbling to the touch. Up close, Fontana could tell by the number of pine needles on top of the car that the scene had not been disturbed in at least a few days. He wondered if it might not have been a week. It had been a week ago, exactly, when they'd found Callahan.

If this had happened the same day, what was the likelihood they were not linked? Fontana peered back through the trees where he could just see the open space he knew to be the road.

He made his way there, marking the site with a stack of small rocks, and hiked back down to the Suburban, where Drummey was sitting. He turned the motor and the heater on, radioed the dispatcher to send the police and the medical examiner, and, ignoring Drummey's pestering questions, drove back to the site.

Alert and eager, Satan remained on the road beside the stack of stones. Fontana placed the truck carefully and aimed the spotlight on the driver's side into the woods until he had it where he wanted it.

"Good boy," he said, kneeling and patting the dog's wet hide. "Good boy, Satan. You did just great, old boy. You haven't lost your touch."

"What'cho got there?" Drummey asked, leaning across the front seat to gaze down into the woods. "God damn! What is that?"

"It's another body."

"Who?"

"You tell me, Larry."

"Hell, I don't know. You think I know?"

■

It was an almost surreal scene, the flashing red lights, which Fontana had turned on to help King County locate him, the rain, the dark trees, the bright beam of the spotlight, and, at the end of the beam, the open car door and the charred corpse, arms raised slightly as if fending off an assailant who'd long since gone home to pad around in slippers and jammies and search the papers to see if he'd been found out.

The vehicle had been just far enough off the road to elude the random snowshoer, hiker, cold-weather mountain biker, as well as the casual police drive-bys, and would probably not have been discovered for weeks had it not been for Drummey's foray into the woods. And for Satan's nose.

Fontana walked back into the charred trees and made a more careful survey of the vehicle and its contents. The front seats were burned out completely, the steering wheel, dash, and air bag melted. There was nothing on the floor except small chunks of charred rubble. In the backseat on the other side of the victim among the blackened seat springs lay an object cracked by the heat. The label was burned off, but Fontana knew it was a liquor bottle.

At the feet of the victim, between the two very thin legs, lay a revolver. The weapon was pointed in Fontana's direction, so by kneeling, he could, without touching it, see that all six rounds had been expended. The fire, of course, would have cooked any leftover rounds in the cylinder.

The scene had some of the earmarks of a suicide. An isolated area. Alcohol. A gun at the feet of the deceased. In fact, had it not been for the other fire a week earlier, he might have guessed it was a suicide.

But so close to the other fire, how coincidental could it be? Had Callahan's murderer finished off Callahan and then driven up here in the snowstorm and committed suicide?

The body was too distorted to tell whether it had taken a bullet, so badly burned Fontana didn't know if it was male or female, black or white.

A few particles of the car seat and a strip of clothing remained discolored but intact behind the corpse. Except for the crotch area, which Fontana had no intention of exploring, this was the only cloth that hadn't either burned away or disintegrated. Taking the heel of his flashlight, he nudged the corpse forward, then turned the flashlight around and swept the beam along the spine.

"What'cho got?" Drummey shouted from close behind Fontana.

"A bra strap," Fontana replied.

"A bitch?"

"A woman. Maybe a girl."

Drummey stood upright and looked around the woods. "She sure ain't going to win any beauty contests."

"No. Not now."

"How long you think?"

"A few days at least. Maybe as long as a week."

"Her sitting out here in the woods all alone. I must have walked right past her."

"Yeah. You must have."

"Spooky, huh? You found one down the road. Now you found one up here. You're the findin'est guy, Chief."

Fontana stood and backed away from the vehicle, wheeling around after it occurred to him not to show his back to Drummey. "What are you getting at?"

"You sure there aren't any more out here?"

"More burned cars?"

"You already found two, man. Maybe these hills are full of burnt cars with people inside. Maybe there's dozens of them."

"Let's hope not."

27

SOME OF
MY BEST FRIENDS
ARE POETS

Fontana turned the scene over to the King County Police and left before Jennifer Underhill arrived. He couldn't account for it, but he felt an odd little lump of guilt over discovering within the span of a week not one, but two badly charred corpses within a mile of each other.

He drove Larry Drummey back to the station, let him take a long, hot shower to warm up, and loaned him some coveralls from the fire department stores. "I want to know everything about the body," Drummey said. "Everything."

"We'll see."

"Was that the way Callahan looked when you found him?"

"What do you mean?"

Drummey stiffened, stuck his arms out awkwardly, and pulled his lips back until his teeth formed a rictus. If it hadn't been so gruesome and if Fontana had not viewed the original, it might have been funny in the same way that all convincing characterizations were funny.

"I think being inside the trunk actually protected him a bit. Plus, when we found him, he was still hot."

"I would have given anything to have seen Callahan still hot."

"For a nickel, you could have had my ringside seat."

"For a nickel I woulda took it."

■

When Fontana drove home, he found the Bounder and the Blazer both in front of his place, no lights on in either. Less than twenty yards away and only slightly below the elevation of Fontana's front door, the river was roaring.

At Mary's front door, he could hear Lou Strange's boisterous voice inside the house. "Ho, you little rascal, you think I don't know what you're trying to put over on me?"

Fontana knocked, scuffed his boots on the mat, and stepped inside. It was sweltering. Insatiably hungry for companionship, and if she couldn't have that, warmth and noise, Mary Gilliam kept the thermostat intolerably high and always made sure every light was on, as well as the radio and television.

Grace Teller was helping Mary wash dishes at the sink. Lou was stooped over a small table across from Brendan, a checkerboard between them. "Hi, Dad," Brendan said, running and leaping into his father's arms. Fontana held him while they spoke, knowing that in another year or so, the boy would be too big to catch.

"How you been, squirt?"

"Fine. Lou's not so hot at checkers. I'm trying to coach him."

"You are, huh?"

"He's going easy on me because I'm a kid, but I'm pretending I don't know," Brendan whispered, squirming out of Fontana's arms. Strange winked over the boy's head.

"So," said Fontana, turning to Mary, who had on paisley stretch pants and three sweaters in various shades of pink. She'd been a beauty in her time, attested to by a wall of old pictures near the front door, but except for her smiling blue eyes, her time to turn heads had come and gone.

Grace wore jeans that had shrunk a little too much, tarnished loafers, no socks, and a sleeveless vest, midriff bare. Her arms were soapy to the elbows and her stomach, while slim, looked full. "You want some help with that?" Fontana asked. It was astonishing and a little frightening—given Grace's history—that Lou and Grace had managed to meet, woo, and flimflam Mary into a dinner invitation in so short a time.

"No, no, Mac," Mary said. "I've got plenty of casserole left over. You sit down and eat."

"Thanks, but I'm not hungry at all. Here. Let me help." He stood next to Grace and rinsed and dried while she washed, taking over the chore that had been backing up on Mary. "You just go sit down and watch TV," Fontana said. "I know you don't like to miss *Jeopardy!*"

Alone in the kitchen with Fontana, Grace smiled to herself and said nothing for many minutes. Finally, choking on her own words, she said, "I had a good time at that dance the other night. It was too bad you had to go home early to take care of Brendan."

Fontana, who had been at Sally's far into the night, could not recall telling her he was going home, nor could he recall the last time a woman had choked at the thought of talking to him. "Yeah, Grace, I had a good time, too."

"Did you?"

The tone of her voice and the moony look in her eyes indicated that she was assembling, collating, and mobilizing implications about the two of them, implications that were wrong. Using only his tone of voice, he tried to put a damper on her enthusiasm, but realized immediately that nuances and hints were never going to do the trick.

"I was wondering," she said. "Do you think you and I could be friends?"

"I thought we were friends."

"No, I mean *friends*. You know. Maybe spend time together? Go out to a show once in a while. Take walks. You like to hike, don't you?"

"I'm not . . . What you're talking about sounds a lot like a date, Grace, and I'm—"

"I didn't mean *that*. We're not going to be here that long. Did you think I meant a date? You thought I was talking about a romantic relationship?" She laughed, but it rode around the kitchen like a car on three wheels. "That's not what I meant. I need somebody to talk to once in a while. I don't know anybody out here, and it gets lonely.''

"Grace, I'm not sure I really have—"

"And I especially need somebody to talk to about my father. Somebody who knows Lou." She was speaking just under the noise of the tap water in the sink. "He's lost everything. I'm all he's got, and I'm not much."

Fontana was vaguely irritated. Here was a human being so starved for compliments she manipulated every conversation to funnel tidbits in her direction. If there was anything Fontana hated worse than manipulation, it was obvious manipulation. It was his major grumble with Mo Costigan.

"Lou lost all his friends, you know. Except for a couple of drinking buddies he's known since high school, everybody he was close to refuses to speak to him. And Lou doesn't drink anymore. To make matters worse, the family always thought of Uncle Harold as the good one, Lou as the black sheep. None of them have been civil to Lou since that book came out. You knew his mother stopped talking to him?"

"It's tough. Your brother dies and people blame you. I don't know what to say."

"Lou thought he was the hero. He ran in with that rookie on his tail, found a fire twenty other firefighters were looking for, tapped it, and walked out as pretty as you please. You know Lou was a born firefighter. Everybody knows that. It's not fair what happened."

"Have you read the book, Grace?"

"No, and I'm not going to."

"Do you know what happened?"

"My father's never spoken about it, and I don't want to hear it from you. The night of that fire Dad went to the hospital for a sprained knee, and while he was gone Chief Callahan got all those people killed. My father had nothing to do with it."

"That's what he told you?"

"It's just what I know."

"It might help your understanding of what he's going through to have a little background. Without telling anybody on the fire ground where he was headed—"

"I don't want to hear this. I don't want to hear any of these lies. I am not listening."

"I'm only trying to give you an understanding of—"

"I don't want to hear. Do *you* understand *me?* I do not want to hear."

"Okay."

"You sound angry at him yourself."

"Maybe I am. Lou was always like a ballplayer who never showed up for practice but could be counted on to hit a home run in the bottom of the ninth. Except this time he struck out. What makes it so heartbreaking is he didn't mean to hurt anybody."

Grace cast a look over her shoulder to see whether her father was listening. "Do you hate him for what happened?"

"I guess for a while I hated what he did, his stupidity, but I don't hate him."

"He thought you were the only friend he had left. He'll yell at me for telling you this, but he was so nervous when we drove out here he asked me to look around first. That's why the King County Police thought I was following you. I was scouting. He was afraid you wouldn't want to see him. You don't know how much he was hoping you would still be friends. He's scared and he's lonely, Mac."

"He puts up a pretty good front."

"And he's going to die. He doesn't want anybody to know, but he's going to die."

"Cancer?"

"You heard? He's got liver cancer. Says it's from all that smoke he took during the early years when you guys didn't wear breathing devices."

"How long has he got?"

"They say not very. Maybe three months. Or less."

"I'm sorry."

"This is going to be our only time together."

"It was generous of you, Grace, to put your own life on hold to take care of him. He looks good. Until I heard, I didn't have any idea."

"He takes morphine at night. Mac? Are we going to be friends? You and me?"

"We're already friends."

He watched her bow her head coyly and wondered how long it had been since she'd washed her hair. Though she acted docile around him, she didn't have a history of docility; and he got the sense that the little-girl voice and little-girl attitude she'd been trying on tonight were an even bigger act.

Laughter broke out behind them—Lou Strange's barking guffaws mingled with Brendan's high-pitched voice that Fontana always thought resembled a spoon rattling inside a bottle. The checkers match was over. Brendan had won.

A few minutes later, when the dishes were finished, all four of them walked back to Fontana's property. At his front door, Brendan went in the house while Grace disappeared into the Bounder, casting a glance over her shoulder as she unlocked the door, an obvious assay to see whether Fontana was watching. He was, and was annoyed she'd caught him.

Fontana told Strange what they'd found in the hills.

"Another one? How many crispy critters you folks got up in these mountains?"

"That's exactly what Drummey wanted to know."

"Drummey? Well, who was it this time?"

"No idea. If we're lucky, we'll find out in a day or two."

"Drummey. That nitwit." Strange patted his stomach and left his hands in place, leading Fontana to wonder how much of his gut was filled with cancer. "You know Drummey's never been wound too tight."

"Maybe not, but he had some interesting speculations. He said you hated Callahan as much as anybody."

"Callahan was a shithead. He would have pimped his sister to the Arabs for the cost of a bus ticket to Bakersfield. If he hadn't bungled that fire and got Harry killed, I'd still be in the department. Heading for a plump little pension, a plump little señorita, and a plump little sailboat somewhere off the coast of Mexico. He killed all of those dreams."

"There were other contributing factors to those deaths, Lou."

"And I was one of them? Is that what you're saying?"

"A lot of people thought so."

"Did you?"

"I thought it was dumb and arrogant what you did."

"Arrogant? I'd rather you said I murdered all nine of those poor bastards than tell me I was arrogant." Strange spat on the ground. "Fuck you, Fontana."

"You asked me what I thought. You don't want to hear it, you shouldn't ask. By the way, I was sorry to hear about your illness."

"Yeah. Well . . ." Strange tugged on one end of his mustache until his pulling distorted that side of his face. "Drummey's nuts. Hell, he's nuttier than Grace." He glanced across the yard at the Bounder. "I didn't mean that. Grace is a good kid. She'll turn out okay. Somebody told me you spoke to Randy Knutson."

"I did."

"You can't take anything he says at face value. You realize that?"

"I can see where you would feel that way."

" 'Sides, if you look at him closely, you'll see he's on drugs. By the way, Mac . . ."

"Yeah?"

"I didn't mean that. What I just said. Still friends?"

"Sure. And I *am* sorry about your illness."

"I know you are." They shook hands. Strange stepped off the porch into the night rain. "It wouldn't kill you to be nice to Grace."

"I'm trying."

"Maybe you could try a little harder. She's had a rough go of it. She's a poet, you know. Jots down poetry when we're driving. She might come across as kind of a tomboy, but she's a virtual poet."

"Yeah? Some of my best friends are poets."

"Who?"

When Fontana could think of no one, Strange smiled weakly and plodded across the yard to his Bounder, found the door locked, and rapped loudly with his ring. Even though her father was only a few yards behind her, Grace had locked the door. What was she expecting? A raid by the authorities?

The phone was ringing when Fontana went into his house, but by the time he'd walked across the living room the caller had hung up. Nine o'clock. He wondered why Brendan hadn't answered but then saw the light on under the closed bathroom door. He considered calling Spain but didn't pick up the phone. It was five A.M. in Barcelona. What if it wasn't Sally who'd called? What if she wasn't out of bed yet? He'd call some other time.

28

IT MIGHT BE NUMB,
HONEY, BUT
LET'S JUST SEE IF
IT STILL WORKS

The phone rang twice more that evening. The first call was from Lawrence Drummey, who said he was in a phone booth in Issaquah and wanted once again, before it went cold in his mind, to compare notes with Fontana about what they'd seen in the hills. Listening politely at first, Fontana cut the conversation off after Drummey fell into a wasteland of conjecture about Joyce Callahan, in cahoots with an unnamed lover, having slaughtered her husband for the insurance.

Mo Costigan called next, initially to chat about hiring more firefighters for the town, but subsequently to sound out Fontana on Lou Strange.

"Don't get too attached to him," Fontana said.

"Why not?"

"Just don't."

"You're not jealous, are you, Mac?" Fontana smiled. Either she had a pretty high opinion of herself or a pretty low opinion of him. How could he be jealous of a woman who offered her charms around as routinely and as indiscriminately as she did? "And by the way. I want you to hand all those photographs over to me in the morning."

"What photographs?"

"There's a scandal of immense proportions brewing in your fire department, Mac, and I want to be in control when the doo-doo hits the fan. You give me those photographs, including the ones you stole from me and Roger."

"I don't have them."

"What do you mean you don't have them?"

"I gave them to Heather."

"You gave them to Heather? You did not."

"I'm afraid I did."

"I don't believe you."

"Ask her."

"Then *she* has to give them to us."

"I don't think so, Mo."

"Why did you do that? You bring them to me first thing tomorrow morning or there'll be hell to pay."

Fontana hung up without saying good-bye, but then the phone rang almost immediately. He counted fifteen rings on the first attempt, twenty-two on the second.

"Dad? How come you're not answering?" Brendan asked, from the other room.

"Just a little joke."

"Is it the mayor?"

"It's the mayor."

"She cheats at board games."

"I know, Brendan. But it's nice of her to play with you once in a while."

"But she cheats."

"She can't help that."

■

Wednesday morning Jennifer Underhill and a second King County investigator called, asking Fontana to go out to the crime scene with them. They met him at the station where he, having stowed it overnight in the safe in the King County Police substation, turned over the Baggie with the cigarette stubs.

The morning produced only a few sun breaks as they drove past the newly built and now-flooded McDonald's near the freeway interchange and headed east on I-90. Underhill told him they'd found no ID on or near the second victim and were still waiting for an autopsy report. The license plates on the car had been removed, but they were attempting to trace ownership through vehicle ID numbers.

Two hours at exit 47 produced no other burned-out cars or bodies, not even a lost wallet. The tire impressions leading into the woods where the second vehicle had been found were not clear even in daylight.

"Mac, I'm going to guess these two fires happened on the same night. This fire here might even have been the same *time* as yours."

"The same time—we would have seen it."

"You sure? With all that snow falling?"

"Well, maybe not. Plus it was getting dark. You may be right. I'm just amazed somebody driving up the freeway saw either fire."

"You think it's possible the murderer was hiding up this road with this other victim while you were putting out your fire? That he waited until everybody was gone and torched this one?"

"Didn't you post a guard overnight?"

"There was an officer here all night. I'll check and see who he was. It's a scary thought, the perp hanging around. And then doing another one with the police right down the road. I wish we could pin these times down better. If these new cars didn't have digital clocks, the hands would be stuck. But listen. If he was up there, he wasn't going to escape by going up toward the pass— way too much snow. He would have had to stay until everybody was gone and go out that way. The tow drivers didn't haul the first car away until nine-thirty the next morning."

"The other thing I was thinking . . . You might get a list of the cabin owners across the creek here. See if any of the names ring a bell. Ask if any of the cabins had been broken into."

"Good idea, but we're already working on it."

■

Later in the day, Underhill called Fontana at the station. Engine 1, Fontana, and the medics had just gotten back from a drowning where the sixty-two-year-old victim had tried to drive his pickup truck across a swollen creek flooding the road to his home. When the vehicle stalled in midstream, he waded part way out, then was washed downstream to parts unknown. Four hours later some kids half a mile away saw a body hung up under a snag. After spending an hour retrieving it with ropes, pulleys, and a volunteer in a wet suit, everybody was feeling pretty sober.

On the phone, Underhill said, "In all the excitement, I forgot to talk to you about Randy Knutson. What'd you find?"

Fontana gave her a rundown of his interview with Knutson, including the fact that, as disheveled and sleepy as Knutson had been, he seemed to know immediately he was under suspicion.

"I guess I'm going to have to talk to him," said Underhill.

"If he'll let you."

"The autopsy came in. You were right. It *was* a woman. Five-five, maybe. One hundred and twenty-five pounds when she was alive. One thirty-five, tops. They're pegging her age at thirty to forty-five. That's from the teeth. No fingerprints, of course. Anyway, they probably wouldn't have been registered anywhere."

"Cause of death?"

"Somebody shot her in the chest, most likely using that thirty-two revolver you found at her feet. We haven't ruled out the possibility that she did it herself."

"Of course there were no powder burns or contact bruising. All that was destroyed by the flames," Fontana said.

"Right. Her nostrils and lungs had smoke stains in them, and there was carbon monoxide in her blood."

"She was still breathing when the car was set afire?"

"Most definitely. She died from shock. Probably a combination of the gunshot wound and the fire."

"Accelerants?"

"We haven't found any traces on the car yet."

"Which makes it a different MO from the other one. What about recent sexual activity?"

"What makes you ask?"

"You find a woman dead in a remote location, it's something you think about."

"Because of the way she was sitting, she was pretty well intact down there. In fact, it's amazing what they found. She'd had sex within twenty-four hours of death. Was fully clothed when she died. Everything except her panties, which we haven't found. Who knows? Maybe she never wore them. Maybe burned up on the seat beside her. But here's the kicker. She had sex with two different men."

"You sure?"

"That's what they're telling us."

"And of course, they can DNA-type the men if there's enough semen, right? So are you running cross-checks to see whether one of the people she had sex with was Edgar Callahan?"

"Already in the hopper. We'll know within a month, or two or three. Depending on the lab. They went up there to meet? Her husband or boyfriend showed up and killed them both? Could be. Except Callahan had a hotel room. Why would he meet a woman up there?"

"I don't know, Jennifer, but if a husband or boyfriend killed them, he probably would have done them together. The way this happened, I think there's another story to it. And the stolen car. We still have to account for that."

"Mac, I'm wondering now if this was even personal. It's beginning to look more and more like some sort of twisted sex killing. Let's say Callahan and some other guy pick up a hooker and drive her up into the hills. Maybe with the intention of killing her."

"What other guy?"

"Well, let's just say there's another guy. And something goes wrong, so the other guy kills them both."

"I don't see Callahan getting into that situation, but I didn't know him well enough to be sure. What about the vehicle with the woman in it?"

"Belongs to a car rental agency out by the airport. Hertz."

"Rented to Edgar Callahan?"

"Bingo."

"So the murders are definitely linked not only by location and MO, but because the woman was in Callahan's car."

"And Callahan was maybe in the woman's car. But the other car was stolen. Women don't usually steal cars."

"But sometimes they hang around with guys who do."

"And there's one other item. Are your friends in the motor home still in your front yard?"

"Sure. Yeah."

"After talking to you the other day, I went over and spoke to them. Did they happen to mention it?"

"No."

"I gave them both a pretty thorough going over. You'd think they would have mentioned it. They were here the day Callahan died, weren't they? Here in town."

"They were in the area. I don't know if they were in town."

"You think about kicking them off your property?"

"I've thought about it. But at one time, Lou Strange was a close friend."

"It's your decision. You think of anything else, give me a jingle."

"Sure."

Fontana was mulling over the phone call when Grace Teller opened his office door without knocking, looked at him boldly for a moment, and then grew suddenly shy. Her hair was wet and she wore the same clothes she'd had on the night before. "Would you like to take a walk with me?" she asked.

"It still raining?"

"I don't think it ever stops in this town. At first I thought it was kind of depressing, but now I see how you get used to it. You like it, don't you?"

"I do, but I can't get free just now, Grace."

"We can talk about whatever's on your mind. I'm a good listener. Or we can just walk without talking. I'm good at being quiet, too."

"Sorry, Grace. I don't have the time."

"How about in an hour?"

"Not then, either."

"Sure." Exiting as unceremoniously as she'd entered, she left his door ajar and slammed the front door.

■

That night when Larry Drummey called asking for details of the investigation, Fontana put him off. He'd begun to suspect that Drummey had somehow led him and Satan to that body.

Filled with pent-up frustration, Joyce Callahan called too, but he told her he wouldn't have anything until Friday afternoon. "There is one question, though, Joyce. It's a little personal."

"Anything."

"Your husband had that accident with the electrical line. You said he was numb?"

"Most of his left side had no feeling."

"What else did it leave him with?"

"From time to time he would get depressed. But as I told you before, never to the point of suicide."

"Yes, well, usually a man like your husband only gets to the point of suicide once. I can't see ever finding any hesitation marks on his wrists. Tell me—and this is the personal part which you don't have to answer if it bothers you—was he able to function sexually?"

"Pardon?"

It was the wrong question, he knew that immediately, yet it was too late to back down. "Was he able to—?"

"I think I catch your drift. I really don't think that's an answer I need to give to a relative stranger."

"No, you don't, Joyce. I said you didn't have to answer it. I'm sorry if the question embarrasses you."

"No, the question doesn't bother me. The impertinence is what bothers me. Are you trying to say there's a woman involved in my husband's death?"

"I'll be able to tell you more on Friday. And I didn't mean to be impertinent."

The person who did not call that night was Sally Culpepper. The more he thought about it, the more he knew it had been her call he'd missed the night before. Exactly at nine.

29

THE CLOWN
IN THE DITCH

Thursday evening Fontana and Brendan cooked supper next door at Mary's: salmon that Fontana had caught in the fall on a fishing trip up to the straits.

After father and son washed the dishes and policed the kitchen, the three of them sat in front of the special news coverage of the flooding, a significant portion of it devoted to the upper valley and the drowning death.

"Hey, Mac? Mac, old boy," hailed Randy Knutson, as Fontana and his son arrived home later that evening. "Mac?"

Slumped like a drunk in the driver's seat of a red Honda Accord, Knutson rolled his window low to give the full effect of his blaring radio and bloodshot eyes. Satan barked until Fontana told him to stop.

Leaving his keys in the ignition, Knutson climbed out, hunch-shouldered and rumpled in dirty jeans, scuffed motorcycle boots, and a white T-shirt with the sleeves rolled up on his thin arms.

"I've got homework, Dad," Brendan said.

"Go ahead on in." The boy disappeared into the house with the dog.

"What's going on?" Fontana asked.

"I heard you found another body up in the hills."

"Where'd you hear that?"

"It's all over the news."

"Come on in," Fontana said, hoping to get Knutson under cover before Lou Strange spotted him. Mo Costigan's red Porsche was parked near the front door of the Bounder, and if there was a commotion, she was bound to create a stink, too.

"Nice wheels," said Knutson, nodding at the Porsche. He traipsed through the front door and at the same time expertly flicked a smoldering cigarette stub into the dormant Exbury azalea outside. He banged into the side of the doorway with his hip as if he'd been drinking, but Randy often walked as if he'd been drinking, stumbling over rugs and bumping into things, partially out of habit, more often as pure affectation.

Fontana clicked on two lamps in the knotty-pine living room and invited Knutson to sit.

Knutson gave him a darting look and said he'd prefer to stand. "So what's with the second body?"

"About a mile from where we found Callahan. A woman in a burned-out car hulk."

"No shit? Rachel's going to want to move. She gets skittery about this stuff. Who was it?"

"Right now, nobody knows. There was no ID, and she wasn't exactly recognizable."

"What do you make of it?"

"It's hard to say, Randy."

"A mile away from the first one?"

"I believe so. Yes. You're going to write about this, aren't you? This is for your next book."

"Probably."

"Go talk to the King County people who are running the investigation."

"No way. They'll put the screws to me."

"You got something to hide?"

"It's a question of personal dignity. I've been through the wringer the last two years, and I don't need any more bullshit."

"Let them put the screws to you. They're not going to throw you in the slammer for asking questions. Maybe they'll even let you in on what's going on."

"Why should I talk to them when *you* can tell me?"

"I can't tell you much. Drummey asked me to show him where Callahan was found. We got to messing around in the woods up there and stumbled across the car hulk."

"Tell me he wasn't the one who found the second body."

"The dog found it."

"Don't you get it? Larry knew it was there. Think about it."

Fontana had already given the idea considerable thought, most of it while he was still in the woods with Drummey. Yet if Larry was the murderer, why would he want the second victim discovered any sooner than necessary?

The very fact that the two bodies had been on a deserted road in a snowstorm hinted that the killer had tried for at least some concealment, either by the location or by the weather; the longer it took to discover the second body, the more evidence would be compromised or eliminated by the elements. And if the killer had been Lawrence Drummey, why hurry it up?

On the other hand, the discovery had confused the investigation. The newspapers were running amok with speculation, and the murders had even made some national newscasts.

Maybe the dead woman was a wild card. Maybe she had nothing to do with Callahan. Maybe she was an innocent victim, a prostitute, a hitchhiker, a cabin owner caught in the wrong place at the wrong time. Maybe she was a suicide who'd read about the murder and gone up the next day to die in a similar manner. No. That wasn't possible. How would she have gotten into Callahan's rental?

"You really think Drummey's involved?" Fontana asked.

"He's been in town over a week, and you and I both know all he thinks about is revenge." Knutson walked to the window and, cupping his hands to the glass, peered out at the motor home for a moment, then turned back. "You bet your ass I think he's involved. I think he came here to kill Callahan and somehow tricked him into a meeting. Maybe that woman was the staked goat. Maybe he got her to lure Callahan up there. Maybe that's why she's dead, too. Because she was a witness.''

''There's no evidence to suggest any of this.''

''You got two dead bodies. What does that suggest?''

Knutson paced as they talked, hands twitchy, his walk erratic, his body in constant motion. Fontana found it hard to imagine he'd been a successful clown, though by all reports he had been. ''Doesn't anybody live up there? Did they see anything?''

''Nobody lives that far up, not in the winter. There's a campground nearby, but that's summer use only.''

''So nobody would have heard anything?''

''Nobody but the participants.''

''And this woman was just . . . what? How did she die? Beat to death? What?''

''Shot.''

''You sure?''

''She was shot.''

''Where?''

''The chest.''

''So she died of a gunshot wound?''

''You're awfully interested in this, Randy.''

''What we've got here is about a book and a half. And it's going to build right on top of the sales of my other one.''

''She inhaled enough smoke to leave traces in her throat and lungs.''

''Meaning?''

''Meaning she was shot, but when the fire was set she was alive.''

He thought about that for a few moments. ''What if the fire was set before she was shot?''

''Who would stay in a burning car, even with a gun on them?''

''Maybe she was knocked out.''

''Possible. But I've seen suicides with the same scenario. A gun at the feet in a burned-out car. Don't ask me why they do it that way, but sometimes they do. Light the car. Shoot themselves. Setting up their own funeral pyre.''

Turning his back to the room, Knutson went to the window. ''Who do you think she was?''

"I don't even want to speculate."

"Whose car was she was found in?"

"Callahan's rental."

"Then whose car was the other one? The one Callahan was in?"

"It was stolen from someplace in Seattle."

"You got an address where it was stolen from?"

"At the station I have. Not here." Fontana had memorized the address, but he wasn't going to give it out to a half-drunk writer who might rush out and attempt to interview the owner tonight.

"Did they tie her up?"

"I didn't spend a lot of time up there, Randy. It was raining pretty hard. The cops came and we left."

Knutson thought about what he'd heard, then laughed a cruel laugh and went out the front door. The Blazer and the Porsche were both missing from the yard now, the Bounder lit but lifeless. Fontana watched Knutson drive out his circular driveway, running over a small evergreen shrub, and wondered what sort of book Randy would get out of all this. Whatever it turned out to be, it couldn't possibly foment as much grief as his last.

Whichever way this unraveled, there was going to be a story in it and Randy was going to make a killing—provided, of course, he could get off booze and drugs or whatever else he was on long enough to do the scribbling. Tonight he'd looked worse than ever, large, blackened circles under both bleary eyes, too antsy even to sit.

Fontana went over Brendan's homework with him until Brendan waved him off. Then he turned the heat up and sat down with the paper, waiting for nine o'clock. At ten minutes after eight the phone rang. "Chief?"

"Yes."

"Chief, we're out here on the old highway on the way out of town where Sutton branches off to go into Snoqualmie on the back side. Chief, you better get out here."

Fontana recognized the voice, Jim Hawkins, riding the aid car tonight with Tolmi. "What is it?"

"You know a guy named Randolph Knutson?"

"He was here at the house not half an hour ago."

"Somebody just beat the crap out of him."

■

They were lined up like toy cars on the dark highway: the Honda Accord, the aid unit, the medic unit, and a King County Police cruiser, the uniformed officer sitting inside working on a clipboard. It was the same officer Fontana had seen Tuesday night in the woods.

Parking behind the medic unit, Fontana stepped up into the vehicle and made his way around the white coats to the head of the gurney. The victim was on his back, one arm in a cardboard splint, his legs in pneumatic MAST trousers. The medics were putting a line into his good arm. "He conscious?" Fontana asked.

Hawkins, a stocky, red-haired, twenty-one-year-old volunteer who lived and breathed the fire department, said, "He's coming in and out of it. We almost didn't have any vitals when we first got here."

"How'd you get the call?"

"That cop out there was checking out a disabled. Found the keys in the ignition and as he was poking around, he heard someone moaning in the ditch. He almost drowned."

Knutson's hair was matted with mud, his clothing, all of which had been scissored off and dumped onto the floor, sopping. "He say what happened?"

"That you, Mac?" the victim mumbled through broken teeth and a mouthful of blood.

Until he spoke, Fontana wasn't entirely sure it was Knutson, but there was just enough healed-over twang from his boyhood in the Carolinas to be recognizable. "What happened, Randy?"

"Stopped my car . . . thought it was an accident. In front of me. Got out and they jumped me."

"Who jumped you?"

"Coupla big, ugly fuckers."

"Did you know them?"

"Beat the piss out of me. No foolin'. I pissed my pants."

Fontana was mildly annoyed when one of the medics took him outside to fill him in and stood right next to the van's exhaust pipe, oblivious of the igloo of toxic gases that had built up around it. "Somebody got him down and put the boots to him," the medic said. "Broken tib-fib. Clavicle. Humerus. A lot of ribs. And you saw his face. There are boot prints all over him."

"You going to give those clothes to the cops? They might be able to get a shoe size. Or type some blood."

"Sure."

Fontana looked up and down the highway. Only one vehicle had passed during the time he was here. Once the assailants had rendered Knutson prone and helpless (and one broken bone would have done that), they could have stopped their beating at the approach of headlights and resumed their labors under the anonymity of darkness.

"Randy," Fontana said, climbing back into the medic unit. "What kind of vehicle was it?"

"Sport utility."

"Like a Ford Explorer?"

"Or small truck."

"What'd these Dugans look like?"

"Didn't see shit."

"I thought you said they were a couple of big, ugly fuckers."

"I guess. Hit me from behind. Didn't see much."

"Either of them say anything?"

"Who?"

"The men who beat you."

"Too busy bleeding to listen."

"Was anybody following you when you left town?"

"Din't see."

While the medics took Knutson to Overlake Hospital in Bellevue, Fontana had Tolmi drive the Accord back to the fire station behind Hawkins in the aid unit. With the medics out of service, there would be only two people on duty, both volunteers, both under twenty-two. Fontana might have spoken to Hawkins about Heather Minerich's pictures, but he had other things on his mind.

It was nine-thirty when Fontana got home. Brendan was in bed, though not asleep. As Fontana washed up and prepared to read him the next installment of the Dave Barry book, Mary came to the bathroom doorway and said, "You got a call. A woman. She didn't give her name."

"Did she say whether she was going to call back?"

"Nope."

"What time did it come in?"

"I don't know, Mac. A while back. Why? Was it important? Maybe I should have asked for her name."

"If it's important, she'll call back," he said, realizing he'd missed Sally three nights in a row now.

30

BAGPIPE CITY, THE PREFACE—OR, MY NAME IS AL SORRENTINO

We go to the Paint Company thinking it's just another fire, Harvey and me. The south end always has a lot of fires so we expect them down there.

We're riding the aid car so we don't even bunk up. We are put on decontamination duty with the garden hose, you know, cleaning off the guys as they come out of the fire building, hosing all the soot and crap off their bunkers and helmets.

They get the fire out in short order and Lou Strange and his crew come over and we wash them off. Strange is laughing and talking doo-doo because his unit came in late, but he was the one who tapped the fire, he and the new guy on their crew, Wickersham.

A few minutes later, Strange comes over to us and tells us we're to take him to Providence Hospital. He's out of his bunkers now and he's walking with a limp so we believe him. We think it's word from some higher source.

He's sitting on the gurney in back, and we're driving up to Providence, me and Harvey, and Lou says to us, "Why don't you guys swing down past Melrose."

"It's not exactly on our way," we say. Neither one of us has any intention of making any detours for Strange. We both know he's got a reputation for doing crazy things on-shift.

"I lost my keys in the fire," he says. "You boys aren't seriously thinking about making me take a cab fifty miles home after I get through with the doc, are you? 'Cause if you are, you're just about the biggest assholes I've bumped up against in this man's fire department."

"We're following orders," we say.

"You're not following nothing," he says. "You got no common sense. You're the kinda guys who'd screw your best friend in the ass without the common courtesy of a little reach-around. Now why don't you two just ease up and drive on over to Melrose where I can get my spare keys from my sister. It's a security building. If she leaves, I'll never get them. Five minutes. Who's gonna sweat five minutes?"

"Let's do it on the way back," says Harvey.

"My sister won't be there on the way back. She might not even be there now if you two jackasses don't get in gear."

So we drive him down by Melrose and he directs us to this brick apartment building and he's smelling like Juicy Fruit gum and smoke and sweat. Strange has always been this legend and to tell the truth, we are just a little bit intimidated. We don't have to go down to Melrose. I'll be the first to tell you we don't have to go down past Melrose.

When we get there, we try to hand him a portable radio so he can stay in contact, but he disregards Harvey, says he'll only be a few minutes, says for us to keep the motor running. Ten minutes later Harvey looks up at the building and says, "Does that look like a security building to you?"

And of course it doesn't look like any such thing. And just as Harvey says this, a couple of college girls prance right through the front door without a key or a code or even a secret handshake. And us sitting around outside like two monkeys screwing a football. "Maybe it just happens to be unlocked today," I say, but we're beginning to get nervous. When Strange doesn't show after fifteen minutes, I say to Harvey, "What unit was his sister in?"

"He didn't say."

So we're looking at this building trying to figure out what Strange has pulled, because now we're thinking he doesn't even have a sister, and to this day I don't know if he does or he doesn't, but if he does, she isn't living there, you can bet Grandma's teeth on that, and now we know there is some other reason Lou is in that building, other than to get car keys. In our guts Harvey and I know we've been had.

There's maybe fifty or sixty units in the building, so we can't go up and start knocking on doors, even if that's what we both want to do, which it is. Harvey's more nervous than I am. Harvey's only got two years in and he likes to do things by the book.

It's about this time that Harvey puts our rig radio on "scanner" so we can check out the other channels and we start hearing reports of trouble back at the Paint Company. It comes on all of a sudden. First the fire buffs report smoke in the building, heavy black smoke coming from the center of the building somewhere, and then the rooftop companies are cutting holes but they're not finding any fire. And then all of a sudden there are flames everywhere. And the voices on the radio are getting excited. And we're stuck there wondering how the heck we're going to get Strange out of that building.

We listen to the frenzy on the radio and we're getting sick thinking about what kind of trouble we might be in. I flick the siren a couple of times, you know, to let Strange know to scoot it along a little, but that doesn't have any effect.

And then we hear some real bad stuff at the fire, Engine 48 reporting they're trapped. But we have Strange right there with us, and he's on Engine 48. So how can they be trapped? It must be somebody else. Callahan is running that fire and Harvey and I are both afraid to get on the air and say we have one member of Engine 48 with us, because we know the first thing they'll ask is our location, and of course, we got no business being down on Melrose. Callahan'll kill us. Then on the radio, one of them says they only have two members on their team, that they're looking for the third member and they've been cut off from their exit by fire and heat. And their hose line is soft. So now Harvey and I are in a blind panic. Afterwards we realized we should have used the radio right then, except we were too scared. I don't know that it would have changed anything. The airwaves were so crowded right then we probably wouldn't have gotten through. A lot of people weren't getting through. And those guys weren't going to suddenly get unlost if they found out Strange wasn't at the fire scene. They were already in trouble.

We're starting to get real scared now, Harvey and me, because it doesn't take a whole lot of mentation to figure out they're probably inside that fire building looking for the man we've been taxiing around on a bogus errand. We turn on the siren, full blast, but the only thing that shows up is about a hundred kids.

Harvey is pacing up and down the parking strip yelling at the apartment building, going nuts. The dispatcher starts cranking up the volume and now they're asking units to report their whereabouts. It stands to reason. They want to know who else might be missing. They're going through every unit that was sent on the initial response, which means in a minute they're going to get to us, ask where we are, and we're somewhere we've got no business being, doing something we've got no business doing.

So when they call our unit number, I get on the horn and say we're en route to Providence with a patient, which isn't exactly a lie, but then, it isn't exactly true, either. That buys us some time. And that is all we are thinking about, buying some time.

Finally, Harvey and I shut off the motor and run into the apartment building. We're listening to Strange's crew on the radio. They're inside the Paint Company looking for him, while we're inside an apartment building ten miles away looking for him, and we're listening to them giving directions for people to come in and rescue them, and we're listening to them, basically, we're listening to them die, because they die right there on the radio with us and everybody else who was working that night listening in. They're screaming that they're trapped. That they're being burned.

We run all up and down the three floors of that apartment building with our radios turned as loud as they'll go, and we're shouting for Strange to come out. And finally he sticks his head out of an apartment door, and we run down to him and we can see he's not wearing anything but a pair of boxer shorts, and this peroxide blonde mop shows up behind him in the door, and she's wearing less than he is, and we say, "Your crew's trapped at the Paint Company."

For a few seconds Strange looks at us as if we're speaking a foreign language, and then he says, "The fire's out."

"Rekindle," we tell him.

Then he's rushing down the corridor with an armful of clothes and only one shoe and cursing us. And we're sick. We're just all so sick we feel like puking.

And you know what? Strange isn't limping at all. Before we can stop him, he jumps in the driver's seat, slams it into gear, and takes off. We barely get on board. He heads straight back up to the Paint Company, slipping into his clothes as he drives, Harvey holding the wheel for him. He doesn't say a word. None of us says a word. Harvey thinks he's lost his job and I'm not so sure what I think. And the funny part is, Strange still smells like Juicy Fruit gum. By this time they're sending in other teams and at least one of them is in trouble, too.

When we arrive, they're doing CPR on Captain Marshall in front of the building but they don't bring him around. And Snyder and Wickersham have stopped screaming on the radio but they're still missing. We're sick. Harvey and I are just sick.

We don't talk about this, Harvey and me. We don't say a word until, maybe a week later at one of the funerals, Harvey comes over to me looking like he's been awake for days, and I guess maybe he has been, and he says, Al, what are we going to do? And I say, what do you mean, what are we going to do? Al, he says, you and I are the only ones who know where Strange was while his crew went in there looking for him. We're the only ones who know about the screwup that started all the other screwups.

And I say to Harvey, I'm not going to lie about it, Harv, but I'm not going to run around shooting my mouth off, either, because Lou Strange will kill us if we do and even if he doesn't, we'll both lose our jobs. And I don't say anything until Knutson calls one day and wants to do an interview, and then afterwards Knutson asks why we didn't come forward earlier and I say to him nobody asked. I mean, what was I supposed to do? I figured Strange would kill me if I said anything. I mean, his own brother died in there.

31

WHAT IF THE DUGAN HAD ONLY BEEN PACKING FOR A TRIP AND ACCIDENTALLY FELL INTO THE TRUNK?

Friday morning while Fontana and Brendan were having breakfast, Jennifer Underhill phoned. "Mac? I hope I didn't wake you."

"I'm just getting ready to send Brendan off to school."

"Can you call me back?"

"I've got some time now. What is it?"

"Great. Okay. Sure. I got your message and I went up to see him late last night. That friend of yours, Knutson. In Overlake Hospital."

"In the middle of the night? How was he?"

"I've never seen anybody worked over quite like that; not anybody who lived. But he wouldn't say much. Knutson was out there to see you. He told me that much. What did he want?"

"Wanted to know about the second body. He thinks Drummey took me up there because Drummey's the killer and he wanted me to find the second body."

"Do you think that's possible?"

"Barely."

"Did you know Knutson was snooping around the crime scene on Wednesday? They stopped him in his car and then later caught him on foot trying to sneak through the woods past the roadblock. I spotted his name in the report a couple of hours ago.''

"A couple of hours ago? What time did you get up, Jennifer?''

"Three-thirty. I couldn't sleep. What do you think he was doing at the crime scene?''

"Either he was working on his next book or he killed both of them and wanted to make sure he hadn't left any incriminating artifacts.'' The line went silent for ten seconds. "You still there, Jennifer?''

"Do you really think that?''

"I think certain people, each with a proprietary interest in those deaths, are hanging around. And they're all suspects in my mind. You got anything on the cigarette butts?''

"Of course not. It's way too early. I did talk to some of the officers who were up there with us last week, and nobody recalled anyone smoking, so it's possible the butts you found were left by the killer.''

"I have a feeling, Jennifer, that if the physical evidence doesn't point directly at a suspect—a fingerprint or DNA or that gun being registered to somebody—we're going to have to fully understand the dynamics of the crime in order to know who did it.''

"Mac, you know as well as I do most of the physical evidence was burned up or washed away. Today or tomorrow we may find out if the woman was shot with the gun you found. There's going to be some DNA from the sperm samples, but all the DNA will prove is that a specific man, two specific men, had sex with her. And even if we get lucky enough to figure out who those men are, placing them at the scene of the crime could be almost impossible. In fact, it'll be hard to dispute a defense attorney who says the woman's death was a suicide. It might even be hard to argue with a defense attorney who says the way it went down was the woman killed Callahan and then went farther up the road and did herself.''

"Maybe that's what happened.''

"That's what one of the deputies was talking about the other night. You think about it, it fits.''

"And she stood around drinking Amber Bock and smoking cigarettes while she was waiting? For what? Was there alcohol in the woman's system?"

"Not much."

"Maybe she sat around talking with Callahan, and he drank the beer. She got the drop on him, put him in the trunk, then lit it. Maybe that explains why we didn't see anybody coming out. She went the other way. But if she killed him and then killed herself, why didn't we see *her* fire? Even in the snow we should have seen something."

"Maybe she waited until the middle of the night."

"I don't think so."

"For a while we were thinking our suspect might be somebody who wanted the chief's job Callahan was up for, because some of those folks were out here for the conference. But they were all on the ferry together the afternoon he died."

"I'll tell you who *wanted* to do it."

"Who?"

"Lawrence Drummey. Louis Strange. For that matter, Strange's daughter, Grace Teller. She has a history of violence and mental instability. But why any of those three would stand around deliberating for ten minutes before torching the car, I can't figure. Maybe there were just the two people involved, Callahan and the woman. Let's face it, there's a hesitation factor here that can't be explained. It seems to me if any of those three were going to do it, they would just do it."

"Mac, murder isn't as easy as people think."

"I know that. But there was a storm up there. It seems like that would have hurried someone along instead of slowing them down. I don't know . . . There were no prints on the bottles?"

"Nope."

"This wasn't somebody knocking on Callahan's hotel room door and blowing him away after he answers. There's a missing story here, Jennifer."

"Assuming it wasn't a murder-suicide, you named three possibles. What about Knutson?"

"Add him to the list. Trying to sneak into the crime scene

doesn't sound to me like . . . I don't know. A murderer might do that. It's no myth that they revisit the scene. I've seen it. Writers do it, too. The deal with Knutson is, he'd already done everything he could do to Callahan. That book was almost like a public execution."

"But an execution he lived through."

"Right."

"What about this, Mac? What if Callahan interrupted some guy or a couple of guys raping the woman, and whoever it was he interrupted, surprised in the act, killed him and then the woman?"

"Then the question is what was Callahan doing up at Denny Creek in the middle of a snowstorm? It's not exactly Fourth and Broad."

"Did he ski?"

"Now *that* I will have to ask his widow. Say he was on his way up to the pass for an evening on the slopes and took the Denny Creek exit either by accident or maybe because he had to take a leak. Who knows? Maybe he thought the road was too slick and he was turning back. Maybe it started right there at the exit. Maybe he pulled over to put on chains and saw something he shouldn't have."

"There weren't any skis in either of those cars."

"He could have rented a pair up at the ski area. And of course, ski clothing would have melted in the fire with everything else."

"And if he ran into somebody up there, there were two of them, of course. Two assailants. That's what you're thinking, isn't it?"

"Two different sperm samples. Yeah, two men. So Callahan came along and saw them, and they detained him and killed him. If we could only work the stolen car into it," Fontana said. "Any reports of missing women since the fires?"

"As you know, the state has no clearinghouse for missing persons. You have to check with each jurisdiction. Unless we get lucky, it's going to take quite a while. The other problem is our description of her is awfully vague. We don't even know the color of her hair or eyes. And when you get down to that sex-crime angle—a woman has sex, an hour or two later she gets murdered—it's possible there's no connection at all, Mac. I had a married friend who was having an affair, having sex with both men, sometimes on the same day. If *she*'d been killed in a burning car, we might have thought *she* was a prostitute or a rape victim too."

"Whatever it was that happened here, I've got a feeling we're not going to be lucky enough to get a walk-in confession."

"No. I don't think so either, Mac."

32

WHAT WE HAVE HERE
IS A FAILURE
OF THE IMAGINATION

After a morning mostly spent dealing with flooded basements, Fontana drove home for lunch and found Lou Strange standing on the dike road with Satan by his side, the moist breeze playing with the thick, unkempt hair of both man and dog. Strange was throwing sticks into the fast-moving river apparently in an attempt to get Satan to jump in, although the dog was having none of it. It was cruel and uncharacteristic of a man who'd always liked animals, Fontana thought.

In the small carport alongside Fontana's house, a pair of short legs in grimy jeans and sneakers stuck out from beneath Strange's Blazer almost as if somebody had been run over. Tools littered the walkway. Grace Strange Teller.

Fontana parked and walked over to Lou, who, upon hearing his footsteps on the gravel, turned and said, "Mac, ol' boy. How you doing?"

"You get that dog to dive in the river, I'll be real upset, Lou."

"Just playing." Strange's face was puffy and blotched, large, swollen bags under his eyes. The river was down some, though still milky with rainwater, silt, and snow runoff. The rushing waters made a noise like an enormous whispering audience. A squall over Mount Washington a couple of miles to the south was creeping toward them, its dark beauty absorbing much of the light in the sky.

"A man could get used to a place like this," Strange said. "Just exactly like this."

"You won't hear me complaining."

"You done good, Mac."

"I know. Lou, I had a visitor last night. You might have seen him."

"I had a visitor, too."

"I noticed the Porsche. You and Mo getting to know each other?"

"She's, uh, one wild polecat you got there, Mac."

"I told you before, there's nothing between us. What I wanted to talk to you about—Randy Knutson dropped by last night. You happen to see him?"

"Why, uh, no. I don't believe I did."

"Did Grace see him?"

"Hell, Mac, if I didn't see him, it stands to reason Grace didn't, now don't it?"

Fontana did not reply.

Strange deliberately walked away. Fontana caught up to him, walking alongside him on the dike road, his clothing clawed at by the bare vines of last summer's overgrown blackberries, droplets of water coming off the thorny vines in fusillades and quickly wetting his right flank.

"Lou, this is serious stuff. On the way home last night, somebody beat Randy half to death."

Strange stopped and faced Fontana. "I cannot approve of a man who does not finish his work."

"Two men faked car trouble, got him to pull over, and hit him from behind."

"I didn't realize Randy was such a do-gooder. That he'd pull over for somebody. You're sure he got hit from behind?"

"Don't mock me, Lou. Did you have anything to do with it?"

"*I'm* mocking *you?* If I had something to do with it, I'd say I didn't. If I didn't have something to do with it, I'd hem and haw just to fuck with you. You know that. Why ask?''

"Which is this? The denial or the hemming and hawing?''

"Well, now, it's a little of both, isn't it?''

"Where'd you go after Mo left last night?''

"What makes you think I went anywhere.''

"The Blazer was gone.''

"What makes you think Grace didn't take it? Maybe I was out with your illustrious mayor. Maybe I was even in one of the empty cells in your little police station making the old double-backed monster with your illustrious mayor. Unless you think *Mo* and *I* did it. Or maybe I asked my date and my daughter to go out and work over Randy's skinny ass while I watched reruns of *The Andy Griffith Show*.''

"I didn't mean anything personal by it, Lou. It just seemed like a peculiar coincidence, him getting assaulted on the way home from my place. Especially after you roughed him up at the funeral.''

Strange took a deep breath and held it. He seemed to be in some pain. "Lou? You okay?''

Slowly, he let his breath out, putting both arms out to his sides as if balancing. "I'm all right.''

It was a while before Strange said anything else. He and Fontana watched the black rain cloud scudding in from the south. "You know, when I got into the fire department I was only twenty-four years old. I'd been jacking off in the army for four years and I was about the saddest-looking little runt you ever saw. Getting in the department was the happiest day of my life. Better even than my first pussy. My uncle was in the department. My brother'd gotten in the year before. My father was still in. Still driving Engine Thirteen. People said he used to drive so fast, if you didn't tie your elbow to the rail you'd fly off when he went over the railroad tracks. Him and Uncle Jack were legends. You still hear stories about them.''

"That's true.''

Strange turned and gestured at the fast-moving river. "You know, if a guy fell into this, he'd go straight on out over the falls and down to the sound and eventually out to the Pacific Ocean. Probably never be seen again.''

"No, Lou, I guess he probably wouldn't."

"Not a bad way to end it. Just let yourself get carried away."

Strange had always lived for the moment, and having an event as final and momentous as his own death dangling over him, listening to a doctor stamp a date on it, leaving him alone with a handful of incomprehensible Latin terms to define it, had to be a form of hell to him. "Lou? Are you okay?" Fontana asked.

"Sure. Just fine."

"Are you *feeling* all right?"

"I take them pills, I feel just as neat and tidy as you please."

"But are you . . . have you—I don't know how to say this—come to terms with it?"

"Have you come to terms with *your* death, Mac?"

Fontana thought about it. "I can't say as I have."

"You ever think about it?"

"After a couple of narrow escapes I found myself thinking about it. But then it sort of faded into the woodwork. I can't say that I've come to grips with it."

"Having old Doc Nielhaus tell me I had five months, tops, somehow didn't do it for me, either. It's still not real. It's supposed to get real when they give you the big number like that, but it doesn't. The only real thing that happened to me in the past couple of years was I quit drinking. Now that was real."

"Have you seen somebody? Maybe a psychologist or—"

"When I find a psychologist who's already died, I'll go see him. Otherwise they can't possibly know what they're talking about. I been afraid of death since I was knee high to a grasshopper, Mac. What do you think all that drinking was about? I lived scared. And I'll die scared. It's like somebody telling you the state's building a road through them hills. When it gets here, we'll see it, but I can't get all worked up over it until it gets here. Maybe it's a failure of my imagination."

"Maybe you *have* come to terms with it, Lou. You always were fearless."

"Me? I was so scared somebody would say I was scared, I

charged into fire buildings in front of them all. Figured being in front was the only place I was safe from the critics. No. I was never fearless. And I've left too many jobs undone. My family life is a shambles. My brother's dead and everybody thinks it's my fault. My own mother doesn't speak to me. My family . . . That's why I'm here with Grace. I'm determined to do as much cleanup as I can in the months allotted me. But come to terms with it? It's not fair now and it won't be fair when it happens. I been cheated and I'd be a damn fool to feel any different.''

When the rain hit, Strange seemed almost stunned by the coldness of it, blank-eyed and oblivious to Fontana's entreaties to take cover. Before Fontana could think of a way to handle the situation, Grace appeared, forcibly taking her father by the arm and leading him along the dike to their motor home. Fontana noticed Strange's knuckles were raw and scraped, contrasting with Grace's hands, which were blackened with grime from working on the Blazer. In a grubby sweatshirt, jeans stretched tight across her thighs, twigs in her hair, she escorted her father to the motor home, and for the first time Fontana saw some actual elegance to the woman, a woman who he'd thought of as cloddish, her name an oxymoron.

Almost as quickly as she'd gone in, she emerged and jogged across the yard to the carport where Fontana had taken shelter from the rain, his mail in one hand, house keys in the other. ''Mac? Are you going to the Bedouin tonight?''

As she waited for a reply, her large brown eyes grew watery with expectation, her body so close he could barely focus on her face. She'd apparently slipped a breath mint into her mouth, because she was breathing on him, purposely it seemed, and her breath smelled exactly like Tic-Tacs. ''I haven't decided.''

''If you decide, I'd like a ride.''

''If I do go, I probably won't be leaving from here.''

''Where then?'' She moved so close her sternum was against his arm, her voice suddenly dull and infused with something he couldn't define.

''I don't know where. Maybe I'll see you at the Bedouin.''

''Did I say I was going to the Bedouin? If you'll remember, I said if you decide to go, I'd like a ride. I didn't say I was going.''

"Yeah, well . . ."

Both her grease-stained hands clamped down on his biceps like the coils of a snake. "Did I say I was going?"

"Grace, I have things to do. Good luck with your truck."

"Don't you walk away from me. I asked you a question."

Using a quick motion, he whipped his arm out of her grip and stepped away, only to have her follow him step for step as if they were chained at the ankles.

"You said you wanted a ride. To me, that means you're going. Grace, I don't know what it is we're talking about here. Okay, sure, you didn't say you were going. It's not that important." Before he could leave, she grabbed him by both arms and hugged him tightly, pressing her rain-dampened hair against his coat. Her body felt stiff and cold, as if somebody had strapped a damp log to him. He couldn't be certain because he couldn't see her eyes, but he suspected she was crying. "Grace?"

Before he could cock his head out of the way, she canted her face up and pressed her wet lips against his, tasting of salt and Tic-Tacs and tongue, then turned and crawled under the Blazer. It had been so fleeting, the argument, the hug, the kiss. He couldn't be sure it had happened at all except that he could still taste her.

33

DUMPED

Fontana went inside, making certain to turn both locks behind him. It was hard to tell what Grace was thinking, or even if she *was* thinking. Clearly she was desperate and disturbed, if not a little batty.

The Bob Packwood move she made on him in the carport bothered him more than anything she'd done till then, even the stalking. Last year, after making a rescue in a high-rise in Seattle, he was kissed by twenty-six women in succession, but that had been an unmatched experience, their motivations relatively pure, primarily ceremonial, an encounter of gratitude and relief that he still recalled with some fondness. But he would have no fond memory of Grace's kiss. It had been voracious, a sneak attack, her own little Pearl Harbor.

Lou was an old friend and he *was* dying, but still, the more Fontana mulled it over, the more he realized Lou had to have been part of the team that waylaid Randy Knutson.

Fontana began to berate himself for letting either one of them loiter around Brendan as long as they had, and determined to have Satan near the boy until he got them off the property. He

walked into the bathroom to brush his teeth, then swished a cap-
ful of Listerine around his mouth. He was going to have to send
his jacket to the dry cleaner to get the greasy prints off the arm.

There were three messages on his machine, but the only one
Fontana returned was to a hotel in Barcelona, reaching an operator who spoke flawless English and who said she'd leave a message
for Ms. Aimee Lee. Fontana did some quick calculating and realized it was just after eight at night there.

When the phone rang midway through a tuna salad sandwich,
Fontana swallowed hurriedly and picked it up.

"Mac? This is Joyce. Joyce Callahan. I phoned your station, but
they said you went home."

"Joyce. I've been meaning to call, but not until later. I wanted
to be organized in my thinking before we spoke again."

"You're not reneging on our deal, are you?"

"I'm not reneging."

"I know you said you'd call in the late afternoon, but it's afternoon now."

According to Fontana's kitchen clock, it was four minutes after
twelve, Pacific time. "Sure, Joyce. Here's what we've got." He told
her about the second car, the second body, gave her a brief rundown on everything that had happened, then answered her questions. As they spoke, he began to get a feeling something was
wrong, that he'd made a terrible mistake and *Joyce* had killed her
husband, had hired him only to keep tabs on the investigation,
but when he swiveled around in his chair, he saw what was giving
him the uneasy feeling. Grace Teller was at the front window,
nose against the glass, staring at him as if he were a particularly
interesting animal at the zoo. Knowing she'd been spotted didn't
faze her. Slowly, he scooted his chair behind a half wall in the
kitchen where he would not be visible.

Joyce Callahan proceeded to tell him in agonizing detail about
the hometown funeral services that had been held that morning.
He listened politely, but all he could think about was whether
Sally was trying to get through, and what might be going on in
front of the house. When she was finished, she said, "Now tell
me if there's anything at all I can help with."

"Just a couple of items. Did your husband ski?"

"He did before the accident. He hadn't been back on the slopes for, oh, I don't know, eight or ten years, I would guess."

"You think he might have tried to go skiing while he was out here?"

"It's very unlikely. He didn't mention it."

"Did he smoke?"

The line was silent for a moment. "Why do you ask?"

"There were cigarette butts at the scene. It's an elimination thing."

"They asked that, too. They called and asked that same question."

He peered around the half wall, but Grace Teller was no longer at the window. When he asked Strange to leave, he'd tell him his daughter had been exhibiting some odd behavior. That should cover it. They'd leave, and nobody's feelings would be hurt. Nobody but Grace's, and hers were already hurt. "Did he smoke?" Fontana repeated.

"Ed used to smoke. Recently he took it up again, but only when under extreme duress."

"What kind of beer did he drink?"

"Ed was more fond of Bloody Marys, but he had a taste for any of the dark beers." The bottles they'd found at the scene had been Amber Bock, a beer that could have satisfied a dark beer drinker.

"Now I'm going to ask you another question, and I don't want you to get angry, but it's come up in our speculation about what happened out here. Which doesn't mean there's anything to it. There probably isn't anything to it. But I have to know."

"What is it?"

"Did Ed play around?"

She was quiet for a few beats. "I've been expecting this since the last time I talked to you. I knew you would ask sooner or later. There's no use trying to hide it. I have to assume he was still at it. After a while, after we'd had a couple of blowups where one or the other of us packed our bags, I thought he stopped. Or maybe I was kidding myself. It was just an out-of-town thing, though. I'm pretty sure of that much. Can I assume this dead woman they found is somehow related to Ed?''

''The other body was found over a mile away and nobody's sure yet if it's related. Probably won't know until they learn who she is. I'll call early next week with an update.''

''I can wait,'' she said, though both of them knew she couldn't. They ended the conversation with some pleasantries about the weather. It had been sunny at Callahan's second funeral, too.

When the phone rang again, he picked it up quickly. ''Mac, did you think I said I was going to the Bedouin? Did you think I was asking you for a ride?''

''Grace, I'm expecting a call. I have to get off the line.''

''Don't hang up on me. Did you really think I was asking you for a ride to the Bedouin? Like I was maybe begging for a date? Is that what you thought? You thought I was begging for a date? Mac, I'm only twenty-three years old. Why would I want to go out with a man who's almost as old as my father?''

''I have no idea. I have to get off now.'' As he hung up, she continued to speak until the phone was racked. It rang again almost immediately and he was tempted to let it, but after five rings he picked it up.

''Mac? I've been trying to get hold of you.''

''Sally. I'm glad you called. I was about to leave. I guess we've been playing phone tag all day. It's—''

''I hope you don't mind that I tell you this over the phone. It's something I'd rather say in person. And it's certainly not something I'd like said to me over the phone. But with the shooting schedule and all, it's the only way.''

''What is it?'' He sat down.

''I've decided you and I should call it quits.''

34

WHERE YOU GOING TO FIND ANOTHER UPSCALE GIRLFRIEND?

Maybe if he'd finished lunch a little sooner, he wouldn't have had to deal with this today. Or maybe if he'd been there for some of those missed phone calls, she wouldn't have come to this decision. The wildest thought of all was that perhaps if he'd agreed to take Grace out, Sally wouldn't have dumped him. Maybe it was fate evening things out. Maybe he just wasn't nice enough for Sally.

"Mac?"

"I'm still here."

"I hate to be telling it to you over the phone and all, but I've been doing a lot of thinking and I just don't feel we're going anywhere."

"*I* thought we were."

"Yes. Of course you did. But we're not."

"Sally, I care about you. I care a great deal."

"I'm happy to hear you say that, but it doesn't really register. I don't mean to come across as cold or heartless, but it doesn't. I guess I'm tired from all the shooting. We've been up half the night the last three nights. I just don't need something like this in my life right now. This relationship. A relationship that doesn't go anywhere. So we're agreed?''

"*You*'re agreed. It just seems a little sudden. Has something happened?''

"Oh, Mac. I like spending time with you. I like the way your mind works. I like the way you are with Audie and with your son. We've always had a good time together, and I know we're going to be friends forever and ever. But this other. It's not working out for me.''

"Sure. Okay.''

"Mac? Are you going to be all right?''

"Fine. I'm just fine.''

"You sound a little funny.''

"How am I supposed to sound when the woman . . . when a woman I've been intimate with tells me she doesn't want to continue the relationship?''

"And you do? Is that what you're telling me?''

"I don't know what good it does for me to say anything, Sally. You've made up your mind.''

"This is not set in concrete. We got along very well for a while, and I thought it was the fairest thing for me to put a little emotional distance between us, maybe because we've got all this geographical distance between us. I called you earlier in the week, but you weren't there. Didn't you know I was planning to call at nine each evening?''

"Believe me, I tried to be here.''

"I got your message. That was sweet. To call back. But I didn't have time to tell you this until now.'' Neither of them said anything for several seconds. "Are you still on the line, Mac?''

"I'm here.''

"Aren't you going to wish me well?''

"I . . . I wish you didn't feel this way, Sally.''

"I told you this didn't mean we won't be friends. I still want us to be friends. You need to know that. I'm just not so sure a romantic relationship with somebody . . . I'm just not sure it's the right thing for me.''

"You were pretty sure it was the right thing when you flew out of here a week ago."

"I was infatuated."

"And now you're not?"

"Now I'm back in the real world and I'm smart enough to know it simply isn't going to work."

"You mean you need somebody a little more upscale than a hardscrabble fireman in a town on the edge of nowhere?"

"Now, you're too sensible to go trying to play head games with me, Mac. We'll always be friends, you and I. You took me through some hard times. I'll always appreciate that."

Friends? They weren't going to be friends. They'd *been* friends and then they'd turned that into lovers and now she'd decided it was over; they weren't going to be friends. They could try but there would always be that uncomfortable void between them, the sharpened stakes of their former intimacy at the bottom of it. He knew it, even if she did not.

He was in his Suburban in the yard when Grace shouted something. "What?" he said, leaning out the door to hear better, dreading what she might say. The rain had stopped. The air was cold. His breath formed phantoms of mist in front of his face.

"I said you probably didn't know this, but when I was twelve I thought we were going to get married." He could see nothing of her except a pair of legs sticking out from under the Blazer.

"I like you as a friend, Grace."

"Friends don't turn their backs on friends, Macky. Friends don't turn their backs on friends and walk into the house and lock their doors. Friends don't do that."

Macky? Nobody had ever called him "Macky" before. And how did she know the doors had been locked, he thought, unless she'd tried them?

35

THE MARQUIS OF QUEENSBERRY'S PROVISIONS FOR FISTFIGHTING WITH LADIES

Fontana drove to Overlake Hospital and waited twenty minutes to visit Randy Knutson, who was in a double room, one bed empty. Somehow he looked worse than he had the night before, his right foot in a cast extending above his knee, right arm in a sling, left wrist and all of his left hand but the tips of his fingers in a cast, bandages around his skull, eyes blackened, face pulpy, nose broken, front teeth missing. The last two fingers on his right hand were splinted. A nasal cannula fed oxygen into his nostrils.

Trying to crack the swelling into a smile, Knutson said, "Hey, pard. Thanks for coming."

"How are you feeling?" Fontana asked.

"I been worse. Not lately, but I been worse." He held up his splinted fingers on the one hand, motioned to the cast on the other.

"This is the test, you know," Fontana said. "This is where you find out how much Rachel loves you." When Knutson didn't even pretend to chuckle, Fontana knew he'd offered up a poor joke. "The police come up with anything?"

"I don't expect them to."

"Why not?"

"I just don't. This is the sort of deal you take care of yourself, anyway."

"What do you mean by that?"

"Nothing. Don't even listen to me. They got me on so many different painkillers I feel like writing a psychedelic comic book. I've been having sex dreams. I'm telling you, this could get addictive. I mean, you can't believe how real they are."

"Randy. You know who did this to you, don't you?"

"I might."

"Why don't you tell the police? King County might not want these of sons of bitches running around molesting our citizens. You coulda died out there, Randy. Or haven't you thought of that?"

"If they wanted to kill me, they would've torched me."

"What does that mean?"

"Nothing."

"No, come on. Talk to me, Randy. *Who* would have torched you?"

"I just meant they hated me, but not enough to kill me."

"So this wasn't a random attack?"

"Did I say that?"

"Don't be a hero. Just give me a name."

"Ah, Mac, I never should have opened my mouth. I'm on drugs. This isn't fair. You know I had this dream? I was a referee in a boob contest. They blindfolded me and I had to feel all these boobies coming by. Almost like an assembly line. I woke up with a hard-on." He made an attempt at a smile that was about as pathetic as a Saturday night dance in the state mental hospital.

"Tell me who did this."

"Strange."

"I noticed his knuckles were all scraped up. Who was with him?"

"Not Lou. His daughter."

"What are you talking about? Grace?"

"That's her."

"Grace whacked you? Are you kidding me?"

"This sport utility vehicle passed me on the highway and then started swerving. I thought they were drunk. They skidded to a stop on the side of the road, and then this woman kind of half fell out the driver's door. When I went up to the car to help her, she hit me in the leg with something."

"Lou and his daughter? Is that what you're telling me? She fell out, and when you went to check on her, he came around behind?"

"Just her. She fell out the door onto the pavement, her hair in this puddle. Made it look so real it was a wonder she didn't bust her skull open. I got to her and she reached around and hit me with something across the leg. Bam! Broke it, I swear, whatever it was. Then she drags me around off the road and out of the head-lights and puts the boots to me like a bouncer ousting an FBI spy from a KKK meeting."

"You're sure it was her?"

"I saw her at the funeral. I'm sure."

"Why didn't you tell the cops?"

"That a woman beat the piss out of me? When I get back on my feet, I'll fix it myself."

"You're going to beat up a woman?"

"I'm going to pull her asshole up over her head and paint it blue."

"Tough talk, Randy, but she used to be part of a renegade paramilitary organization. She's had cops and the FBI chasing her all across the country. She's been in an institution. Don't mess with her."

"If that's all true, everybody'll be glad when I zip her face into the dirt."

"Did she say anything during the beating?"

"Just cussed up a storm."

Knutson pushed his head back into the pillows and sulked, ex-hausted, as if the confession had sapped his strength as well as his pride. Fontana said, "So I tell the cops, you're going to deny it?"

"Of course."

"What are we going to do?"

"Here, Mac. Let's do this. You don't tell the cops, and I'll re-consider how I'm going to handle this. I won't make any promises, but I'll think about it. And you don't tell Rachel. Hell, she'll probably have us living in Singapore in a week anyway, that's how jumpy she is. Bargain?"

"I don't tell the police. And then you think it over."

"Right."

"Okay."

"Thanks, Mac."

"But I *am* going to tell the arson investigator. She needs to know."

"I'll deny it."

"I figured you would. By the way, Randy. Did Grace know you knew it was her?"

"She looked right into my face. I don't see how she couldn't. You know, now that you mention she was in some terrorist gang, it kinda makes sense. I was trying to help her one second, and the next I was on my back feeling the most excruciating pain of my life. I mean, it hurt so bad I didn't even care if I drowned in that ditch."

"Tell me something, Randy. Do you always handle the law yourself?"

"What are you getting at?"

"You and Edgar Callahan had a knock-down drag-out argument the day before he was murdered."

"Sure, we yelled at each other. He tried to tell me I didn't have any right to show up at the convention. He said he'd already proved in a public forum that my book was pure dee horseshit. Believe the balls on that man? But that's all it was. An argument. What are you trying to do? I was with Rachel. I was with her all day. Hey, listen. Can you hang around till she gets back? We'll play cards, man. It'll be like old times."

"Wish I could, Randy. I have to pick up my kid at school. Maybe I'll come by the house after you're released. Let me ask you something else, though. What do you think happened up there in the hills?"

"Callahan got his ass in a sling and somebody fired him up. Punk kids, probably."

"A minute ago you seemed to think if Grace Teller wanted to

kill you, she'd have torched you. That sounds like you think she torches people. Think she torched Callahan?''

"I'm on drugs."

When Fontana left the hospital, all he could think about was the phone call from Sally Culpepper. He wasn't even clear on what he and Knutson had agreed to, though he vaguely recalled having settled some minor issue. He'd tried to go straight back to work, but the depth of her rejection and the power with which it had affected him had swamped his thoughts and overwhelmed his afternoon. He'd been in a haze talking to Knutson. In fact, he could barely recall driving to the hospital. That single phone conversation was going to blight his week, discolor everything he'd said or done for a month.

He'd deluded himself into thinking his liaison with Sally was one of those relationships he could take or leave; had envisioned the end of it, should it come to an end, as something he would himself promote. He didn't know why he'd been so overconfident, for in other relationships he'd fully expected to get dumped right from the beginning.

Sally had been different. He'd been her pillar, her strength; she'd said as much, and he'd had the feeling all the short while they'd been together that she needed him more than he needed her. And then somehow he'd been fooled into believing that sex had cemented their togetherness into a place it had not been before. Now that she'd declared their relationship at an end, he wondered if maybe the sex, instead of being the glue, hadn't been the solvent.

"Hey, old boy," Fontana said, slapping Satan's hide heartily when he got back into the truck. "Hey, old boy."

There were times when your dog really was your best friend.

36

A STRANGER'S
TEARS ARE ONLY
SALT WATER

By Friday evening the temperature had dropped precipitously, the weatherpeople were predicting snow, and those who'd been flooded out were gaining new hope.

Dark and silent, the Bounder sat in Fontana's yard, the crippled Blazer still in the carport, a salad of used auto parts garnished with Fontana's borrowed tools strewn across the yard. Grace had gone missing all afternoon.

When he wasn't mulling over the devastating phone call from Sally, Fontana was thinking of ways to get Lou and Grace off his property, a task he'd necessarily postponed until he could locate them.

Though it crossed his mind, he refused to tape a note to the door. Not only would a note be tactless and rude, but he had the feeling if Grace found it first, she would dispose of it without telling her father, and that would cloud the issue even further.

That evening, after making arrangements at the fire station for a pair of volunteers to deliver Knutson's Honda to his home in Seattle, Fontana dawdled in his office for a half hour thinking dark thoughts, not one of which he could have put into a sentence had someone asked.

Some careless volunteer had left a *National Enquirer* in the station, an issue featuring Aimee Lee in an apparent romantic tryst on the beach near Barcelona with one of her male costars. In the photo spread, Sally wore a skimpy bathing suit, her hair wind-tossed, and her costar displayed the sculpted ribs and abdominals of an underwear model.

For the first time in a couple of years, Fontana began reevaluating his general position in life, particularly his vow to eschew material goods and the prestige attached to them. He'd come to this town intending to adopt a quiet life, to become a nobody in a town of nobodies, to work a little and relax a little, and to raise his son in peace. In some respects, he'd succeeded.

But his relationship with Sally Culpepper—their friendship followed by their hurried love affair and her desertion, first to Spain and then into the arms of another man—was depressing for what it implied about the way she viewed him and about the way others probably viewed him, too.

For whatever else Sally claimed, he knew that his humble career, poor salary, lack of possessions, and somewhat precarious position in life had influenced her decision. As Aimee Lee, she was a world-famous actress, while he was a fire chief overseeing two paid employees and a crew of half-trained, gossipy volunteers. A man who in the past had displayed uncommon investigatory skills. A man whose ambitions had dwindled to frequenting a dark dance palace on Friday nights, fishing when the river was low, and spending evenings and weekends playing board games with his son. Sally, on the other hand, was filming a movie in Spain and cavorting on exotic beaches.

Together they were an old shoe alongside a diamond tiara.

Had it been too embarrassing for her to tell people she was romantically involved with a fire chief in a rainy, one-horse town in the Pacific Northwest? Or had distance so quickly diminished him to the point of irrelevance?

■

At the Bedouin that night, Fontana tried to hang out with his cronies, but as he was plowing through the thin spread of random local couples, Mo Costigan accosted him and asked him to dance.

"Sure, Mo," Fontana said, taking her into his arms. The jukebox worked through a series of love ballads: "Unforgettable," "Cry," and then a sappy version of "Strangers in the Night." Neither of them spoke. Fontana was still thinking about Sally. Mo was humming along to the melodies.

Finally, Mo said, "Your friend is really something."

"Which friend would that be?"

"Lou. He knows more details about the world and more stories about weird people than just about any man I've run across."

"Lou's a talker."

"He said you and he were practically best friends."

"Practically."

"Did you know he had a big crush on your wife when she was alive?"

"I'd gathered something like that."

"He told me he took her death almost as hard as you did."

"That's a silly thing to say. Nobody except Brendan took her death as hard as I did."

"Is that because of the affair?"

"What affair?"

"The affair you had the month before your wife was killed."

"Lou told you about that?"

"Your wife found out. You fought. She went out for a drive and never came back."

"Lou really told you this? Why doesn't he write a piece for the paper?"

"Lou and I have talked about everything. He's wonderful. He's good-hearted and sweet, and he has a self-deprecating sense of humor. In fact, he's the first man I've run across in a long while that I could just possibly consider settling down with."

Fontana wasn't going to ask, but he had the feeling from the note of hope in her husky voice that Mo wasn't aware that Lou Strange was dying. "Lou shouldn't have told you those things."

"I certainly don't think any the worse of you for it, Mac. In fact,

it's rather touching, carrying a torch for your late wife. All that
guilt really is rather touching."

More than a little miffed, Mac changed the subject. "Have you
seen much of his daughter?"

"Grace? Now there's a queer duck. We had dinner a couple of
nights ago, just the three of us. Grace didn't let out a peep."

"Be careful around that one. She can get physical."

"I can get plenty physical myself."

"Don't test her, Mo."

"I could kick her butt to Tacoma and back with my hands tied
behind my back."

"I said, don't—"

"There is a matter I need to discuss with you though, Mac.
Those photos. The ones you've got laying around your station.
What did you do with them?"

"I told you before, I gave them to Heather."

"Not possible."

"I'm afraid it is."

"Read my lips, Mac. *That is not possible.* Don't kid around. This
is official business. As mayor, I am demanding those pictures.
Also, I want a written explanation of where they came from, how
they got into your hands, and who took them. And I want it on
my desk first thing Monday morning. The pictures? Those you
hand over tonight."

"I don't have them, Mo."

"You'd better rethink this, Mac, because we heard from her
lawyer this afternoon. Heather is suing."

"She was at work not five hours ago. She didn't say a word
about suing."

"They're filing suit."

"On what grounds?"

"Those pictures you were passing around constitute a serious
case of sexual harassment. You embarrassed her behind her back
and in front of her coworkers. It was despicable behavior. Even
you have to admit it was despicable."

"I didn't have anything to do with those pictures, Mo, and you
know it! And I never showed them to a soul. You and Truax are

the ones who were flashing them around. And I embarrassed *her?* I'm the one who gathered them together and gave them back. She embarrassed herself. I cleaned up that mess. Now all she has to do is lay low and forget about it. And she's going to sue? Why doesn't she just have Lou put the whole thing down in the piece he's going to write about me? Or put a billboard up at the edge of town: 'I posed naked for a bunch of drunken firemen.' "

"I'd sue, too."

"Shit."

"That sort of language is not going to endear you to the power structure. You're really like a little boy, Mac. You know how I know you're lying?"

"No, Mo. How?"

"Because her attorney told me those photos are still in your possession."

"I'm not even going to think about this, Mo. My head will explode."

"Does that mean you're not going to write the letter? We're going to need a letter."

"Tell me something, Mo. In all this chitchat you two had, did Lou ever talk about the murders up at Denny Creek?"

"You're going to change the subject, aren't you? You're going to change the subject and try to sweep this other matter under the rug."

"What other matter?"

After a few moments of stewing, Mo said, "He and Callahan got into the fire department together, he told me. They were in the same recruit school. In fact, Lou says Callahan barely made it in, that he was kind of a wienie. Lou was the top of the class; Callahan was the bottom. Then, every time Lou had some sort of contact with Callahan over the years, Callahan tried to screw him over. When he got a chance, he transferred him or nixed some time off he had arranged. I read that book. You were at that fire. That Paint Company fire."

"We were the ones who found Snyder and Wickersham."

"The two who got chased up the stairs and into that room by a fireball?"

"You must be quite taken with Strange if you went to all the trouble to find that book and read it."

"He didn't want me to and I certainly am not going to admit to him I read it, but I had to. Is it true?"

"True enough, Mo. Strange's crew was inside looking for him without telling anybody because they knew he had a penchant for lone-wolf exploits and they thought he'd gone back in alone. They didn't want him to get hurt or get in trouble because the fire was beginning to flare back up. They knew the incident commander didn't like Lou, so they were afraid to say anything. But he wasn't even at the fire location by then. He was across town getting laid."

"Lou have a lot of girlfriends?"

"Lou used to meet women he'd slept with and not even recognize them."

"But it wasn't his fault all those people died, was it? He was just the scapegoat. Lou never meant any harm. Lou was the man who initially put the fire out."

"The deaths were a combination of Lou's irresponsible behavior, Callahan's foul-ups, and bad luck."

"Speak of the devil," said Mo, standing on tiptoe to peer over Fontana's shoulder to where Strange and his daughter had been dancing together. Without a word, Mo slipped out of Fontana's arms, paired up with Lou, and danced out of reach.

It was an uncomfortable moment for Fontana, who stood in front of Grace without knowing what to do. If there had been one plan in his mind for the evening, it was to not dance with Grace, to not *see* Grace. He'd been hoping she wouldn't show up, but now that she had, she looked forlorn and pathetic and bruised, a perfect visual image of the way he'd been feeling since Sally's call. Against his better judgment, he held out his arms and immediately regretted it after she stepped into them with a smug little look on her face, as if she'd been expecting it all night.

In a black vest over a long-sleeved white blouse, pink slacks, and high heels, she was looking better than Fontana had ever seen her. Her hair was clean and swept back over her shoulders.

She moved closer to him, trying to paste herself against his hips while he struggled to keep her at a distance.

About halfway through "It's All in the Game," Fontana said, "You get your truck fixed?"

"Not yet. Thanks for asking." Her voice was unnaturally prim and small and polite, as if he were the ventriloquist and she the dummy.

"What's wrong with it?"

"The muffler. Must've run over something in the snow."

"When were you driving in the snow?"

"A few weeks back."

"Grace. Do you know Randy Knutson?"

"I believe I may have seen him at the funeral talking to my father, but I wouldn't say I know him. No, I don't believe I do." Her words said no, but the sudden tension in her limbs said yes.

"He took a beating last night—just out of town here. I spoke to him in the hospital, and he said you administered the beating."

"*Moi?*"

"It's not anything to get cute about. He could have died."

"He must be out of shape to let a woman beat him up."

"Did you do it, Grace?"

"If I ever did do anything like that, I would certainly have a reason for it."

"And what would that reason be?"

"I didn't say I did it. I said if I ever did, I would have a reason."

"And I didn't say you did, either. I just said, what would that reason be."

"For starters, he wrote *Bagpipe City,* the book that destroyed my father's life."

"So you beat the crap out of him?"

"You have the right to do whatever you *can* do."

"What does that mean?"

"It means, I'm here and he's in the hospital."

"And your father's life is back together?"

"You know it isn't."

"So what's been accomplished?"

"To me, it makes sense. If you can't see it, that's *your* problem."

Without another word, Fontana left Grace in the middle of the dance floor and walked over to the bar and ordered a beer. When he turned around, she was up against him, her face tilted ferociously up at his.

"Mac, a stranger's tears are only salt water. You ever hear that expression?"

"I can't say that I have." He tried to move, but she moved with him, pinning him against the bar, arms at her sides. "Grace, back off! Just back off."

"My father's tears were only salt water to Knutson."

"Yeah, Grace. Thanks for setting me straight. At least I know *why* you did it."

"You're not listening. I never did anything."

"Have it your way. Just move away from me."

Still tethered to him by her angry brown eyes, she backed away and then disappeared among the dancers.

37

MÉNAGE À TROIS
WITH A
CRISPY CRITTER

Later that night Lawrence Drummey showed up at the Bedouin with a white man who looked as if he molested kindergarten teachers when he wasn't sticking up liquor stores. The two of them watched the dancing for a while, importuning various women and being rebuffed, danceless both, when Drummey spotted Fontana nursing a beer with Mrs. Kilpatrick in a corner lit by an orange neon sign in the shape of a Chihuahua.

Mrs. Kilpatrick was a congenital flirt and the perfect companion for Fontana tonight, for she could puff up any man's ego without hardly trying. When it became apparent to her that Fontana knew Drummey, she left, clearly uncomfortable with the way Drummey's friend was leering at her. Fontana wasn't comfortable with it either and came close to saying something before deciding to let it pass.

"Hey, old man," said Drummey, sitting down at the table. "I heard you been up to see our old buddy."

"Who would that be?"

"Randy, of course. Randy, Randy, Randy. He's up in the hospital, ain't he? I been thinkin' about him. I been thinking about you, too. There's some things I maybe forgot to tell you.''

"And what did you maybe forget to tell me, Larry?" Fontana noted that Drummey's friend did not sit and was pumping down his beers as if they were nutrient instead of refreshment. He was dressed modestly, but his shirt, coat and slacks were wrinkled and out-of-date, as if just that afternoon he'd been released from prison and taken his clothing out of a wire basket where they'd lain for twenty years. Fontana noticed that the uniformed security guard across the room was also keeping a close eye on the guy.

"I told you about Callahan and them conspiring against the brothers?"

"You mentioned your theory."

"No theory, man. It was an out-and-out conspiracy, full-blowed. You don't think so, ask your buddy, Strange. He'll confirm it. And then I told you about Strange deciding to come out here to Washington State after I told him Callahan would be visiting?"

"You didn't mention that."

"I told him two months ago. He went right out and bought that motor home the next day. You don't think that's a coincidence, do you?"

"Hard to tell."

"I tell you about Callahan having dinner with Knutson and his wife the night before he died?"

Fontana sat up straight and pushed his half-empty beer bottle away. "You didn't mention that either."

"They had a cozy little dinner together. Just the three of them. A ménage à trois, if ya-know-what-I-mean."

"How do you know this?"

"I followed 'em. Randy and his wife. I hang out at their place and I watch. Lots of times. Sooner or later somebody's going to try to do them, and I want to be there. I get tired, sometimes I go inside and visit. I don't know how she ever hooked up with that bum."

"Where'd they have dinner?"

"Place called Tulio's. Italian food. It's not far from the hotel downtown where everybody was staying. They were in there for a good two hours. Randy didn't mention it to you? Seems like Randy would have mentioned having dinner with a dead man twenty or so hours before he got fried. Randy didn't mention that?''

"Anything happen at dinner?''

"I wish I knew. For two years Callahan and his wife have been running around talking trash to the papers about Randy. Maybe they were trying to work out some sort of personal truce. You know, man. Something that wouldn't make them want to shoot each other?'' Drummey glanced around the room. "Did you know it was snowing at High Point when we drove out? Could hardly see the road. Cars fishtailin' all over the place. Then we got here in town—nothing.''

"It'll hit here soon enough,'' said Fontana. "Why'd you wait until now to mention this dinner, Larry?''

"I thought you knew. I told the cops. Then tonight with Maurice here, I got to rehashing everything and I began to wonder what all I *did* tell you. So we came out to check. Also to bring back them clothes I borrowed.''

"Anything else you want to tell me, Larry?''

"Sure. Okay, man. I fried his ass. I lit up old Edgar just so I could hear him sing inside that old car trunk!'' Drummey began laughing raucously.

"Did you, Larry? Did you light up that car?''

"I don't know, man. You tell me.'' He was still laughing when Fontana left the Bedouin.

A smattering of snowflakes was drifting out of the sky as Fontana walked to his truck. Drummey. Grace Teller. Randy Knutson. Everybody was lying. And who the hell was Drummey's friend Maurice?

The streets were vacant, and although it was midnight, because of the dusting of snow on everything, it was fairly light out. On the roads the snow had accumulated so that the only color that showed through was where another vehicle had left tracks. The wind had died.

A mile from the Bedouin his headlights picked up a figure walking alongside a deserted stretch of road, a woman, no coat, her arms folded in front of her for warmth. Fontana's immediate thought was car or boyfriend trouble or both. And then as he came abreast of her, he recognized Grace Teller.

He stopped and waited until she reached the passenger door, rolling the window down after it became apparent she wasn't going to use the door handle. Cold air filled the truck. Snow drifted onto the sill with a tiny, barely audible whisper.

"Grace, get in. I'll give you a ride."

"You're not interested in me."

"Are you all right, Grace?"

"What do you care?" Now that she had stopped moving, he could see that she was shivering violently.

"Grace, get in."

"I'm walking." Despite her statement, she remained in place.

"Get in before you get hypothermia."

"I'm not getting in. You don't like me."

"I like you fine, Grace. Now get in."

38

FURTHER DISCOURSE ON THE MARQUIS OF QUEENSBERRY RULES: FISTFIGHTS BETWEEN MEN AND WOMEN

When Grace climbed into the truck, snow cookies fell off the top of her head and the back of her blouse. He rolled the window up and turned the heater on high, but still she shivered. He'd seen patients with hypothermia and recognized the early to middle stages. One good sign was that she could still talk.

"You hate me," she said.

"Why were you walking home?"

"The Blazer's out of commission. I was hoping somebody'd give me a ride, but you were more interested in your friends."

"You came out tonight without a coat?"

"I forgot it at the Bedouin."

"How on earth could you do that?"

"I was mad. I rode to town with my father and his slut, but they're busy getting drunk together. I didn't want to be a bother."

"I thought your father was on the wagon?"

"He *was*."

Fontana's house was dark except for a lamp in the living room where Mary liked to sit with a blanket on her lap and read potboilers. Fontana lined the passenger door up with the motor home and came to a stop in snow that felt like a mattress. Waiting for Grace to get out, he said, "You going to be okay?"

"What do you care?" The words were barely audible.

She left the truck door ajar when she got out. He parked in front of his house, shut both truck doors, and went inside without glancing at the Bounder.

"You have a good time?" Mary asked, as she laboriously got out of the chair.

"Reasonable."

"You were down in the mouth when you left."

"I was, wasn't I?"

After he'd walked Mary home, he was back at his front stoop stamping the snow off his shoes when he noticed a figure across the yard on a plastic chair in the cold in front of the Bounder. "Grace?"

There was no reply.

He went into his house, checked on a sleeping Brendan, spoke kindly to Satan, who'd been following him around the house, then cracked a blind. Using his nose, the dog clumsily cracked a blind lower in the same window. It was still snowing. The figure in the chair in front of the Bounder hadn't moved. Satan whined softly and remained at the window long after Fontana had turned away.

He telephoned the bar at the Bedouin, could hear the jukebox playing "Just a Dream" in the background as Velma searched the dance hall for Mo and Lou. "Can't find 'em, honey. They were just here a minute ago. I don't know where they went. Bad night. The place is clearing out early. People don't want to be on the roads."

"Thanks, Velma."

He deliberated five more minutes before calling Mo Costigan's house, where he left a message for Lou on the answering machine, hoping somebody would pick it up as he was talking. No one did.

When he checked the Bounder again, Grace hadn't moved. It had been fifteen minutes since he'd let her out of the truck. If she hadn't been hypothermic before, she was now.

By the time he reached her, she was in some sort of shivering trance. He brushed snow off her shoulders and hair, tried futilely to get her to walk, and then carried her up the steps into the Bounder. He fumbled for a light and sat her on a cushion near the driver's seat. "Grace? You going to be okay? Listen, Grace. You need to go back there and take a warm shower, okay? Not too hot."

"M-m-m-e?" Though he had no sure way to diagnose it, he had a feeling her behavior was a lot more than mere bullheadedness.

"Grace, you're in trouble here. You're very cold and that's dangerous. I want you to walk to the back of the rig and take a nice warm shower. I'm going to wait."

"W-w-wait?"

"I'll be right here."

When he'd helped her up, she tottered to the stern of the motor home, and after a few minutes of grunting and door banging, he heard a weak shower. When he got up enough nerve to look down the central corridor, she was out of sight. After a while he could hear her bumping against the walls in the shower stall. He peeked out the window at the snow falling like shreds of paper in the cone of light under his porch. He was struck by the contrast between the peace in the yard and the storm back there in the shower.

When she finally came out in a thick, white terrycloth robe, Grace was moving softly, toweling her hair, rosy-cheeked, weak and sleepy-looking. Her makeup had been smudged but not scrubbed. Soap bubbles hung off one ear like melted jewelry.

She walked directly to where he was sitting in the passenger's swivel seat and pulled his face hard against herself.

When he tried to disentangle her arms, she fought him for many seconds. She was stronger than he thought possible. It was such a bizarre contest he almost laughed into her chest, but then he finally freed his head and said, "Grace, don't do anything else like sitting out in the snow, okay?"

"You really care about me, don't you?" She followed him to the door.

"I care that you don't get into trouble."

"No. You care more than that."

And then she was on him, kissing him full on the mouth, arms twined around his neck in a stranglehold, and all he could think of as he struggled was her tongue, her muscular tongue as it infiltrated his lips and pushed up against his clenched teeth. It was after midnight, and he was in a motor home with 135 pounds of tongue. He wrenched out of the hold and pushed her away.

"You don't love me, do you?"

"No, Grace, I don't."

"You don't even like me much, do you?"

"I guess I don't, Grace."

Because of the dim lights and the sudden movement, Fontana didn't see it clearly, but he had his hand on the door, his back partially turned away from her when she slapped at him with something white. It appeared to be a rolled-up newspaper. Thinking it would be harmless to let her get away with, he almost let her have a free swat at his head. But at the last second he ducked.

He'd been trying to get the door open, but now he was on the floor under a seat, eyes burning, a loud pulse pounding in his left temple. Grace was swinging again, striking the metal base of the seat as she tried to break his leg. Each time she struck the seat with the rolled newspaper, the metal rang out like a bell.

"You sonofabitch!" she said. "You sorry motherfucker!"

He had a lot to think about, but one thing he knew for sure was that she had a blunt weapon inside the newspaper, a pipe or something. She was going to beat him the way she beat Knutson. She'd gone after his skull and was now trying to fracture one of his legs. He thought he'd ducked the blow to his skull, but if he'd ducked he wouldn't be on the floor.

He lay still, feigning more serious injury than he felt, and when she stooped over him again, he kicked suddenly at her mouth, which made a slapping sound as the blow forced it closed.

By the time Fontana had righted himself and shaken the cobwebs off, she was up again and charging, blood inking the spaces between her teeth. She brought her weapon down hard toward the top of his skull—he was on his knees now—but he sideslipped and the heavy blow grazed his left shoulder. She swung horizontally, and he arched his face away from her so that she missed completely. On the backswing she cracked a window, splitting it open, letting a puff of cold air into the cabin, which still had not quite righted itself in Fontana's mind. Taking the next blow on his upper back, he dove forward and tackled her around the legs.

For a moment he thought her blow might have broken his spine, but he climbed up her furiously kicking and clawing form anyway and threw a hard right cross at where he thought her jaw should be. The last time he'd hit a woman he killed her. It was his first thought. She stopped moving instantly.

Breathing heavily, he picked up her weapon and examined it, the icy breeze through the hole in the driver's side window chilling him. He was holding twelve inches of heavy steel that looked as if it had been sawed off the end of a weight-lifting bar.

Kneeling at her side, he checked her vitals. She had a bounding pulse and was breathing steadily, half snoring. Her pupils were equal and reactive. He rearranged her robe, which had fallen open during the fracas, gathered the belt and knotted it at her waist, picked up Strange's cell phone and dialed 911. While he was waiting for the authorities, he went to the back of the motor home and examined himself in the steamed-over bathroom mirror. A lump was already forming inside the hairline on the side of his head. His shoulder was bruised and he could barely lift it.

The aid crew came first and treated Grace, who regained consciousness quickly and locked herself in the bathroom. When the first King County Police officer, H. C. Bailey, arrived, she gave Fontana a dirty look. "What's going on?" Fontana went over the events of the last half hour. "Does hypothermia do that to you?" she asked, when he'd finished.

"No, I don't believe it does."

H. C. Bailey knew about Grace, so she smirked when Grace came out of the bathroom and said, "He beat me up because I was dancing with other men." Bailey let her get dressed, then manacled her and hauled her away. Fontana noted she'd put on the same damp clothes she had on earlier.

■

Twenty minutes later Mo Costigan dropped Lou Strange off in front of the Bounder, then spun out of the driveway in the snow. "What happened?" Strange asked, after pounding on Fontana's front door.

"Lou, you're drunk. You're a suspect in a murder. Your daughter assaulted Knutson. Tonight she assaulted me. You're out of here. Both of you. Gone. I'm sorry. I don't care if you have to stay up all night doing it, but I want you and your vehicles gone when I wake up."

Strange was genuinely offended. "What'd I do?"

"Nothing, Lou. Nothing at all. It just has to be this way. But answer me one question before you leave."

"What's that?"

"Did you have anything to do with Knutson's beating?"

"You're kicking me out 'cause of that? I never laid a finger on him."

"Your daughter needs treatment, Lou."

"Don't you think I know that? She claims she's talked to my ghost. *My* ghost. I ain't even dead yet. She's been stealing my meds."

Half an hour later Fontana heard Mo's tires spinning outside when she came back to help; heard engines being revved in the cold, vehicles moving, tires ripsawing in the snow and gravel. Despite Grace's claim, the Blazer was running just fine.

After a few minutes, Mo's Porsche was the only extraneous vehicle left in the yard. Fontana hoped nobody would see it and assume she was sleeping with him. He considered getting dressed and throwing a tarp over it, but fell asleep before he got nervous enough to actually do it.

39

THREE THINGS
TO DO WHEN YOUR
COAT IS ON FIRE

It snowed part of Saturday and most of the afternoon on Sunday. By Monday morning there was enough accumulation to keep the buses off the roads and the schools closed. Fontana took Brendan with him to the fire station, meaning to check in and take the day off, and that's what he would have done if Jennifer Underhill hadn't phoned. "Mac, can we talk?"

"I was going to get in touch later, Jennifer. Friday night I spoke to Lawrence Drummey, who claims Randy Knutson and his wife had dinner with Callahan the night before Callahan died. He said he already told the police."

"We knew. I've got some other information I wanted to discuss with you. You going to be around this morning?"

"I was planning to go sledding with my son."

"I'd *really* like to see you. I think you were right. This is one of those cases to talk out."

"Can you get out here right away?"

"Is forty minutes soon enough?"

"I'll be here."

It took over an hour, her calculations thrown off by slick roads and motorists with more horsepower than sense. The sky was pocked with white clouds, blue patches to the south, the sun emerging from time to time in a blinding veil of light that radiated off the snow and made squealing children, trudging old men, and cautious dogs squint against its refracted glare. The air was warming up, and snow was beginning to forsake rooftops in large drips and to slide off parked cars in chunks.

Brendan watched *Cool Hand Luke* in the beanery with Heather Minerich, Kingsley Pierpont, and a pair of volunteers, normal firehouse activities having been suspended until the weather modified. Fontana hadn't mentioned Heather's lawsuit to Kingsley, knowing Kingsley already thought she was out of her league as a firefighter.

Clad in dress slacks, a white shirt and tie, and his fringed buckskin jacket, Roger Truax had been hanging around all morning, quizzing Brendan on remedial fire safety, giving the stop, drop, and roll lecture, pontificating about the importance of not doing anything stupid when confronted by an emergency, which was funny, because Truax had brought with him from the Tacoma department a penchant for panicking during an emergency.

For a long while, Brendan did his best to conceal his annoyance, but when Truax said, "Okay, Brendan, now tell me what you would do to keep from getting burned if your coat was on fire," Brendan replied brusquely, "If my coat was on fire, I wouldn't put it on." To Truax's consternation, the quip generated a roar of laughter in the room.

Later, Truax, whipping his long strands of blond hair across his bald spot with a practiced toss of the head, lit up like a Chinese lantern when Jennifer Underhill came through the front door. Even though everybody in the department knew about his schoolboy crush on the arson investigator, Truax still believed it was a secret.

Fontana turned to Brendan and said, "I'll be in the office if you need me."

"Sure, Dad." On the tube, Paul Newman was getting ready to swallow a batch of hard-boiled eggs.

Eyes on Jennifer Underhill, Truax stepped forward, his fleshy cheeks wobbling, and said, "Mac, you need any help?"

"Uh, I don't think so, Roger." Behind him, Pierpont wore a smile of commiseration for the obvious and painful cravings of Truax, who was married to a living doormat with perpetually hurt eyes, a woman rarely seen in public.

When he closed the door, Jennifer was in his office sitting in the straight-backed chair against the lockers, a briefcase on her lap. "Mac, how are you?"

"Good. How are the roads?"

"Not bad in town. Worse the farther out I got. I saw about eight cars in the ditch. There was a tractor-trailer rig off the road right outside of town here."

"It's supposed to snow again tonight."

"At least it stopped raining. So. What did Drummey say to you? When I spoke to him, he was so full of cock-and-bull stories, I put that dinner thing on the back burner. Plus, Knutson wouldn't corroborate anything. We finally traced Callahan's American Express card and learned he'd paid for a three-party dinner the night before he died. Nobody from the convention had any idea who he dined with, and except for Drummey's allegations, neither do we. If it's true, what do you think it means?"

"I don't know. Actually, right now I'm more interested in Knutson's relationship to Lou Strange and his daughter than I am in his relationship to Callahan."

"I spoke to Knutson at Overlake again this morning. They're releasing him at noon."

"What'd he tell you?"

"He said he was standing by his statement that two men attacked him and he didn't see their faces."

"It was Grace Teller with a length of steel tubing wrapped inside a piece of newspaper. The same thing she used on me Saturday morning."

Underhill gave him a concerned look. "She attacked you?"

"Some lovesick thing going on in her head. King County Jail's got her."

"A steel bar? That's bizarre. And she did Knutson?"

"I'm certain of it."

"Why would Knutson cover for her? Do you think she has a lovesick thing for him, too?"

"I think it's something else with him. And he didn't tell you because, besides being embarrassed about having the stuffing knocked out of him by a woman, he's plotting revenge."

"He's going to beat up Grace Teller?"

"I believe that's what he has in mind. Although if I were him, I wouldn't be that anxious for a rematch. He didn't get in too many licks the first time."

"You don't think there's any possibility *she* lured Callahan up there last week, do you? What would her motive be?"

"Grace figured Callahan was to blame for her father's ruined career."

"But I thought it was Knutson who ruined her father."

"In one sense, by exposing him. But Strange blames his downfall on Callahan too, and so probably does she."

"I don't get it. Strange didn't get canned after that fire for dereliction of duty or whatever? For running off like that? I just assumed he had."

"Before Knutson's book came out, only those two in the aid car knew he hadn't been at the fire."

"And they didn't tell anybody? Didn't they have a moral duty . . . I mean, why didn't they tell? I can't believe that."

"Telling somebody wasn't going to bring any of those people back. Those two Dugans on the aid car, what were they going to do? Rat out a fellow firefighter? It was easier to say nothing. Besides, they had reason to think that if they came forward, Lou Strange would come after them. He had a reputation. A guy'll do a lot to keep his job. Then too, they weren't exactly guiltless. They were both new to the department. Weren't sure they wouldn't get fired themselves. They knew they should have gotten on the radio the moment they heard Engine Forty-eight was in trouble."

"So they didn't tell anyone?"

"Maybe their wives. No one else until Randy Knutson started digging."

"And Strange didn't tell anyone."

"After a while, self-justification kicked in and Strange started blaming the whole catastrophe on Callahan, who *did* run a bad fire. And of course Grace Teller's attitude toward Callahan was shaped by her father."

"The trouble is, if Grace Teller killed Callahan, who was the dead woman?"

"The dead woman's been the problem since we found her."

Underhill shrugged. "Did you know Callahan had a habit of hiring call girls when he was out of town?"

"How'd you find that out?"

"On his credit card there was a two-hundred-dollar tab to Sunset Limos, a Kirkland outfit. It's a call-girl ring, but out-of-towners don't mind using their company's credit cards for a limo service."

"Did he hire her after the supposed dinner with the Knutsons or before?"

"Just after he flew in. I've been thinking the second body up in the hills might have been a Sunset Limo worker. Or somebody from another escort service. We don't have any other credit card charges, but maybe he was paying cash. The husband and wife team who run Sunset Limo clammed up and called their lawyer, but I did manage to wheedle the name of the woman who visited Callahan. Francine Snodgrass, working under the name of Cherry LaTrice. We tried to talk to her, but she's at Disneyland with her kid. Nobody seems to know when they'll be home or even if they're staying in Anaheim. The one detail that bothers me is that one of the bellhops said when Callahan asked for a hooker, he asked for somebody 'special.' "

"What did he mean by that?"

"The bellhop seemed to think he meant someone he could get rough with, but he didn't pursue the subject with him. It fits the evidence, doesn't it? Two different sperm samples? She was a hooker. So assuming he was up there in the hills with somebody from Sunset Limo or some other escort service, what happened? I mean, we have *him* locked in the trunk of the stolen car. The *woman* with a bullet in her chest in his rental. Both cars set on fire. What happened?''

''Maybe none of this revolves around Callahan. Maybe we're going at it backward, Jennifer. Maybe it revolves around the woman. A jealous boyfriend, another customer, a pimp, some nut case. He steals a car and follows her up into the hills. He finds them together and kills them, leaving the stolen car and the rental and driving the woman's car back down.''

''But why were they in the hills, Mac? A man wants a woman, why not go to his hotel room?''

''Maybe he had some sort of fantasy he needed to play out that required a rural setting. Maybe that's why he needed somebody 'special.' ''

''The whole thing sounds like a serial killer asking his victim to drive around and help choose a dump site. I don't see a savvy hooker doing it.''

''How about a dumb hooker?'' Fontana said. ''I bet there's a few of those on the loose.''

''On the other hand, Mac, there's no reason to assume this was anything other than a random murder. Callahan's out there with a woman. Two men come by in a stolen car. Lock him in the trunk. Rape and kill her. Then kill Callahan. Drive off in her vehicle. That's the most plausible explanation.''

''I'd be more comfortable with any of these ideas if we knew who the dead woman was.''

''Unfortunately, we didn't get much out of our missing-persons checks. There's a woman missing from Tukwilla, reported by her husband, but she weighs close to two hundred pounds and is taller than our victim. They're looking for a woman in Olympia they think drowned down at the mud flats when the tide came in, but she's in her eighties.''

''Another thing that's been puzzling me is why was the car still burning so fiercely when I got there? A gasoline-fed fire burns pretty hot, and if somebody saw smoke and called us, by the time we got there it should have died down at least a little from what we saw. It took us twenty-seven minutes to get there. But if some-body called *before* the fire was set, it would account for County getting only one call on it.''

"Are you saying the caller made the call and then set the fire?''

"Maybe.''

"Which would mean we have the killer's voice on tape. I'll tell you what I'm going to do, Mac. Tomorrow I'll get that tape out and play it for you; see if you recognize the voice. It might be somebody you know.''

"Fine. There's something else that's been bothering me. There seemed to be some hesitance before Callahan's death. Somebody sat around and thought about it. The cigarette butts. The beer bottles. What was the uncertainty about? There was no hesitation at the scene where we found the woman. The bullet, the fire, the concealment. And also, with Callahan there was no attempt to hide the crime. The stolen car was in the center of a narrow road. Why all the dillydallying and then no attempt at concealment? Why was that so different from the way the woman died?''

"Who knows?''

"You get any ownership off the gun?''

"It's a thirty-two-caliber police special,'' Underhill said. "About forty years old. Could have come from anywhere. Not registered. I like this call girl theory. I think we might have figured out the how and the why. And if so, it was a coincidence that Callahan was a fire chief and burned to death. It wouldn't be the first time we've had a coincidence like that.''

"A hell of a coincidence. Another thing. We should be looking for an abandoned vehicle in the area. If there isn't a missing woman, maybe there's a vehicle that's been towed or ticketed or junked, her vehicle.''

"We'll start looking.''

"Also, somebody might have seen a car thief in Seattle.''

"The owner of the car was in the shower, saw zilch. None of his neighbors saw anything.''

"You mind if we visit him?''

"This morning? Sure, Mac. Then I've got to run out to Lake City on another case.''

Before he could take a disappointed Brendan home, Fontana was ambushed by Mo Costigan in the fire station. She grabbed him by the sleeve and dragged him toward his office. "What is it, Mo?"

"I need to conference with you and Roger."

"Roger? Is that why he's been hanging around all morning?"

"I told him to meet me here."

"Sorry, Mo. It's a snow day at school, and I'm taking a vacation day so I can run a few errands and spend the rest of the day with Brendan."

"Spend the rest of the week with him. Starting this morning, I'm replacing you as chief. Roger will take over." As if he'd been cued, Roger Truax left Jennifer Underhill at the front door, where it looked like he'd been trying to make his normal constipated small talk, and walked toward Mo and Fontana. His face was completely devoid of expression, not even a hint of triumph. He was good.

"Mo, you replace me, the city council will reinstate me Thursday night, like they did last time."

"Maybe so, Mac, but this department is out of control. You've got those car burnings up in the hills that everybody's talking about."

"Nobody's talking about them, Mo. Nobody but you."

"You've got your refusal to hand over those materials last night." Mo lowered her voice. "You've got the allegations of sexual harassment. The lawsuit. I can't let it go on, Mac. As of now, you're suspended."

"Mo, you keep screwing with me and I'm going to run for mayor."

Nervously, Mo patted her disheveled hair with her stubby fingers and said, "I'm sorry. This is the way it has to be."

"See you Thursday night, Mo."

"I look forward to it," she said, though uncharacteristically her voice betrayed both a lack of confidence and a lack of enthusiasm. It was interesting that she avoided Fontana's eyes while Truax fixed on them.

"What was that all about?" Underhill asked after Mo and Truax went next door to the mayor's office.

"Business as usual. Can you do me a favor? I suddenly need to meet with our rookie today, and I'd like a witness. It'll only take a minute or two."

"Sure, Mac." Underhill went back into Fontana's office while Fontana called Heather Minerich, who walked into his office and leaned hipshot against the edge of a low file cabinet by the door, swishing Coca-Cola around in the bottom of an aluminum can just in front of her crotch.

40

SWEATY PALMS

Fontana closed the door, went to the other end of his desk, and leaned against the second metal filing cabinet across from where Underhill was sitting. "Heather. Are you suing the fire department?"

"Me? No."

"The mayor said you were."

"I don't know how she got that idea."

"She said your attorney called Friday."

"My attorney . . . oh. Well, maybe . . . I guess that could have happened."

"So are you suing, or are you not?"

"Not. I'm not."

"Maybe you want to tell that to your attorney."

"Yeah, sure."

"Were you thinking about it?"

She nodded.

"For sexual harassment?"

She nodded again.

"Heather, do you think I've sexually harassed you?"

"Well . . . You asked me where those pictures came from."

"That was harassment?"

She nodded, although she had turned her attention toward the door, was studying it with a focused concentration she usually reserved for the glow at the tip of her cigarette.

"The mayor seems to think I still have the pictures."

Heather Minerich turned her head back around, a look of inquiry in her doe-brown eyes. "The pictures?"

"I gave them to you. Remember?"

"Sure."

"You agree I gave them to you?"

"Yeah."

"Your lawyer seems to think I still have them."

"I don't know why that would be."

"Is there another problem, Heather? Something I don't know about?"

"I don't think so." Heather was one of the few people Fontana knew who could let silence magnify itself within its own framework; someone who could listen and stare and say nothing until you cracked. She would have made a hell of an interrogator, though he had a feeling her silence was closer to a teenager's insolence than to a disciplined technique.

"Thank you, Heather. By the way, Roger Truax will be taking over the chief's duties for a few days. I'll be back on Friday. Now could you send in Jim Hawkins, please?"

"Certainly, Chief."

After she'd gone, Jennifer Underhill said, "What was that all about?"

"I'm not sure I know anymore."

Hawkins looked nervous, his red hair combed into a sharp swatch over his brow. He was a short, freckled youth who wanted nothing else but to be a firefighter, though sadly would probably never get further than the volunteers. The competition these days was fierce, one applicant in five hundred, sometimes one in a thousand, outlasting the gauntlet of written tests, obstacle courses, interviews, and affirmative action demands.

"What's going on?" Hawkins said, with blustery false cheer. "If this is about the mirror, it was dark and we already got the wrong address once, so we were late to the alarm. The driveway was dark and I thought I could clear the side of the car, but then I heard glass breaking. We took the aid cases and went in. When we got back outside, this man was standing there with the broken mirror in his hand. I know I shouldn't have, but it was just a mirror.''

"Shouldn't have what, Jim?''

"I offered him twenty bucks. I didn't want to write all those accident reports. And I sure didn't want to get in trouble with you. I offered the guy twenty bucks. It was just a mirror. He said it would take fifty, so Tolmi loaned me the other thirty. I thought that was the end of it.''

"And?''

"Some old lady called this morning and wants to know what we're going to do about her mirror.''

"Who'd you give the fifty to?''

"I don't know.''

When Fontana had finished laughing, he said, "What I wanted to talk to you about are those pictures last week. I thought I recognized some of your mother's furniture, Jim.''

"Oh, God.'' Hawkins began rapidly chewing the inside of his cheek, his lip, then the tip of his left thumb. He scurried across the room and sat on the edge of Fontana's bunk. "The party pictures?''

"Them's the ones.''

"What'd'ya want to know?''

"I want to know how they got to the fire station.''

Hanging his head so that Fontana could see hair but no face, Hawkins said, "I don't know how I get into these jams. I really don't.''

"Tell me about it.''

"I brought them in.''

"Where did you get them?''

"I guess I took *some* of them. Tolmi and Chavarria took the others.''

"When did this happen?''

"A couple of weeks ago. Remember the night of the big rainstorm? My folks were out of town, so we got some beer and had a party. We had some girls over and what's-her-name showed up."

"What's-her-name?"

"You know. Heather."

"And?"

"We had both wood stoves going, and it was real hot in the house and we were drunk, so I guess some people started taking their clothes off. I was going around with the camera pretending there was no film in it. Like it was a game."

"Only there *was* film in it?"

"Right. We were laughing. Having a good time. After a while everybody just went home. Nothing happened, really."

"You have any more pictures?"

"A few."

"I want you to go home, gather up everything you've got—everything—along with the negatives, bring them here, give them to Heather in private, and then I want you to apologize. Do you understand?"

"Apologize?"

"For spreading them around like hunting trophies. You should be ashamed of yourself."

"I'm sorry."

"Not me. Heather."

"Yes, sir. I will. But I am sorry, sir."

"I hope so, Jim."

"Can I still be a volunteer here?"

"I'm not sure. Maybe if you promise never to take any more nude shots of my firefighters."

"Yes, sir. I promise. But can I still be a firefighter?"

"I'll have to think about it."

41

THE RAT IN
THE LAP POOL

The car had been stolen from Thirty-third Avenue South in Seattle, an avenue that ran along the top eastern edge of a hill overlooking the Lake Washington basin.

It was a pleasant neighborhood in the Mount Baker District, remodeled or enlarged homes, many of them positioned on lots so small the living room windows were butted up against a neighbor's bedroom or bathroom window, a district fashioned for gossips, hard-of-hearing eavesdroppers, and agoraphobic Peeping Toms.

Jennifer Underhill had trouble finding it, backing carefully out of more than one snowy dead end, until she arrived at a wrought-iron gate anchored by a brick colonnade. She got out, tiptoed from one clear spot on the street to another, pushed a button in the colonnade and spoke into a recessed speaker. Underhill walked briskly back to her car and shouted, "He's home. I thought he would be. He works second shift at the shipyard. She's a school principal. I thought they'd be in."

"This is a pretty big spread for this neighborhood," Fontana said, surveying the long brick driveway beyond the gate, the ornamental cherry trees and sculptured shrubbery.

Underhill walked over to his car window. "Yeah. I asked about it. Her uncle left it to her. He was a judge and hated everyone in the family except her."

"Some people get all the breaks."

"I don't think so. Huddleston claims the uncle sexually abused her from when she was little."

The gate opened on an electronic mechanism and slowly swung wide. The property sloped down the hill, but the drive was almost level, cutting across the hillside. Fontana followed Underhill's Dodge along the driveway and parked behind her in four inches of trackless snow near a black BMW next to a lap pool. Broken plates of ice were floating in the pool, along with a dead rat on its back. A Subaru sat near the front door of the house, the windows defrosted and clear. Fontana left Satan in the Suburban.

He met them at the door, Arthur Rembrandt Huddleston, a man whose bald head resembled a bowling ball with fringe. He looked to be around forty, a tad younger than Fontana, with thin arms and legs and a stomach that protruded like a pregnant woman's. He was in his socks, wore jeans, no belt, and a white crewneck T-shirt under a shirt that seemed ready to shoot buttons across the yard; Fontana was tempted to ask for eye protection.

"Oh, yeah," Huddleston said, nodding to Jennifer Underhill. "You find out about my car? Come on in. What'd you find out?"

As they stepped into the warm foyer, Underhill said, "Nothing. Actually, I've brought along the fire chief from the district where your car was found. We'd like to ask you a few questions."

Huddleston led them into a messy kitchen that smelled of burnt toast and black coffee. Underhill accepted his offer of a cup; Fontana did not. Underhill also accepted a chair at the table with Huddleston while he dug into a heaping plate of scrambled eggs and sausage.

"Excuse me, but you caught me right in the middle," he said through a mouthful.

"No problem," said Underhill, sipping from her gold-rimmed cup.

"What did you want to ask me about?"

"That gate out there for one thing," said Fontana. "Is it always locked?"

"It is now. It never was before. We're so hard to find here and it's such a goddamned long driveway, we never thought we had anything to worry about. Down the street there were some burglaries a couple of years ago, but never up here. I'm gonna get that pool spruced up too and start swimming as soon as the weather turns around. You see our fitness rat? Did one lap and froze up. Been a shitty winter, don't you think?"

"Not the greatest," said Fontana. "You ever have prowlers before your car turned up missing?"

"Us? Nope. Nobody comes to this neighborhood unless they're looking for one of our neighbors or they're lost. Nobody ever comes up here."

From the kitchen window Fontana could see traffic racing across the new floating bridge on Lake Washington, below on the hillside the tops of leafless trees, a few random roofs, and a man shoveling his sidewalk. There were paintings in the living room, originals. An Oriental rug. Antique furniture. Delicate vases. These people didn't have kids.

"Hey," said Huddleston, talking around a conglomeration of eggs and ketchup. "You didn't happen to find a couple of envelopes on the dashboard, did you? I had some mail."

"There wasn't anything left except metal," said Fontana.

"No harm in asking."

"Mr. Huddleston," said Underhill, glancing at Fontana, "could you go over the events of the afternoon your car was stolen?"

"Nothing to go over." He sat back and made slurping noises in a mug of coffee. "I started it up, stepped into the house to take a shower, and when I came out it was gone."

"You didn't see anything?" Fontana asked.

"Not a dad-blamed squirrel. Not a mosquito. Not a leftover fart. 'Course, that Grand Marquis always did run silent."

"And how long were you inside?"

"Twenty minutes."

"You have any friends or acquaintances who might drop by at that time of day?"

"You mean like they might have seen whoever stole it?"

"Something like that."

"I told everybody I know about this. Nobody saw a thing. It's ridiculous. I warm my car up and somebody steals it. Makes you wonder where they were hiding. After what I read in the paper, I wonder I'm not lucky to be alive."

Fontana said, "This might seem like a strange question, Mr. Huddleston, but do you know anybody who works for or have you ever had occasion to patronize an escort service?"

"You mean hookers?"

"Yes."

Straddling his chair like a man on a tractor angling for a better view, Huddleston stood and glanced past Fontana into the other end of the house, then sat back down and spoke in a softer voice. "Not here in town. I wouldn't know who to call here in town. Maybe on the road once or twice before I met Martha."

"How about your friends? You have any friends who might patronize an escort service?"

"If I do, they don't talk about it."

They went over the make, model, and year of the car, whether there had been any firearms in it, whether Huddleston owned any firearms—three hunting rifles, all accounted for—and then they asked him to speculate on what might have happened. He had no idea.

Jennifer Underhill looked at her watch, announced she had a meeting in Lake City, and left. Fontana remained, chatting with Huddleston about the house, the changeable winter weather, Huddleston's job at the shipyard—trying to get a feel for the man.

He knew Underhill would check Huddleston's finances to see if he could be traced to any of the local escort services. It was possible he'd faked the theft of his own car to cover up the fact that he'd killed somebody in it, and Callahan had somehow stumbled upon him disposing of the body. Of course, he probably would have needed a confederate to get out of a snowstorm in the mountains.

As far as the alibi, it wouldn't be the first time somebody had been clocked into a factory without setting foot on the premises.

"Your wife around?" Fontana asked, as Huddleston showed him to the door.

"Uh, yeah. She took some aspirin and went back to bed. Say, that reminds me. You heard the one about the husband and wife going to the costume party? She gets a headache and tells him to go on alone?"

"Yeah, I'm pretty sure I did hear that one. Was your wife out driving in the Subaru this morning?"

"Naw. I warmed it up. I like to have a rig warmed up." He looked down at his white socks.

"One last thing," Fontana said. "I got twisted around driving in here. Could you tell me how to get to Thirty-two twenty-four South Plum?"

"Thirty-two twenty-four?" Huddleston said, trying to conceal a smile. His fingers were jammed up to the knuckles in the front pockets of his jeans.

"What's the matter?"

"It's right up there," Huddleston said, nodding at a thirty-foot embankment on the west end of their property. Ivy from above cloaked the top two thirds of the concrete wall. Along the rim stood a picket fence and part of a large house. It was the place Knutson was house-sitting.

"You know those people?" Fontana asked.

"The guy owns the place is in Bermuda or someplace working on a land deal. Somebody's staying over for him."

"You know *them?*"

"Caught him looking down here with a pair of binoculars once. Seems like a prick."

"You're sure that's Thirty-two twenty-four Plum?"

"Yep."

"Your wife know them?"

"She knows fewer neighbors than I do. Two days ago she

called the police on the guy down below because she thought
he was stealing ferns from the woods. Turned out he owns
the woods.''

''Thanks for your time.''

''My pleasure. Hey? You have any trouble on the roads?''

''The main ones are pretty good.''

''I figured.''

The wrought-iron gate swung closed as soon as Fontana's rear
bumper cleared the grounds. He circled the block and parked in
front of the place the Knutsons were house-sitting. When he got
out of the truck, the sky was a solid gray overcast and seemed as
flat and low as a basement ceiling.

42

STEPPING
IN YOUR OWN BOOT PRINTS

Fontana let Satan out for a stretch, then walked up to the front door and knocked. Nobody answered.

The Accord was in front of the house but had made no tracks in the snow. Fontana peeked into the window, worried that if she were home alone, he might frighten Rachel Knutson.

Walking noisily through snow that still had a frozen crust on top, he strode through the backyard and over to the fence where he could see down into Huddleston's estate, the long brick drive, the lap pool, the BMW, the floating rat. Though it had been only minutes since he'd left, the Subaru was gone.

Fontana turned and looked back up at the Knutson house, tracing a direct line of sight from Knutson's living room window to Huddleston's parking area and front door. He vaguely remembered the same view from his visit with Randy a week earlier, but he hadn't paid much attention to it then. Surely, Randy and Rachel had witnessed Huddleston warming up his car; surely they knew the routine, as might any of Knutson's guests.

After he walked back to the front of the house, stepping in the same prints he'd pressed into the snow earlier, Fontana spotted the German shepherd directly opposite a Nissan Pathfinder half a block away.

Fontana walked up the street, scratched Satan behind the old wound on his floppy ear, said, "Good boy," then turned to the Pathfinder. "You been there all morning, Larry?"

"Hey man. How ya doin'?" Lawrence Drummey rolled his window down and bared all his teeth in a savage grin. "I was afraid you mighta been jobbing me about that dog of yours. You know, man? Like he really didn't like black people only you were telling me he did."

Fontana continued to stroke Satan's head. "He likes everybody, Larry. He's just scared of black people. You here to visit Knutson?"

"Not to visit really. I told you before, I come up here once in a while. I just mostly look. He's scared of us?"

"I don't suppose the neighbors have ever called the police?"

"They did once about two weeks ago, but I beat the rap, man." He grinned at the humor of it. Until the Paint Company fire, Drummey had always seemed content, pleased with himself, amused by the world.

"You waiting for them to come home?"

"They're home, man. Car's right there. I seen you knock, but they gotta be home. The car's right there."

"I don't believe he'll be released from the hospital until noon."

Drummey shrugged. "It don't matter. I got nothin' else goin' on."

"See anything?"

"Haven't seen anything except some kids and a sour old man out here shoveling off that sidewalk. He broomed it. Then he came out with a big old shop vac. A *vacuum* cleaner. I think he's the one called the cops."

"You going to talk to the Knutsons when they get home?"

"If I'm here, I just might."

"Why are you here, Larry?"

"God, sometimes I feel like an apple core trying to work my way out of an elephant. Nobody ever hears what I'm saying. Don't you get it? He's the center of everything."

Fontana turned around and went up the vacuumed walkway.

"Hey! Where you goin'!" Drummey yelled from his truck window.

"Some Dugan shot at the house a while back. Neighbors might have seen something."

"You're going to ask about me, aren't you?"

"Right off the bat, Larry." Fontana went up an inclined walkway, up two concrete steps worn smooth and painted red.

A cautious old man who looked part black and part Asian answered the buzzer. He was wearing slippers, baggy brown trousers, and suspenders as red as the ones on Fontana's bunking pants; his shirt was buttoned tightly to the folds of his slack neck. He said his name was Ramos. After Fontana displayed his chief's badge and told him he was investigating a sequence of car arsons, the old man stepped out onto the stoop in his slippers, closing the door behind him to keep the heat in. "That fella out there in the car? I thought he looked like a firebug. Most likely a dog snatcher, too."

"No, sir. I don't believe so. He's afraid of dogs. What can you tell me about the people who live in the next house down?"

"They snatch dogs?"

"They knew somebody I'm interested in, that's all."

"She came over and introduced herself, brought us brownies and told us all about themselves. She claims he's a famous author, but all he does is ride that motorbike up and down the street."

"Have you noticed anything unusual about them?"

"Just that fella sitting out there in his truck watching their house."

"Does he come here often?"

"Couple days a week for maybe the last two or three weeks. Sometimes way into the night. We called that nine-one-one number, but they didn't roust him. Didn't do a thing. Now you tell me, young fella; you have a man just sitting there in a car outside your house at twelve o'clock at night, don't you think you've a right to be skeptical?"

"Anybody loitering outside your house would be worrisome."

"Mama sits up here and waits for him to break in or something.

I'm afraid to leave her alone. We take the dog with us when we go out."

"In the past month or so have the Knutsons had any other visitors?"

"Some young gal sits out there sometimes, almost where that fella is."

"What does she drive?"

The old man took half a step, peered over the snowcapped rhododendrons in his yard and said, "I don't know. She's not there now."

"You see Mrs. Knutson this morning?" Fontana said, stepping down off the red stairs.

"Haven't seen much of her for a few days. Now that you get me thinking, I haven't seen much of him either. Are they moving out?"

"Don't get your hopes up. I don't think so."

Fontana found three other neighbors at home, nobody with anything noteworthy to add, although a widow with a clear view of Knutson's place had been disturbed over Lawrence Drummey's loitering, wanted to know whether to call the police.

"I were you, I would," said Fontana.

43

DOES GOD
WEAR SANDALS
OR LOAFERS OR WHAT?

Engulfed in a blur of cigar fumes, wearing a starchy, white chief's shirt, complete with collar insignia, Roger Truax overwhelmed the tilt-back chair in Fontana's office. Fontana thought he looked like a drunk in a child's plastic wading pool.

"Hey, old man," Truax said, propping his boots on the edge of Fontana's desk. " 'Bout time you showed up. You realize that if you lose the chief's job, you give up that Suburban, too."

Fontana flicked the keys at Truax so hard they bounced off his chest, struck the wall, and slid along the floor into the corner. Stalking angrily out of the station, he walked the slushy streets home with Satan tagging jauntily alongside. It was a surprise, this anger, because he'd thought he had been at peace with Mo's usurpation of his title. It wasn't the first time a sudden anger had informed him of what he was really thinking. Sally had dumped him. His life had been complicated by Lou Strange and his disturbed daughter. Joyce Callahan was ragging on him to find out who'd immolated her husband. He had tried and failed to spend this free day with his son.

Each time he passed a pile of snow, he kicked slush in all directions, and each time, Satan hopped aside and then looked up at his master curiously.

Two people stopped to offer rides, but he declined, knowing that if he made it too easy on himself he wouldn't be as angry. He wanted to be angry.

He spent the remainder of the afternoon blowing off steam by pulling Brendan around their vacant, snowbound neighborhood on a sled, then, after a flurry of back-and-forth phone calls, drove the boy over to a friend's log cabin home on the Mount Gadd road, dropping him off with a sleeping bag and a toothbrush, chatting five minutes with the boy's mother amid a pack of barking dogs. Fontana was a little uneasy around the Andersons, mostly because he had the feeling that Marti, who had always been standoffish, thought he was on the make for her, which he definitely was not, but secondarily, because he always had the sense that they felt sorry for him and Brendan.

Pity wasn't a trophy he needed. Perhaps Marti Anderson had been comparing her new Jeep Cherokee with his 1960 bucket of bolts. At least he didn't boast about sleeping in a bed with five dogs, one of which he had just seen rolling in stale roadkill out on the street.

At home he popped a TV dinner into the oven for himself, fed Satan, and made a phone call to a man who worked at the King County Dispatch Center. Dave Walls. Fontana had never met him, though they exchanged messages earlier in the week.

"Dave? Mac Fontana here. From the Staircase Fire Department. We responded to that car fire up at Denny Creek Tuesday last. You remember the one?"

"Sure. Underhill was asking me about it."

"I've seen the transcript of the call, but I was wondering what your impressions were."

"I was talking to Angie about this. I mean when you think about it, he might have been a firefighter, the guy who called. I don't know what it was exactly, because I've listened to the tape again myself and I can't see anything there, really, except I had this feeling. You know the connection was obviously a cell phone and pretty bad."

"Refresh my memory. Did he describe the smoke?"

"Heavy, black smoke. Said it looked like it'd been burning awhile."

"Was that on the transcript?"

"No. Like I said, it was real scratchy. Whoever transcribed the call probably couldn't figure out what that part was."

"It was roaring when we got there twenty minutes later. Twenty-seven minutes later. Even with gas poured over it, I've been wondering how it could burn so hot for so long. He didn't give a name?"

"I think he was going to, but his phone cut out. That happens up toward the pass. But the tone of voice sounded like he knew what he was talking about."

"And he never called back?"

"Not while I was on shift."

"Thanks, Dave."

A fire burning out has a certain look to it, the smoke less black, rising slower, gobs of older smoke smudging the sky. A fresh car fire, on the other hand, gave off fast-rising, rich, black smoke with nothing above it. Two different looks.

Fontana suddenly realized they hadn't gone up there responding to the burning Mercury Marquis. They were sent to Callahan's rental with the woman in the backseat, which had burned out before they got there. While looking for that car, they encountered the second burning car with Callahan in the trunk, the fire set sometime between the phone call and their arrival. It had to have happened that way. First the woman in the rental, then Callahan in the stolen car. Being certain of the sequence—something he should have figured out right away—made the picture clearer.

Fontana phoned Overlake Hospital and asked for the floor nurse on Knutson's wing, explaining to her he was a friend of Knutson's and was compiling a list of his visitors so he could send thank-you cards.

"Oh, gosh. We don't keep any kind of list. But I was here all three days. Let me think. There was a fire officer from somewhere. A short black man came in. Then there were two women.

The tall one was an arson inspector or something. The other one must have been his wife? I guess she was luckier than him. Only a black eye. She only came the once."

"That was it? Four people?"

"I'm pretty sure."

■

Taking Satan with him, Fontana headed for Seattle in his old truck. It was supposed to snow again, but the only signs were a chill in the air and a high cloud cover that had crept in over the last few hours.

At Knutson's place, all the lights were on. The Honda had not made any fresh tracks in the refrozen snow. Drummey was gone.

Fontana let Satan out to piddle and sniff for cats, then put him back into the truck before he found one.

"Mac? Mac?"

Grace Teller slammed her Blazer door and crossed the dark street. Surreptitiously, Fontana unlatched the passenger door on the ancient GMC so that Satan, should he feel the need to defend his master, would have free access. Teller wore a ski coat, jeans, hiking boots. Her hair was uncombed and greasy, and she wore no makeup, a massive bruise obliterating the top part of the left side of her face. He hoped it ached as badly as his sore shoulder did. There were no obvious weapons in her pockets, and her gloved hands were empty.

"Grace."

"Mac, what are you doing here?"

"I came to visit Randy Knutson. You realize this is his house, don't you?"

"Here? Yeah. Why are you seeing him?"

"No, Grace. The question is, why are you sitting in the dark outside the house of a man you beat half to death?"

"No reason, really."

"You better leave."

"You don't have to play mind games with me, Mac."

"This isn't any kind of game. You leave or I call the cops."

"Mac, I don't hate you at all."

"Grace, you didn't beat up Knutson just to confuse the issue, did you? Maybe to mix things up so we'd lose track of your father?"

"What about my father?"

"Why was he here in the Northwest at the same time as Callahan? Why did he run out and buy a motor home the day after Larry Drummey told him Callahan would be at this conference?"

"Maybe he wanted to take a trip."

"Maybe he wanted to dog a fire chief he blamed for ruining his life."

"You don't use logic, Mac. You don't reason things out the way a normal person does. Why would my father want to lock Callahan in a trunk, drink beer for twenty minutes, and then light the car up?"

"Did he drink beer for twenty minutes? I thought he was on the wagon until just the other night. And how do you know it was twenty minutes?"

Grace shifted her feet, glanced at the ground, then began systematically crushing a tiny ridge of frozen snow on the parking strip with her boot heel. "I wouldn't know."

"When did he start drinking again? Before Tuesday a week ago?"

"I don't know when."

"How did you know somebody was up at the crime site drinking beer?"

"It was in the paper. Listen, you mess with my father, you'll get what Knutson got." Issuing the threat seemed to calm her for a few moments. "Mac, have you ever had an epiphany? Something that happens that's like a spiritual revelation? That's what I had the other night when we were together."

"While you were trying to break my face with that pipe?"

"I don't know if it was during or after. Or if it was because I got so cold, but I felt as if I wasn't in my own body, as if I was looking at *me* from outside, from somewhere up high. Have you ever had a gut feeling that you just knew was true in the real world? And then later on you discovered it really was true? And there was no way you could have known?''

"Not recently, Grace."

"It was actually, if you think about it, a true spiritual experience. I feel like I've seen God. Or maybe part of God's house. Are you following me? Maybe not a big part of his house. Maybe it was only a small room or a closet. And maybe I didn't even see all of that. Maybe just one of the shoes in the bottom of the closet. But I've seen it. I know I have."

"You've seen one of God's shoes? Was it a sandal or was it a loafer?''

"Don't make fun of me."

"What are you doing here, Grace?"

"I'm telling you about my epiphany."

"Are you here to hurt Knutson again?"

"You said we were going to be friends."

"We're not going to be friends, Grace. We're not ever going to be friends."

"You said we were."

"I was mistaken."

"You broke this bone in my face. Did you know that? They X-rayed me, and you broke this bone."

"You come at some Dugan with a pipe, darlin', they tend to do things like that."

She stared at him, eyes bulging, incredulous at his answer. "Do you know I'm thinking about suing?"

"You might get a group discount if you look around. Maybe a class action suit. You better think about getting out of here. Knutson here, he finds you're in front of his house, he's likely to stick a hunting rifle out one of those upstairs windows and squeeze off a round."

Using her hands to brush her bangs away from her eyes, Grace scrutinized the house. "There's no rifle up there."

"Why are you here, Grace?"

"I was thinking about my spiritual and emotional life. I was thinking about you, actually."

"That's a good thing to do, Grace. Ponder your life. Because your life is screwed up. You *should* ponder it. But don't do it here. Good night, Grace."

He watched her walk back to the Blazer. She was confused, slovenly, and deep in the throes of some mental illness he could not identify. Fontana felt an emotion that, when he analyzed it, turned out to be a second cousin to pity. His charity might have run deeper except for a premonition he had that she was about to shoot him in the back of the head as he proceeded up the walkway to Knutson's front door.

44

IT WASTES FUEL
AND KILLS BIRDS

When Knutson swung open the front door, it banged against his wheelchair. Fontana assisted him back to a clear spot in the living room not far from the couch where he'd been sleeping on Fontana's first visit, a locus surrounded by rogue newspapers from the past three days, crumpled beer cans, an ashtray with a hot butt in it, and an ice bucket scummed over with discarded candy bar wrappers. The furnace was pumping tropical air through all the vents, and there wasn't a light bulb in the place that wasn't too hot to touch.

After he locked the front door, Fontana stepped behind the coat rack and peered out a tall rectangular window at the street. The Blazer hadn't moved.

Knutson wore only a T-shirt, sweat pants with one leg scissored off for the cast, and a gray wool sock on his uninjured foot. His hair stuck out all over his head. Though the swelling in his face had gone down, it hadn't gone down much. And he couldn't have had many friends because there wasn't a single get-well message on the white plaster cast on his leg.

"Where's Rachel?" Fontana said.

Still breathing heavily from rolling himself to the front door and back, Knutson gave him a sideways look. "We had a fight."

"She left you alone here in a wheelchair?"

"Yeah. I don't know if she's even coming back."

"What'd you fight about?"

"Some stupid shit."

"There aren't any car tracks in the snow outside your garage. That Accord hasn't moved."

"Then she's got the Jeep. Took a cab. How the hell do I know?" Knutson reached down with his better hand and drained a beer can, gulping loudly. His face was pale, his broken nose taped, his eyes bloodshot, at least what Fontana could see of them through the puffy slits. He had been bragging about his Jeep ever since Fontana had known him, but it had not been in the street earlier and nothing had gone in or out of the garage. "Have a beer?"

"No thanks."

Knutson looked at Fontana for a moment or two. He wasn't completely drunk, but he soon would be.

"What? You wanna know how I'm feeling? My balls are swollen out to the size of coconuts. I can barely see out of either eye. I been beat to crap by a girl, and my wife has left me. I got a headache that feels like Mount Rainier about to erupt. How do you think I feel?"

"I think you've been feeling badly for a week or so. I thought you were on drugs."

"I am *now.*"

"I called the hospital. They said you had four visitors."

"I didn't do a head count. I was doped up most of the time."

"A fire officer. That was me. A black guy. That was Drummey—"

"I don't really care what you found—"

"And two women. A tall one from the fire marshal's office and then your wife. The first woman was Jennifer Underhill, who's investigating those murders at Denny Creek. But your second female visitor was Grace, wasn't it?"

Knutson stared at him through the slits that were his eyes.

Fontana continued. "Grace has a shiner. That's why the nurse assumed she was in the same accident you were in. Called her the lucky one."

"You know when she was a kid, she was kind of winsome. Now she's about as cute as a pinch of cold shit. Yeah, she came up there. I don't remember hitting her that night, but I musta got in at least one good shot."

"Sorry to disappoint you, but I'm the one who hit her. What did she want in the hospital?"

"Asked me how I was. Like she had nothing to do with putting me there. It was weird."

"So you spoke?"

"Not really. She came in. Made a stab or two at conversation and left before I could buzz the nurse."

"You think maybe she came to kill you and changed her mind?"

He thought about that. "Now that you mention it, yeah, maybe so."

"Two women visitors. Underhill and Grace Teller. Where was the third?"

"Who are you talking about?"

"Your wife."

"My wife was there the whole time."

"I don't think so, Randy."

After some wandering, Knutson's eyes finally came to rest on a fish tank along one wall. "She was there all night. Afterwards she went over to a motel in Bellevue and crashed."

"I can go back and ask them again, but they said you had four visitors. Not five. Four. A chief. A short black man. And two women. One of the women—"

"Okay. Well, yeah, I didn't want people to know. We've been on the skids. Rachel's gone off to see her mother in Texas."

"When was this?"

"A week ago."

"Then why tell me she was just here?"

"Didn't want anybody to know."

"I don't think so."

"You don't think what?"

"I don't think she's in Texas."

"Where is she then?"

"In the medical examiner's office. Your wife is the woman we found up at Denny Creek."

Knutson lit a cigarette and began blowing O's into the room. Soon there was a blimp of smoke over his head. It was an unusual conversational gambit for him, saying nothing.

"You want to tell me what happened up there, Randy?"

"I don't know what you're talking about."

"Sure you do. We have a dead man up there who had a major grudge against you and who had been put into a confrontational position with you that neither of you liked but neither of you was going to back away from. And then we have an unidentified dead woman who's about the right height and about the right weight to have been your wife—who is now missing and being lied about."

Knutson reached down, groped for another can of beer, popped the tab, and swished a mouthful of liquid through his teeth. He swallowed, placed a fresh cigarette between his lips, and let it bounce while he spoke. "My wife never visited the hospital because she left me."

"Left you just about the time that woman was getting herself killed up near the pass."

"Rachel's in Texas visiting her mother. Maybe her sister in North Carolina."

"We'll call her mother. We'll call her sister. After I tell the medical examiner my suspicions, they'll run a DNA test on the body. They get blood from her mother, they'll know it's Rachel."

"Run your tests." Knutson picked up another unopened beer and tried to wheel out of the room with it. Fontana stepped in front of him. "How do you figure it, Mac? What would my wife be doing up there?"

"That's what had me stumped all afternoon. The car Callahan was found in was stolen from your neighbor down the hill. Not two hundred feet from your stash of beer here. You stole your neighbor's car, and then you went up into the hills to meet with Callahan. I don't know how you talked him into going up there, but you did. Rachel went too. She might even have taken a second car. Probably your Jeep. You got into some sort of beef with Callahan. While you two were struggling, Rachel got shot. You locked him in the trunk and then she died, so you rolled the car she was in down into the woods and burned it. It must have destroyed you to learn later that she was still alive when you set fire to it."

Knutson reversed the wheelchair and rolled back to his spot under the reading lamp, where he eyeballed Fontana through lowered and swollen brows. It occurred to Fontana that his theory, while it seemed to have goaded Randy Knutson, did not account for the two different types of semen in the victim, or explain why the three of them were meeting out in the woods.

"Or maybe you took her up there thinking to get rid of them both. Maybe she was playing around on you. Callahan was threatening you. Kill two birds with one stone. Why'd you steal the car?"

"I didn't steal any goddamned car, although God knows, I should have."

"What do you mean?"

"You can't be warming a car up for twenty, twenty-five minutes every goddamned day. Besides being a waste of fuel, it ruins the valves. Birds were falling out of the trees from the fumes. We could smell that stinking exhaust all the way up here."

"After your wife was shot, you drove him part way out on that road, and then decided to stop and talk it through with him. Or kill him."

"You're not even close."

"I can prove she was your wife. I can prove that much."

"With the DNA?"

"With the DNA."

"What makes you think I was up there when it happened?" Knutson's argumentative instincts were coming to the fore.

"Because you knew that was your wife before I told you. I saw it in the way your body collapsed when I brought it up. That's why you've been moping around looking like you were on drugs."

Knutson chewed that over for a moment or two, and his shoulders sagged even further. "Rachel disappeared the day you found

Callahan. I knew where that stolen car came from. Knowing all that, it made sense that she stole the car and went up there and killed him."

"Why didn't you tell anybody?"

"Because I wasn't sure. And I would have been sending the cops after my own wife."

"You must have been worried."

"Damn straight I was worried."

"Is that why you went up there poking around the scene of the crime?"

"I went up there a couple days later."

"You'd like to think you can talk your way out of anything, Randy. But you can't talk your way out of how you feel."

"What do you mean by that?"

"We all thought you were on drugs, but it wasn't drugs. You've been operating on one hundred-proof guilt. You killed your wife, and you're being eaten alive by the guilt. It's like that flesh-eating bacteria. Trust me. I'm an expert on guilt. I know exactly what's going on. I bet you didn't even defend yourself during the beating."

"I loved Rachel. She was my life."

"You loved her, why'd you kill her?"

"I didn't!" he screamed, tears streaming down his face. "And you don't have any idea what's going on with me." The yelp of emotion took Fontana by surprise. Even in the midst of his most vociferous arguments, Knutson had handled himself calmly, had always remained in control of his feelings. But something had changed here.

"You shot her and burned her alive. Your own wife."

"Bullshit! I got there too late. He killed Rachel. That stupid bastard." Knutson dropped his face into his chest and sobbed, drool and snot and teardrops darkening his white T-shirt. "He killed her. That sonofabitch. He killed her."

"Tell me what happened, Randy."

"I wasn't up there." He wept.

"Come on, Randy. This is Mac. Explain it to me. How did he get her up there?"

45

THE REAL TRUTH, OR,
DO YOU HAVE
ANY LAST WORDS?

"It was all Rachel's doing. I figured I hurt him bad enough with that book, which is still selling all over the world. Whenever he said anything about me in the papers, I brushed it aside, because I knew the next day those papers were going to be lining the cat box. It was Rachel who couldn't stand it. Rachel was a nervous wreck. She used to pull all the drapes and hide in the back of the house, thinking bullets would come through the walls.

"You should have heard all the veiled threats he made at dinner that night. The way she figured it, we would knock him off and it would be self-defense. Get him before he got us. She was so damn nervous. That's what made it all happen. If he'd known how nervous she was, he would have kept his mouth shut."

"So the two of you concocted a plan?"

"I told you. She made the plan. I nixed it."

"Tell me what happened."

"I don't know what happened."

"Tell me what you think happened."

"She went up there to meet him. She locked him in the trunk and killed him. Then she felt so bad she drove farther up into the woods and shot herself. You found the gun at her feet. She must have shot herself, and then the car rolled into the woods and caught fire."

"I don't think so, Randy."

"Why not?"

"For one thing, you just told me you thought *he* killed *her.* And the fire in her car happened before his. It was reported by a motorist, but it burned out by the time we got there. We saw the second fire and thought it was the one we were dispatched to."

"No. She burned his car up, and then she was hiding up there. Later on she killed herself."

"It didn't happen that way, Randy. It was her car fire that was reported. She died first." Fontana paused before continuing. "The medical examiner said she'd had sex with two men."

Knutson became incredibly still.

"I figure one of those men was you," said Fontana. "The other had to be Callahan."

"That bastard! That sonofabitch deserved to die. That goddamned county investigator, Underhill, told me the dead woman had sex with two men prior to her death. God. You guys thought Rachel was a whore. Don't you get it? Callahan met her up there expecting sex, and when she didn't cooperate, that pig raped Rachel and then he killed her."

"Is that why you killed him, Randy?"

Knutson wheeled his chair over to the small table the phone was on, took a tape out of the drawer and inserted it into the answer machine in his telephone unit. It was the second time he'd played a recording for Fontana.

It was a woman's voice, timid and rather sweet:

"Randy? This is Rach. I know you're in the house. I'm glad you didn't hear the phone, because now you won't be able to talk me out of it. I'm up at Denny Creek. Exit forty-seven. You know? Where Rickie and Bert showed us their cabin last fall? I've talked Callahan into meeting me up here. He thinks I'm leaving you. He thinks I'm interested in him. God, he's such an egomaniac. You better get up here, Randy. I can't do this by myself. If you leave right now, you'll get here in time. Randy? I love you. I know you told me this was stupid, but this all has to end, otherwise we're never going to have a life. I love you."

Knutson shut the tape off and looked away.

"She snookered him, and then he got the jump on her? Is that what happened?"

Knutson nodded, his head tucked into a shoulder.

"What'd you find when you got up there, Randy?"

"Christ!" Knutson wheeled himself back to the stash of beer without realizing he already had a can in his lap, another half-finished can on a coffee table. He was staring at the carpet. "I wrecked the Jeep on the way back. It's been in the service station down the street ever since. I was *so* shook up."

"What happened, Randy?"

"I went up as fast as I could, snowstorm or no snowstorm. I just kept thinking about Rachel and Callahan. She didn't know what a pig he was with women. I got up there and went up that narrow old road toward where all the cabins are at Denny Creek. I figured they'd be there somewhere parked along the side of the road in the snow, but I couldn't find them. Finally, coming at me on the road was this car. I didn't recognize it at first with the headlights in my eyes in the middle of the afternoon. I'm blocking the road. I get out and lo and behold, Ed Callahan is driving our neighbor's car. Rachel's not there.

"So I says to him, 'Ed, old boy, what's going on?' 'Nothing,' says Ed. 'Nothing at all.' But Ed is lying. I can tell. And he's *real* nervous. At first I can't tell if it's because I have a Luger in my hand or if it's something else. Where's Rachel, I say. Rachel? He hasn't seen Rachel. He doesn't know anything about Rachel. But I can see he's got a scratch on his face and it's bleeding. So I make him get out. I ask him why he's bleeding, and he says he was out in the woods and walked into a branch. Now this, I almost believe.

"But what's he even doing up there if he hasn't seen Rachel? He says he was supposed to meet her. He admits he was supposed to meet her. But she never showed. So he was on his way back.

That might fly, except he is driving my neighbor's Mercury Marquis. I recognize the plate and the KVI radio sticker in the back window. I wonder if my neighbor is up there.

"I ask Callahan what he was supposed to meet her about, and he won't say. So I make him hop into the trunk. The trunk of my neighbor's car."

"He got in? No struggle?"

"Oh, there was a struggle, but Ed had been sitting at a desk too many years. He didn't have much fight in him. In my wildest nightmares I couldn't have imagined what he'd done. At the worst I thought maybe he'd slapped her around. You know. And she was up there crying. Anyway, I lock him in the trunk and take my Jeep around the Marquis and up the road. It's four-wheel drive. It'll go anywhere."

"You weren't afraid he'd escape while you were gone?"

"I had the keys. He might have gotten out of the trunk, but it was highly unlikely he knew how to hot wire a car."

"You had the keys?"

"That's right."

"Then what happened?"

"I saw smoke. I followed it and found a car in the trees. I went down in there, but it was burning pretty good. There was a body in the backseat. I was hoping it was my neighbor. It wasn't a car I could recognize and I couldn't even tell if it was a woman. I kept looking around in the snow for Rachel. She had to be somewhere. I knew that wasn't her in the burning car. Later that night I waited for my neighbor to come home from work, and when he did, I threw up."

"Because you knew then that it had been Rachel?"

"I guess I knew before. I knew."

"What about Callahan?"

"I waited for the fire to burn down, thinking I'd be able to tell whose body it was, but the longer I waited, the more worried I got. Pretty soon I wasn't going to be able to do anything, so I went back. God. I should have made it worse on him."

"I don't see how."

"I drove back down the road. I had two five-gallon cans of gaso-

line on the back of the Jeep, so I took one and emptied it all over
the car, inside and out. He smelled it from the trunk and started
yelling. Ordering me to let him out.''

"But you didn't."

"I opened the trunk and made him throw all his money out,
you know, to make it look like a robbery. For some reason it
calmed him down. Then I threw the keys in and slammed the lid.''

"You threw the keys inside so you couldn't back out?''

"Something like that. I went over against a tree and had a couple of brewskies. I had all kinds of theories about what had happened and who that was in the burned-up car. Part of my mind
was telling me it was Rachel, and part was saying it couldn't be.
He sure wasn't going to tell me. I let him ramble, though. Hell,
he talked himself hoarse. He tried every song and dance you ever
heard. Offered money. Threatened me. Told me Rachel had
come at him with a gun and they'd struggled for it; that she'd
driven away. Said there was somebody else up there. He claimed
he didn't know anything about a fire.''

"And?"

"After a while I realized sooner or later somebody was going
to come up that road and discover I had some bastard locked in
the trunk and that I'd poured gasoline all over him. Figured it
was time to shit or get off the pot. That's when I asked him if he
had any last words.''

"Did he?"

"Did he what?"

"Have any last words?"

"No. He was real quiet. So I lit him up. He didn't let out a
peep. I don't know what he was doing in there. Trying to get out,
I suppose. I got out of that road just in time because I saw your
red lights coming up the freeway as I was going down.''

46

TODAY IS
THE TOMORROW YOU
WORRIED ABOUT YESTERDAY

"You must feel relieved," said Fontana.

"Telling you? I don't know. I guess it wasn't until now that I've really faced the fact that Rachel's dead, that she was in that car. For a week I've been sort of half expecting her to come walking through the door. I almost expected her to be here when I came home from the hospital. It's going to make a helluva book. Of course, the tour will be a little restricted. Maybe they'll let me do some teleconferencing from my cell. Say, Mac, I've been reading true-crime books the past week. The Mounties don't always get their man. Neither do the locals."

"What are you trying to say?"

"He killed my wife. I killed him. You know about it, so what? Can't you just say justice was served and leave it at that?"

"I'm no judge and jury, Randy. This has to be handled by the authorities."

"Oh, come on. You couldn't possibly be that much of a tight ass. You're kidding me, right?"

"No, Randy. I'm not. Maybe a jury'll let you off. Maybe a prosecutor will figure they can't prosecute. But you know I can't keep this to myself.''

"Okay. Shit. Before you do anything . . . you know . . . before you call that lady investigator or tell anybody about this, can you do me a favor? Let me call my dad? I don't want him to find out I'm a suspect from the TV. And I don't want Rachel's mother to find out Rachel's dead on TV. Can you give me that?''

"I'm—''

"What am I going to do?" he said sarcastically. "Run for it? I can't even walk.''

"Okay, Randy. Sure.''

Knutson took a pack of cigarettes and a lighter and slowly wheeled himself into a first-floor bedroom. Before he went inside, he looked at Fontana and said, "I never should have written that book. I figured, well sure, it was going to hurt some people. But I never really thought past that. That fire ruined so many lives. And then my book ruined the rest. I never imagined Lou Strange was going to get raked over the coals the way he did. And Callahan? He should have been run out of town on a rail. Instead, they make him the chief. How do you figure?''

"There's no figuring, Randy.''

Fontana waited on the couch in the living room and wondered how to proceed. If he called Underhill, there was an off chance Knutson would repeat his confession. On the other hand, if Knutson denied everything, there wasn't much they would be able to do. It would be Knutson's word against Fontana's, and as far as hard evidence connecting Knutson to the crime scene, there might not be any. One slim chance involved the gas can. Knutson had left a five-gallon can at the scene, and because the can had probably been strapped to the back of his Jeep for years, there would be scratch marks, abrasions, rubbings that a good forensics specialist could match to the Jeep.

After ten minutes Fontana approached the bedroom. "You okay, Randy?''

He had almost reached the door when a shot rattled the plaster walls.

Standing to one side, he touched the doorknob and called out again. "Randy?" No answer. He turned the knob and slowly pushed the door open. Knutson was in his wheelchair facing the door, a Luger in his lap next to a beer can and an ashtray with a live butt in it.

"Fooled ya," said Knutson, grinning. "I sure thought about it. Tell you the truth, I'm just not there yet. Besides, I don't think you're going to prove anything, and I'd kind of like to stick around and watch you flagellate yourself trying."

"Mind putting that gun away, Randy?"

Knutson flung the pistol across to the bed, where it vanished in the rumpled bedding. "Just tell me one thing, Mac. When did you first suspect?"

"At Callahan's funeral. You were far too complimentary. People who kill often go through a period of remorse where they flatter the dead. Whatever. You felt bad about killing him. You wanted to say something nice. It was way out of character for you."

"I'm that much of a fool that I said something nice about the guy and you immediately thought I killed him?"

"It was the first hint. After that it was the stolen car and the sequence of those fires."

"I don't know why Rachel figured she needed a stolen car. Or why she took it from down there. Sooner or later they would have tracked it to us. You did. It was stupid. The whole plan was stupid. Believe it or not, that dinner was the first time Rachel had met him face-to-face. In the middle of the meal I went to the restroom and left them together. That must have been when she arranged to meet him, because later on I realized he acted funny after that."

"Why do you think he left her in his rental?"

"I know why. He panicked. I found out firsthand, you kill somebody, you panic. You can't believe what panic is. Twice on my way back I ran that Jeep off the road. Lucky I didn't kill myself. I figure he shot Rachel and then got so flustered he destroyed his rental with her in it. Wanted to burn the body to make identification harder. He was probably headed back to town to claim some black guy swiped the rental. But Rachel wasn't thinking either.

Sooner or later somebody was going to figure out we were Huddleston's neighbors. Rachel, Rachel, Rachel. You know, she was wonderful. She came in here that afternoon before she left and took a nap with me. I know now she was saying good-bye. Hey. You ever see my picture of her?''

''I believe I did.''

''She was so goddamned beautiful.'' Knutson took the picture out of his wallet and was in the midst of offering it to Fontana when he slumped across one arm of his wheelchair. Fontana went across the room and found blood trickling down the inside of a blanket Knutson had wrapped around his shoulders. He checked for a pulse and found none. He'd shot himself in the chest, stalling with small talk until he could die. Removing the hot ashtray, Fontana put it on a table and then picked up the photo of Rachel and looked at it for a long while. In the end, he placed it back in Randy's wallet, then put the wallet on the nightstand next to the smoldering ashtray.

47

NONE THE WORSE
FOR WEAR

"It was just a screwy deal," mused Fontana, after Jennifer Underhill showed up. "She didn't have to go up there and pull that stunt. After the conference Callahan would have gone back home and they never would have seen him again. She'd just built it up so big in her own mind she couldn't let go of it."

"But you said Callahan had been threatening them."

"He threatened everybody. It was a way of life with him."

"It caught up to him. You know, Mac, it must have been the bravest thing she ever did, as well as the dumbest."

"It's surprising how many people combine those two."

"It had to have been awful for her," said Underhill. "Up there in that storm hoping her husband would come to the rescue and then getting raped when he didn't. By the very man she'd come to kill. She must have gotten to the gun at some point. And either she didn't have the nerve to pull the trigger or was overpowered by Callahan before she could, and then he turned it on her. The whole thing was too disorganized for him to have thought it through."

"And Randy. Through little fault of his own he steps into a

situation that turns him into a murderer. And to make it worse, the clues that led us to him were left by his wife. He spent all that time pondering whether or not to kill Callahan because he couldn't be sure that was his wife in the first burning car. Callahan wasn't going to confess, and Randy had no way of checking."

"He must have known on some level, or he wouldn't have burned the man to death."

"I think he knew on *every* level. He just didn't want to admit it."

"Why did he kill himself? Surely he knew he had a real chance of getting off, maybe a couple of years, depending on what sort of evidence we could work out of that crime scene."

"He felt guilt for what he'd done. Then too, he was in deep mourning over his wife. They'd been together since high school, and I have a feeling he couldn't stand the thought of going on without her."

■

It was snowing lightly by the time Fontana left for Staircase. When he got home his yard had two inches of new, the town clothed in an anonymous, all-encompassing purity.

Thursday night at the monthly town council meeting, Fontana's job was returned to him amid a serious round of squabbling between Mo Costigan and several council members who chastised Mo for being high-handed. It didn't faze Mo, who had never been wrong about anything.

On the way out of the meeting, Fontana overheard two of Mo's neighbors talking about her: "Hey, how come I never see Mo out on her front porch playing that accordion of hers no more?"

"Ah, she don't do that since she stopped drinkin' whiskey."

"Hell, I kinda liked it."

■

When he finally got the chief's Suburban back from Roger Truax two days later, he found it had been serviced by one of Truax's cousins in his home garage to the tune of $493.87, despite the fact that Truax knew the vehicle was under contract to be serviced by Opal and Les Morgan. Nor had the Suburban been due for servicing. He had also used city money to have the windows shaded all around and a row of blinking lights installed in the back window. The swivel chair in Fontana's office was broken, too. Roger was the type of man who would borrow your dog and bring her back pregnant.

Five weeks later Lou Strange ended up in a hospital in Yakima. On his second to last day, he opened his eyes briefly, saw Fontana, tried on a limp smile, and said, "I ever tell you the one about the guy slammed the chicken's head in a chest of drawers?"

"I think you did."

"Why did he ever have to write that damned book? You ever figure that out?"

"I don't know, Lou. Maybe because he knew a truth and he thought he had to tell it. Sometimes the truth'll burn a hole in your pocket, like five bucks in a kid's pants."

Grace Teller seemed to have disappeared, taking with her most of Lou's pain medications. Strange had no idea where to locate her, and so it was without any family members present that he passed away in his sleep at ten o'clock on a bitterly cold Thursday morning. Even dead, he looked none the worse for wear.

Sally telephoned from the movie set in Spain once a week, asking for updates on her property, which Fontana was safeguarding, and telling him repeatedly she wanted to remain friends. She confessed a romantic involvement with her younger costar and admitted they were thinking about marriage. Watering her house plants twice a week was painful for Fontana, who felt as if the house were full of ghosts, his and hers and others, as if he and the house were somehow in another dimension. He felt sorry for himself, all the while wondering why he was taking it so poorly.

Jim Hawkins was suspended from volunteering for three months. He dutifully apologized to Heather Minerich, and then to everyone's amazement, they began dating each other. When Tolmi pressed for details, Hawkins said only, "Heather's a very nice girl."

Heather, for her part, had dropped her lawyer and her lawsuit against the city, although it was rumored she was still taking notes on the day-to-day activities around the station—just in case.

The day after Knutson shot himself, Joyce Callahan phoned Fontana at home, a call he had been dreading. As promised, he laid out the story for her. When he'd finished, Joyce Callahan said, "This is why you were asking about our sex life?"

"Yes."

"My husband would never rape anybody. And he didn't kill that woman."

"I'm just telling you what I know."

"You realize I'm not going to pay you for this drivel."

"I had a feeling you weren't."

"I didn't hire you to hand me a load of garbage. This is the worst fabrication I've ever heard. And you're the biggest gas bag I've ever met."

"I'm sorry you feel that way," he said, before realizing she'd already hung up, "but it's the truth."

The day after Joyce's call, Staircase received another foot of snow. Fontana spent the day building a snow fort in the yard with Brendan. It was the day Brendan started talking about Christmas. "If I only ask for two things, I figure you'll have to give me one or the other of them. Right, Dad?"

"What two things?" Fontana asked.

"A fish or a pig."

They'd had a fish once, but Satan had eaten it. "How about a turtle or a pig?" said Fontana.

"That would work," Brendan said.

"You got a deal, kid." Satan should have a much harder time with a turtle.